PENGUIN BOOKS

The Green Fool

Patrick Kavanagh was born in Inniskeen, County Monaghan, in 1904, the son of a cobbler-cum-small farmer. He left school at the age of twelve, apparently destined to plough the 'stony-grey soil' rather than write about it, but 'I dabbled in verse,' he said, 'and it became my life.' He was 'discovered' by the Literary Revival veteran, AE (George Russell), in 1929 and his poems began to appear in Irish and English journals. In 1936 his first book of verse, *Ploughman and Other Poems*, was published, and in 1938 he followed this up with *The Green Fool*, an autobiography. He spent the lean years of the war in Dublin, where *The Great Hunger* was published in 1942. After the war he published the novel *Tarry Flynn* (1948) and two further collections of verse: *A Soul for Sale* (1947) and *Come Dance with Kitty Stobling* (1960). The bulk of his verse was included in his *Collected Poems*, and some of his prose in *Collected Pruse*. He died in 1967 and is buried in his native Inniskeen.

Patrick Kavanagh

The Green Fool

Penguin Books

PENGUIN BOOKS

Published by the Penguin Group
Penguin Books Ltd, 80 Strand, London WC2R 0RL, England
Penguin Putnam Inc., 375 Hudson Street, New York, New York 10014, USA
Penguin Books Australia Ltd, 250 Camberwell Road, Camberwell, Victoria 3124, Australia
Penguin Books Canada Ltd, 10 Alcorn Avenue, Toronto, Ontario, Canada M4V 3B2
Penguin Books India (P) Ltd, 11 Community Centre, Panchsheel Park, New Delhi – 110 017, India
Penguin Books (NZ) Ltd, Cnr Rosedale and Airborne Roads, Albany, Auckland, New Zealand
Penguin Books (South Africa) (Pty) Ltd, 24 Sturdee Avenue, Rosebank 2196, South Africa

Penguin Books Ltd, Registered Offices: 80 Strand, London WC2R 0RL, England

www.penguin.com

First published by Michael Joseph 1938
This edition published by Martin Brian & O'Keefe 1971
Published in Penguin Books 1975
Reprinted in Penguin Classics 2001
9

Printed in England by Clays Ltd, St Ives plc
Set in Monotype Times

ISBN-13: 978–0–14–118420–3

www.greenpenguin.co.uk

Penguin Books is committed to a sustainable future
for our business, our readers and our planet.
The book in your hands is made from paper
certified by the Forest Stewardship Council.

Contents

TO MY BROTHER

1 Angelhood

When I was about two years old I was one evening lying in the onion-box that had been converted into a cradle. I looked up and saw for the first time the sticky black-oak couples of thatched roof. If I did not see stars it was my child observation was at fault for the blackbirds had pecked holes in the thatch – to the very bone in places. The blackbird was a great enemy of old thatch and in its search for the little red worms in the decayed straw would stop at nothing. At three or four o'clock of a summer's morning he would begin his attack and by six, narrow sunbeam ribbons like wedding festoonery would be stretched from roof to floor in peasant homes, or as happened more often, spitting rain would startle the sleeping faces of children in their beds, and indeed I often heard father tell of a wet night when he had to hold an umbrella over himself and my mother in their bed.

The house where I was born was a traditional Irish cabin, wedge-shaped, to trick the western winds. It was surrounded on three sides by a neighbour's field, which was inconvenient as unless we were on good terms with the owner of the field – which we were not – the back could not be thatched except by hanging a ladder across. It had a tiny back window, about a foot square, but through this window, it appears, we were not entitled to let in legal daylight. Once upon a time the owner of the field had built a cock of hay against the window, thereby leaving the occupants of the house in the plight of Diogenes when Alexander the Great cast his shadow on the bung-hole of the Sage's tub.

The bog over which my young eyes strayed, and through which I often waded in the search for ducks that layed out, was a twenty-acre waste from which the peat had long been cut; in some of its clear pools greedy pike survived, but only the eels could be said to have security of tenure. Beautiful blue and

white and pink flowers grew on the bog and more magical
flowers I have not seen since; they were exciting as a poem and
had a different beauty for my changing moods.

Around our house there stood little hills all tilled and tame.
Yellow flame-blossoms of the whin lit bonfires all over the landscape; the whin was as persistent and as fertile as sin and disease.
The sunny side of the hills was good soil and boasted some tall
thorn trees, but the black side facing the north was crabbed and
poverty-stricken and grew only stunted blackthorns and sorrel
plants. There were no trees to speak of except the poplar and
the sally; here and there a cranky old elm which had survived
the crying of a cold kitchen spread about his trunk and tried
to look a forest. From the tops of the little hills there spread a
view right back to the days of Saint Patrick and the druids.
Slieve Gullion to the north fifteen miles distant, to the west the
bewitched hills and forths of Donaghmoyne; eastward one could
see the distillery chimney of Dundalk sending up its prosperous
smoke, or, on a very bright day, one could see the sun-dazzled
tide coming in at Annagasson. To the south stood the Hill of
Mullacrew where once was held a fair famous as Donnybrook
and it had as many cracked skulls to its credit too.

The name of my birthplace was Mucker; some of the natives
wanted to change it to Summerhill which would have been worse.
All who could do so without risking the loss of their scant mail
cut 'Mucker' out of their postal address altogether. The natives
of the place were known far and near as Muckers, which in
after years was rhymed obscenely by corner-boys. The name was
a corrupted Gaelic word signifying a place where pigs were bred
in abundance. Long before my arrival there was much aesthetic
heart-aching among the folk who had to put up with, and up
in, such a pig-named townland. In spite of all this the townland
stuck to its title and it was in Mucker I was born.

Astrologers anxious to read my stars have now and then
queried the hour and date of my birth. I always gave them
somebody else's stars to read so that the horoscope mightn't put
me out of humour with my dreams. But to those who may desire
to cast for me my horoscope now I will say: My stars are events
in time, things that happened and could not have happened to

one born in the sixteenth century. The date of my birth is cut on the tablets of common existence.

The railway line to Carrick was visible from our back window. One hundred yards from our house was the railway gate-house and level-crossing where the Mucker Road joined the county highway. The railway was important: we set our clock by the three-thirty train. My father said the three-thirty was the only train you could depend on. It was the only train that had a connection to make. The other trains started just when the driver felt in the humour, and made no important connections except the pubs, where the driver, fireman, and guard quenched their smoky thirsts. We possessed the only clock in the townland. It was an old clock, father bought it second-hand for half a crown thirty years earlier, and the old woman from whom he bought it had herself bought it second-hand forty years earlier still. That clock was as touchy as a spoiled child; it would only go for father. Not even Jock Brickle, the wandering clock-repairer, could make it keep time. Once indeed father did let Jock try his hand at the old timepiece. Jock took it asunder. When he reassembled it there was one wheel for which the clock-repairer could find no place. He tried to fix the wheel in sideways, angle-wise, and turban-wise, and while so engaged the old clock started tick-tock, tick-tock.

'There was a wheel too many in yer clock,' Jock said.

The clock continued to go but when the hour came to be struck there was no response. Father disassembled the clock again and reinserted the extra wheel.

'That finishes me with Jock Brickle,' he said. Of course father had a watch, but that was a private affair, and had no communal importance. All the neighbours passing our house called in to inquire the time.

At the other end of the Mucker Road, out of sight of the railway, was another clock. It wasn't very reliable as it was set by the bread-cart. The 'Bumper' Rooney, the bread-server, was sometimes late and sometimes early. Our clock was dependable, never more than a half-hour fast or slow. In any case time hardly mattered much. The sun rose and set in a land of dreams whether the clocks were right or wrong.

My part of Ireland had a poet at one time, a poor ragged fellow whom no respectable person would be seen talking to, but he left doors open as he passed. The peasant folk knew the lore and strange knowledges of God and Greece that they didn't know they knew. From the lips of simple old women I heard phrases of whimsical prophecy and exciting twists of language that would delight the heart of a wheelbarrow or a modernist poet.

When I was born the people weren't expecting a poet. They already had one, self-styled the Bard of Callenberg, and his satiric rhymes were about as much as they could stomach.

'Tailor Magrane putting in the long buck stitches
  And Carpenter Hamill cutting his timber out of the ditches.'

That was how the Bard of Callenberg summed up the local tailor and carpenter.

The people didn't want a poet, but a fool, yes they could be doing with one of these. And as I grew up not exactly 'like another' I was installed the fool.

I was the butt of many an assembly. I hadn't then read the wisdom of King Cormac Mac Art. 'Never be the butt of an assembly.' At wake, fair, or dance for many years I was the fellow whom the jokers took a hand at when conversational funds fell low. I very nearly began to think myself an authentic fool. I often occupied a position like that of 'The Idiot' in Dostoevsky's novel. I do not blame the people who made me their fool; they wanted a fool and in any case they lost their stakes.

Being made a fool of is good for the soul. It produces a sensitivity of one kind or other; it makes a man into something unusual, a saint or a poet or an imbecile. I often used to regret not having been born among the mountains or by the sea. Then I might have been brave enough to drink to excess the wild wine of fantasy. And I thought, too, that it would be a fine thing to be reared in a workhouse – fatherless, motherless, and so free from the net of love.

Many of my neighbours treated me with cruelty and derision, but against that I have had – not friends – lovers. Anybody who cared for me cared a great deal for me.

When I arrived in Mucker the natives were beginning to lose faith in the old, beautiful things. The ghost of a culture haunted the snub-nosed hills.

The Parish Priest was the centre of gravity, he was the only man who was sure to go to Heaven. Our staple diet was potatoes and oatmeal porridge. Porridge had only recently taken the place of potatoes and buttermilk as the national supper.

Though little fields and scraping poverty do not lead to grand flaring passions, there was plenty of fire and an amount of vicious neighbourly hatred to keep us awake. Most of the neighbours had at one time or another gone to law chiefly for trespass.

'Show me good fences and I'll show you good neighbours,' is a saying we had. The fences in Mucker were bad stone-ditches that a lame duck could cross. Neighbours often went to law over the right-of-way to a well. Never was there a case for abusive and threatening language. There was language abusive enough though. Each person was keeping up spite to at least two of his neighbours.

We had two families that we didn't care a great deal for, though in the end everybody got too lazy for hating.

My father was a shoemaker in the good days when a pair of shop boots were an insult to any decent man's feet. He was a small, lively, intelligent man and had among the people a reputation for learning almost as great as the schoolmaster. He played the melodeon till he was forty. He then got married. His passion for music was strong and even after his marriage he found crevices in among his cares in which to play. He was fond of reading but – peace to his soul – he never really got beyond the stage of *Tit Bits* and *Answers*. I am sorry when I think of all the creations of the mind that he could have enjoyed.

My father loved me and I loved him, but he didn't like my day-dreaming way of living. He said I'd end my days in the workhouse if I didn't change my gait of going. Like Solomon he was a firm believer in the virtue-giving qualities of the rod, except that he used a strap, and many's the flogging I got from him, most of which I deserved; for I had none, or very few, of the qualities that go into the making of a perfect child. I was a bit of a lazy-bones, a bit of a liar and a bit of a rogue.

'Let me at him,' father would say. 'Let me at him till I knock the daylight out of him.' He wouldn't be very well pleased if he was let at me. As our kitchen was his cobbler's shop there was always someone to stand between me and my father's anger. I was only afraid of my father when he had his spectacles on. He is dead a good many years now, yet as I write these words I know he is beside me, encouraging me to go on and win to be a great writer. I can see him smile and he isn't wearing his spectacles.

My mother was a simple peasant woman, twenty years younger than father. She was without any schooling but was very shrewd, a good judge of men and animals, and the best measurer of unknown quantities I have ever known. From my father I have inherited the spirit, from my mother the material garment of wisdom. In our house the two most important subjects were the saying of the Rosary each evening and the making of money. Ours was a united house, there was only one purse, let it be full or empty. In other houses the man held to what he could make from cattle or corn, the wife would have to supply the kitchen from the proceeds of butter and eggs. Everybody was poor and proud. My parents didn't know anything to be proud of, so they just carried on. All the small farmers had as income was the price of a pig or a calf every twelve months. We had no land but into our house came what is known as the 'dropping shilling'. My parents were great experts in making the hens lay in winter – the hens of the neighbours only laid when the birds in the bushes were laying and prices at their lowest.

There were nine children in our family. All our names are to be found in the calendar of the Saints: it was to that calendar father went in search of a name when a child was born, and not back to some dubious ancestor with a name like a gnarled stick.

My father wrote the history of his family for me on a sheet of foolscap. I have often wondered since if he hadn't some instinct that I should some day give it the permanency of print. It was a romantic story of his father who had come out of the West to sow the wild, vigorous seed of Connaught among the little hills of South Ulster.

Because I knew I had the manuscript to read any time I only

scanned it once. I put it in what I thought a safe place in the bottom of a large delf jug – a preposterous heirloom that was never in use. When my father was dead a month I looked in the jug and it was empty: and whether it was the handmaid of Prudery or Cleanliness swept it away I do not know. I was filled with grief as I never now could have a copy.

All my early memories are evening memories close to bedtime. The haze of years is kind to sharp jutting stones.

I was in my mother's arms clinging with my small hands to the security of her shoulder. I saw into a far mysterious place that I long associated with Wordsworth's Ode on Immortality. I believed for many years that I had looked back into the world from whence I came. And perhaps I had.

But examined in the light of honest reality what I had really seen was the secret side of a cupboard. It was a sort of press which only opened one door, and the end of the not very accessible top-shelf was filled with rent receipts and curtain rings and such like.

Not very long ago I have looked into that same cupboard where it lies in an outhouse discarded, and the rent receipts are still there, a good deal yellower than they were and their corners mouse-eaten, and the curtain rings are there, too, though the rusty base metal has eaten away most of the brass veneer.

Of such is the Land of the Immortals.

An old white-whiskered man stood on the laneway outside our house. As I ran in to tell, I heard the gate open and his footsteps following. He came in.

'Ah, Garret dear, you're as welcome as the flowers of May,' my mother said, running to meet him.

My father looked up from the boot he was stitching. His welcome wasn't showy ever but there is no doubt he was glad to see Garret back again.

Garret Plunket, he was one of the journeymen shoemakers who worked for my father off and on as he travelled the roads of Ireland, sampling the porter of the pubs and the black bread and tea of the workhouses and jails. For the journeymen shoemakers were men who took life as it came and it sometimes came hard. Garret was one of the most lovable of them all; he looked more like a priest than a tramp, he had an air of gentility and even in drink carried himself with unaffected nobility.

'And where have you been since we last had a sight of you?' my mother asked.

Garret, who was sipping a mug of tea, turned round on his stool.

'Where was I?' he said. 'Aye, that's the question, where was I?'

'Were you down seeing Tumelty?' my father inquired. It was a professional query.

'Tumelty has a man working,' Garret said. 'Dan the Butt is with him.'

Tumelty was a shoemaker and Dan the Butt was a journeyman. Garret called me to him. 'When are they going to put trousers on you?' he laughed.

My mother laughed and said: 'When he knows how to loose his buttons.'

I felt ashamed. I was wearing the petticoats over which hung one of the most winsome remembrances of my childhood – the Pink Bib. The pink bib was a flowery cotton overall of which I was terribly proud. I wore it by the bog-side and it blended with the pink bog-flowers so perfectly that one could hardly pick out of the pattern the floral design that was me.

When Garret had finished his tea he went to one of the spare cobbler's seats and started unwrapping the bundle of tools which I hadn't noticed before. In his cobbler's apron they were wrapped. Hammer, knife, awl, etc. He picked them out gingerly and laid them in a row on the seat.

My father didn't tell him he needed a cobbler but Garret didn't mind that. A poor man doesn't wait for a royal invitation. At any rate, my father wasn't that kind of a man. If a cobbler came he told him straight if he hadn't work for him. There wasn't much romantic glamour about the business, it was a case of bread and butter, though cobblers more than any others do not live on bread alone, but by every word that proceedeth from the mouth of God.

The western sun, without regard for the laws of men, peeped through our small back window.

'The sun never comes in that window save one month in the

14

year,' my father said. It must have been midsummer then for the sun passed our little window completely before he went behind Rocksavage Hills.

Garret put on his basil apron that was holed and knife-scarred and sat down to work. Then he began to fumble in his waistcoat pocket as though looking for something important.

'What's the bother?' my father said.

'Where I put me specs is a mystery to me,' he said.

'Think of where you last were sure that you had them,' said my mother, trying to be helpful.

'Think, think, think,' he repeated, almost exasperated.

I had my back turned and as I was keeping very quiet it aroused suspicion.

'What is this blackguard doing here?' my mother said, coming close to me.

I was fitting on Garret's spectacles; they had fallen out of his pocket while he was having his tea. Neither Garret nor my father took my trick in good part, to take a tool off a cobbler's seat was one of the most heinous offences known to the trade.

My father and Garret sewed and hammered and talked, dry practical talk, good bony talk of kips and uppers and toecaps. Sometimes it turned romantic or political.

'Paddy Hanlin is getting married next week,' my father said.

'Poor Paddy,' Garret sighed.

'Do you think Ireland will get Home Rule?' my mother said in a sort of lofty appeal to Garret the profound traveller.

Garret was pulling hard at a wax-end and didn't notice. He was grunting too and I often heard my father say grunting was half ease.

Customers came in, some with basketfuls of old brogues and some with them hanging on their shoulders.

'Let us have a look at the hard cases,' my father said, spilling the contents of a basket without ceremony on the floor. He ran through them very quickly, then gathered all into the basket and made to go out the door with the basket of boots.

'Where the divil are you taking the boots to?' the customer shouted.

15

'To the deepest bog-hole I can find,' my father said, as he ran close to the bog.

'For God's sake, James, don't drown the boots,' my mother called.

He returned with the boots.

'Do you know,' he told the customer, 'a man wouldn't make salt for his praties mending boots like yours. You may thank herself here that I didn't give them the bog-hole.'

For weeks and weeks after his arrival each evening Garret would take me with him for his limb-stretching stroll across the hills, and he would point out to me all the places around for miles and their history. Away over in Armagh the village of Forkhill where they kept a good pint, and Dundalk that had a distillery, two breweries, and a jail.

'Were you ever in Dundalk jail?' I asked.

'I was,' he replied, 'and it's a bad one.'

'Is it indeed?' I commented.

'You were nearly as well working for a farmer,' he said. 'Dundalk jail is the worst in the world.' And he pointed out to me the Hill of Slane though he made no mention of the fire Saint Patrick lighted there.

'I never was in an unluckier spot than Slane,' he declared. 'A month without the option of a fine I got.'

Garret would surprise a person in the habit of taking a book by the cover. Such a one would say that Garret was a saint and a mystic and poet, yet he was none of these things but a plain philistine with a kind heart and a prophet's beard.

It is still evening time but dark now it is the winter of the year. I was going to bed and as I stood in my naked innocence I noticed that my skin was spotted and I felt sick. The measles were going on their rounds and the smell of burned whisky and boiled nettles was in every house. At that very moment my father began to play the melodeon in the kitchen and he sang with it:

> 'A starry night for a ramble
> Through the flowery dell
> Beneath the bush and bramble
> Kiss but never tell.'

From that day *A Starry Night* became for me the greatest song in the world: whenever I sing it or hear it sung I am back again in childhood, where my father is playing the melodeon and my skin is measles-spotted.

2 Break with Tradition

The old thatched house in which I was born was knocked down when I was about five years old. I remember the masons coming in the mornings. I stood on our dunghill watching out for them. I could see them when they crossed the railway. They wore white moleskin trousers, and were very sour men. That is about all I knew of their characters. The black-oak couples came down and were thrown in the garden before the door.

It was summer-time. My father removed his benches to the back-garden. The noise of his hammering on the last echoed across the bog. My mother did the cooking at an improvised fireplace in a shed. The masons were good quick tradesmen, but they couldn't work without porter. Each day father went to MacNello's pub with a big hamper and carried home two dozen bottles of porter. The masons drank this quantity. The two builders' labourers must have got an odd bottle, but as far as I can remember from experience and hearsay it was the two masons drank the most of it.

When the boys would be coming from school they would climb up on the scaffolding. One of the masons didn't like this. I remember him pushing a lad off the planks, he fell ten feet. That affair was all the talk for years afterwards. On Sunday afternoons the neighbouring children came to our half-built house and made see-saws of the long planks that were lying around.

A girl got up on the new wall and gave a recitation. I remember it:

> 'I went to the fair of Dungarvan
> It being on a market day
> And I bought the finest ram, sir
> That ever was fed upon hay
>   With me iddle de umpty arby
>   And me hokey dokey day
>   He was the finest ram, sir
>   That was ever fed upon hay.'

There was a good deal more and though I only heard the ballad once I can recall it from the graveyard of almost a quarter of a century. That ram was a remarkable beast if only because of the footprints he made on the sands of my memory.

> 'The horns that grew on this ram, sir
> They grew up to the moon
> For I went up in April
> And I didn't come back till June.'

When the new house was finished Peter Hamill, a dear friend of father's, came to see it. I heard him say to father: 'Ye'll have to be taken out the window if ye die upstairs.'

Father said he didn't care how his coffin was taken out. The landing top of the stairs was too short on which to turn a coffin.

People in Ireland never forget that they have to die. Even at the building of a new house the thought of the last going out was in somebody's mind.

Father didn't mind. He was like that. He was too busy living life to give over consideration to death.

I often heard him say that he wouldn't care if he was buried in the corner of a field. He was a practical man and a practising Catholic.

'It's the way you live that matters,' he often said.

We had a new house. A two-storied slated dwelling in a town-land of thatched houses.

It was more imposing on the outside than the other houses, but it was colder inside. The walls were plumb and level. There were no secret nooks where one might find an old prophecy or a forgotten ballad or the heads of old clay pipes. A modern dwelling cut off from the Gaelic tradition.

The new house was healthy. There was plenty of room for children; not like the old house which had only two rooms and the kitchen.

The journeyman shoemakers slept in the settle-bed in the kitchen. The settle-bed was a great place for a drunken man, he couldn't roll out.

'The Kavanagh is a great wee man,' I heard people say. 'Built a new house! Why, we're all sleepin'!'

'Aw sure, they got a legacy,' another said. 'Oul' Micky left a batter of money.' Old Micky was my father's uncle. He was a professional stone-breaker.

'Oul' Mickey was rotten with money,' the people said.

All he left after his death was the sum of thirty-five shillings. Father told us. He didn't bother telling the neighbours. They wouldn't believe. Mickey had the name of having money and as we would say, 'When you get the name of early rising you may sleep till dinner-time.'

Father had a good trade. At one time he had three and four journeymen working. Customers had often to wait five or six weeks for a new pair of boots.

Late to bed and early to rise was his motto, and his practice. From six o'clock in the morning till twelve at night was his working day. That was how he made his money. He used to say that he never could have a penny to call his own till he married my mother. After that full and plenty walked with him. My mother was said to have 'the luck of the money'. The hens and animals my mother tended prospered well. She was a perfect partner for father. Every penny she got her hands on was a prisoner till the ransomer – whether of the market-place or the field – proved that the prisoner on release would work well for our household.

Mother wasn't a miser, neither was father. They both believed in eating well and giving their children good food.

They were wise in this. They knew that all the good things of the earth are the cheapest, and the least thought of. They didn't know that the National Galleries and Libraries, being free to all, have the fewest customers. They didn't know, but had they known would have understood. A pound of tea would do our house for a long time. I – being a spoiled boy and an only son during my early years – got tea in the morning. Porridge was the staple diet. It is the recognized supper all through Ireland. We got it in the mornings and called it our supper. None of us would admit having eaten porridge for breakfast. It was something to be ashamed of. I remember a lad coming in one morning and finding me delving into a porringerful of porridge. I quickly slipped the porringer behind my back while I blushed to the two ears and beyond them. All the children of the nobs at school had white bread. We envied them; all we had was plain wheaten bread. The children of the nobs called their white bread 'lunch' and nibbled at it with aristocratic finger-tips. We had no lunch, just bread which we ate greedily and washed down with a mug of water.

My father didn't smoke. I heard him say he smoked for one year and then gave it up. A great deal of tobacco-smoke arose from our townland. It was easy keeping poor people poor.

> 'That's the way the money goes
> Pop goes the weasel.'

Father sang *Pop Goes the Weasel*, but not at all labouring the moral of the song.

Children kept coming to our flock. I occupied the middle berth in the family ship.

I used to hear people saying that God never sends a mouth but he sends something to fill it. A true saying only that it seemed to me – God sometimes sent the mouthful to the wrong address. In our case such a heavenly mistake never happened.

I knew the secret of birth before I was five years old. I picked up stray bits of old women's talk. 'And when is it due?'

'In a month.'

The small children at school and on the lanes debated the whereabouts of the finding of the latest baby. 'Under a stalk of cabbage he was found.'

'Lord, and do ye know where I was found?'

'Where?'

'Under a stalk of cabbage.'

Nearly all the children seemed to derive from the caterpillars. I didn't mind the lie but the lack of originality and variety may have annoyed me.

When I was near six years I could stand it no longer.

'Head of cabbage,' I jeered at a fellow. 'That's not where ye came from.'

He looked at me surprised that I should presume to doubt the authenticity of the legend.

'Mary Duffy said so.'

'Mary Duffy is telling a lie,' I said.

The little fellow whom I was about to lecture on obstetrics was no more than five.

'Was I not found in Brennan's cabbage-garden?' he said.

'You were not,' I said. 'Your mother had you.'

'Mother had me,' he repeated. I can still see him scratching his fair curls as he knelt on the dusty road.

One day I overheard two young women talking. From that day I have never been puzzled or curious about what young women talk of.

'Oh, he's a lovely fella.'

'How long is he goin' with ye?'

'Two months.'

'Does he mane business?'

'What?'

'Is he a marryin' man?'

And then they giggled loudly. I didn't see the joke but my education was going on. I learned quickly to read. Upstairs in a trunk was a pamphlet on midwifery. I read it from all angles. I spelled out the hard words. Nobody knew how much I knew, though once I smiled during a discussion on the physical capabilities of a newly-wed husband. One of the talkers gave me a side-look.

'Did ye see the smile of him?' she said. 'There's more in that thing's head than a comb could take out.'

On summer evenings we kicked a rag-ball in a meadow beyond the bog. We kicked with our bare feet. We let our toe-nails grow long – not to kick the rag-ball, but to tear each other's shins. We hung our shirts over our trousers so that modest people passing would be shocked. They couldn't see our trousers and thought we were playing in our shirts.

At seven o'clock when the play would be only getting going I would get the call:

'Patrick come home.'

There was a lad among us who could mimic me. He would shout back.

'No I won't, ma, ye can go to hell.'

'Wait till yer da hears this,' mother would say.

'Tell da to go to hell, too,' the mimic would add. I'd be then on my way home much too much out of breath to explain.

About this time father bought a field which ran to within twenty yards of our door.

I was coming home from school when I heard the news. A boy standing on top of the wooden stile at the railway gate-house was announcing the news to all passers-by. 'Kavanagh's bought a farm, Kavanagh's bought a farm.'

I was unmoved.

The farm cost two hundred pounds. Its area was nine acres, four of which were bog. The man who was father's rival for the field was disappointed and his wife was worse. When he entered his house his wife was standing facing him with the tongs raised. She knew that he had let the field slip from his grip. She flung the tongs at her husband's head. He screamed.

'Shut up,' she cried. 'We're shamed, you let a cobbler best you.'

Where father got the money to purchase land was a mystery. He built a house and now had given two hundred pounds for a farm. In those days and in that country two hundred pounds was a 'quare handful'.

The mystified people fell back on the legacy theory.

'Divil a other but 'twas a legacy.'

'Divil a other.'

There was another poor man who suddenly became rich. People said he robbed the Mail-coach.

'That's how I got the money,' the man told one of these people, 'and now let you go and rob another Mail-coach.'

We had many callers, congratulating my parents.

'Why, yer as good as any of us now,' they said. And to me they turned saying: 'Yer a farmer's son now.'

I didn't feel different.

Previous to buying the farm my parents had invested in a cow. She was a strawberry cow with one broken horn and due to calve in a week. I cannot say if there was much jubilation in our home. There was jubilation I am certain. For years mother had to travel two and three miles for a can of butter-milk. She got it for nothing, but all the same it was dear enough at the carrying.

23

We always kept two goats. One of them, a white horny, I am not likely to forget. Many a time she sidled up behind me and before I'd have time to do anything I'd be lying on my mouth and nose in the middle of a nettle-forest perhaps. That goat was as nimble of foot as a champion feather-weight boxer. Goat's milk was very good when one got used to it. In the winter the goats didn't give any milk and until we got the cow mother had to travel for milk.

As soon as we got the cow father disposed of the goats. Apart from the injuries they inflicted on the unheroic side of my anatomy they were a heart-scald. 'Whenever you meet a goat give her a kick,' people would say, 'for if she's not going to harm she's after comin' out of it.' Father agreed with this theory of goats though I'm sure he never put it in practice.

While we had a goat about the house we couldn't have a rosebush or a lilac or a ridge of cabbage. When our first cow was bought we had no place to graze her except on the Long Acre, which was the name given to the grazing along the country road. Mother grazed the strawberry cow on the road during the early hours of the summer mornings and after rain. In midday the grass would be dusty and rank poison for a cow. Worse than that, the police in those days were very officious. The second morning on which mother was herding the cow Constable Kinsella of the R.I.C. caught her. 'Don't you know you have no right to trespass on the public highway?' he said.

Mother very humbly admitted that she had no right. 'I'll summon you,' he said, and he did. We were fined a half-crown.

'Kinsella was a bad article,' one of our neighbours said.

'A bad pill surely,' was the reply.

Constable Kinsella joined the Army at the outbreak of the War and was killed the first week.

'It was the price of him,' people said, 'he couldn't have better luck.'

The cow was only a short time about our house when she took ill, a mysterious disease. None of the numerous quacks could say what was the matter with the cow. Even old Willie, who was master of every complaint from ringworm to a broken leg, was puzzled. She hadn't swallowed the water-beetle or she'd have swelled up, so there was no need to send for the Cassidys. Father lost faith in the power of the quacks. He threw off his apron and walked into Carrick to consult the veterinary surgeon. This was an unusual thing to do. People had little confidence in professional men. When father came back he had a dose with him for the cow. 'She has the red-water,' he said dramatically.

'Nonsense,' one man said.

The cow got well. It was a nail in the coffin of quackery. When neighbours came to see the cow they said: 'The right man is the right man in the long run.'

As I lay in bed two days later I heard moaning outside. I looked out the window and saw the cow giving birth to a calf. Two neighbour-men were taking the calf, they were groaning almost as loudly as the cow. The calf was still-born.

3 Schooldays

I was sent to school at four. I didn't want to go, for I had heard stories of Miss Cassidy, the principal teacher, and the assistant, Miss Moore. Once I had caught a glimpse of Miss Cassidy walking to her school, and I didn't ever want to see her again. She had a bundle of yellow canes, with crooks on them, under her arm, and she looked like a girl that could use them for all they were worth. She was a big woman with a heavy, coarse face, and across her round, massive shoulders she wore a small red shawl. In winter she wore heavy hob-nailed boots of my father's making. She liked my father because he wouldn't object no matter how hard she used the cane on any of his children. She didn't like our neighbour, John Gorman. 'Gorman,' she said, 'beats his children with a straw.' Miss Cassidy was around fourteen stone in weight and about five feet in height. The assistant mistress, Miss Moore, was thin and wiry. I heard enough about her to make me want to go to America.

'Miss Moore,' George Maguire said once, 'she could cut cowld iron with her tongue.' George was my friend; he put nicknames on the teachers and advised me not to go to school. He called Miss Cassidy 'Sally' and Miss Moore 'Cutty'.

'Sally and Cutty will rise welts on ye, Paddy,' he told me. 'The schoolin' is no good for anybody that has to make a livin' at worm-cuttin'.'

I liked George very much for these words as well as for the fairy tales he told me. I have good reason to remember the first day I went to school. I am always good at creating a first impression, and afterwards going flat.

One of my sisters dragged me into the school. I was wearing the pink bib. I was put sitting on a seat near the door till such time as Miss Cassidy could come to me. A little girl beside me spilled ink over my hands. When Miss Cassidy came and saw my hands she went into the tantrums.

'Go outside at once and wash your filthy hands,' she commanded.

There was a pail of water outside the door which I knew nothing of. What I had was a vague notion of water being under a railway bridge somewhere. I found the bridge but not the water, so I sat down in a cranny among slaty stones and spat on my fingers. When I didn't return to the school and couldn't be found outside it, there was a great commotion. My sister Mary was hurried home after me.

'Of course he went home, the little rat!' Miss Cassidy said.

The assistant mistress agreed with her. I wasn't at home, and my mother and father were nearly frantic as they made for the school.

In the meantime all the boys and girls had been turned into sleuth-hounds. I was discovered at the end of a half-hour by two big boys. I heard them prancing down the railway slope on the farther side of the bridge. I peeped around the corner and withdrew my nose quickly again. I thought I saw one of the boys look under a whin bush.

'Where in the name of Moses did the cobbler's gossoon go?' one asked the other.

'The fairies must have taken him,' said the other.

'What will the Kavanagh say?'

I put my nose round the corner again but didn't withdraw it in time. They eyed me.

'Did you spot anything?' the tallest boy queried.

'The little bastard,' the other fellow replied. 'Trying to play hide and seek.'

They were very proud of their capture. As they led me down towards the school gate I saw my mother facing up to Miss Cassidy. Miss Cassidy was shivering in her shoes, and my mother wasn't using very lady-like language.

'They'll tear the livers out of other,' one of my warders said.

'It'll be worth watching this,' said the other. There was no fight after all. My discovery settled the whole thing. Miss Cassidy wept and my parents didn't try to stop her, I think. Miss Cassidy was past her prime when I went to school; she had taught some of the fathers and mothers of my companions.

I was a rather bright pupil, though my brightness didn't save me from the cane. Seven or eight hard slaps on each hand was a common thing, and on top of that maybe a bonus of a box on the ear or – it is quite true – an ungracious kick on the behind.

Miss Moore didn't ever use the boot on us. She depended entirely on the cane, and it must be admitted she could put sting into her blow.

The most important subject on the curriculum was the catechism. At cramming children with religion our teachers had few equals. For weeks before a religious examination nothing was taught but the catechism; which same had the result of nearly driving all orthodox piety out of me for ever.

Once when the religious exam came round I let down my teachers disgracefully. They expected a lot from me, too, and had me perched in the middle of the front desk right beside the crucifix on the priest-examiner's breast.

'What is a publican?' he asked me.

'A man that keeps a pub,' I answered. He laughed a priestly laugh and expected everyone to join with him.

Miss Cassidy or the assistant mistress didn't laugh, they were furious.

Three or four girls giddily put up their hands.

'Well, what is a publican, you?' he said, pointing to one of the girls.

'A tax-gatherer,' she answered proudly. Miss Cassidy was released from her agony. She shook her fist at me from behind the priest. 'You'll get it, you'll get it,' that shaking fist said.

The priest didn't compliment the girl, I think he thought my answer best. It was more up-to-date, anyway.

'The only thing you're good for, Patrick Kavanagh, is a bit of arithmetic,' she declared as she spat on her hand and balanced the cane.

Miss Cassidy hadn't an ear for music. Miss Moore did the singing lessons, though she had no knowledge of tonic sol-fa or the technique of the business. She gave us the music of a song by singing it, and we picked it up that way. Along the walls during singing lessons stood a row of non-singers, the Crows they were called. I pitied the Crows for one thing. At the end of the school-day, just before we got out, all the singers sang a hymn, the same hymn always:

> 'Hail, Queen of Heaven,
> The ocean star,
> Guide of the wanderer
> Here below,
> Thrown on life's surge
> We claim thy care.
> Save us from peril
> and from woe.
> Mother of Christ,
> Star of the Sea,
> Pray for the wanderer,
> Pray for me.'

It had a lovely air. I am sure that Queen has prayed for me and has guided my wanderings.

No matter how poor I have been I have had a song and a prayer, *A Starry Night*, and *Hail, Queen of Heaven*.

When I had discarded the pink bib and had been let into the secrets of trousers and their buttons I soon showed what I could do in the business of clothes distinction. My mother was a careful and thrifty woman and she kept the holes patched, patch on top of patch of every shade and pattern, till I had a coat as many-coloured as Joseph. There travelled a beggar around our place in those days whose wearables rivalled mine in their improvised melodies. Myles Courtney was the beggar's name. Miss Cassidy thought it would be a good joke to call me Myles Courtney. My father heard of it; he wasn't just pleased. To put a nickname on a person in Ireland was ever the most terrible weapon in use. The old poets did it and the names never came unstuck for seven generations.

My father accosted Miss Cassidy on her way to school. She went down on her two knees in the gutter and cried for mercy, which was forthcoming. The name wasn't well gummed on the back and I lost it.

Miss Cassidy wore a heavy black frieze cloak during the winter.

The nap had hardened a good deal so that the texture of the black cloak resembled a board well tarred. It was a good waterproof, and would keep out a year's rain.

One wet morning, when we were all a good deal older, the black cloak was hanging a-drying on a pair of high stools by the fire.

Around the cloak, trying to dry our wet skins, we, the five members of the top class, stood. We were enveloped in the mist that was rising from the black cloak like the mist from a dark horse-pond on an evening in July.

Miss Cassidy herself was teaching in the lower end of the school those pupils who had already dried themselves; we were the last batch.

'Oh, look!' one of the girls in our class exclaimed. We all looked towards the exclamation mark.

'Ha, ha, ha, he, he, he,' the laughter burst from us like sun through fog.

'Oh, isn't it great,' someone else said.

'What will she say when she sees it?'

'There'll be fun.'

'Ha, ha, ha, ha, he.'

The truth is Miss Cassidy's beautiful black cloak was on fire, and a hole was spreading from its centre, slowly spreading outwards.

Miss Cassidy was at the bottom of the schoolroom; she must have been teaching the catechism; no other subject would have shut her senses off from some inkling of this disaster. We now and then gave a look from the cloak to its owner. She hadn't noticed or sensed anything, though there was a fine flavour of burning wool in the place.

She heard our laughter.

'I'll be up with you in a minute,' she said, without turning round, 'and I'll make it salty for ... no, it's not the Fourth Commandment, missy. What is the Fourth Commandment? What are you children laughing at?' she cried, turning her attention, but not her eyes, towards us.

'My God! is it my cloak?' she moaned, as the tragic truth dawned on her at last, and she came running up.

'My cloak! My God!' she moaned again, this time reversing the order of preference. The cloak was all but fire-proof; though the flames had had it in their grip for almost ten minutes, only a hole about three feet in diameter was burned in its back.

'My cloak! My God!' she kept repeating.

She didn't give us the cane: the thing was too serious for that, it was something on which an endless feud might be based.

If God appeared to Moses in a burning bush, a merry pagan god surely appeared to us in Miss Cassidy's burning cloak.

Miss Cassidy was curious as a London policeman. I remember one morning how she lined us up and asked us what we had for dinner the previous evening. 'What had you for your dinner? And you? And you? And you?' just like it was a lesson. As luck would have it, the first to be questioned was a girl whose people – to use their own expression – were 'tryin' to build up a bit of dacency'.

'What had you for your dinner?' Miss Cassidy asked.

'Potatoes and meat and vegetables,' the girl replied. It must have been at that moment that 'Sez you', incarnate in the womb of language, cried out to be born. No other comment would be worthy to follow this girl's answer.

We all took up the cue, save one girl.

'And you?'

'Potatoes, meat, and vegetables.'

'And you?'

'Potatoes, meat, and vegetables.'

And so on till she came to one of the Carson girls. This family had been reared in a North of Ireland town in some sheltered spot so that they hadn't developed a deceit-resistance to curiosity. We knew when to tell the truth – whenever a lie wouldn't fit in.

'And you?' Miss Cassidy said.

'Please, miss, praties and gravy.'

The plain unvarnished truth of this girl's answer has remained in my memory these long years as a pearl of great price. It was so pitiful, so beautiful, not one of us laughed, and Miss Cassidy felt as if somebody had caught her stealing from a blind man's hat.

When I was six years old or thereabouts I went to confession.

Nobody told me to go. The children didn't all go in a body as they do now. The initiation rite wasn't organized. I can't say why I wanted to confess my sins and I don't think they weighed heavily on my soul.

Father MacElroy, an old white-haired and deaf priest, was in the confessional.

'What sins do you remember?' he said.

'I committed adultery.'

'You committed what?'

'Adultery,' I said out loud.

After a pause he continued.

'Any other sins?'

'I stole.'

'What did you steal?'

'Sixpence.'

'Who did you steal the sixpence from?'

'From the press,' I explained.

'Well now, you mustn't steal from the press any more,' he advised me tenderly. 'And for your penance,' he hurriedly summoned up, 'for your penance you'll say ... No, you'll come in and serve my Mass on Sunday.'

My father taught me the Latin, and the next Sunday I began to serve Mass. I was very poor at the business, and tripped and stumbled against all sorts of projections.

'That's the fella was breaking stones on the altar,' some fellow sneered as I was going home.

Father MacElroy was an old-time priest. The people looked upon him as a saint, though they'd have been better pleased with him if he'd used his power. He would have then come in very useful in times of sickness among both cattle and Christians.

Father Pat, the curate, did go in for cures. He was an old priest, too, From the altar he was in the habit of using very strong language such as 'A pack of flaming faggots'. This was what he called the designers of the low-necked blouse which the women were beginning to wear.

The whole congregation laughed.

'Yes,' he said on another occasion, 'when you have a child sick you'll come for the penny doctor.'

The penny doctor was himself.

Sometimes he lectured on theology, his lecture consisted in repeating that 'The people that are going now are as ignorant as box-barrows.'

Father Pat was a hard man on Mass-servers, so hard that in the end none of the lads would serve for his Mass.

If we talked while he was vesting he knew punishments that would have taken the light out of Torquemada's eyes. He would make us lie on the floor with our noses on the tiles without moving for five minutes. We were like faithful Moslems at sunset, except that we didn't face Mecca. He addressed me as Cobbler, and had me face the congregation one Sunday and demonstrate how to draw a waxed-end.

A priest can't say Mass without a clerk, and there came a morning which found Father Pat in this dilemma.

Up and down through the aisles he marched, peering in and out between the legs of big men where he knew he might find a truant clerk. And he spotted me.

'Ha, Cobbler,' he grinned, 'come out here,' and he put over his hand and caught me by the ear. He led me up to the altar by the ear as a man would lead an unhaltered colt.

Father MacElroy made long, long sermons on all sorts of subjects. If he had lived he might have given a tight race to Huey Long for the speech-marathon championship of the world.

The patient hearts of his hearers were broken, but what could they do?

Going home on his side-car, he would shout:

'Did I do that well, Biddy?'

'Oh, it was grand, Father, God bless you, it was grand.'

On Candlemas Day, 1916, I was serving mass for Father MacElroy. I think I had helped him to bless the candles, though I'm not sure, but at any rate I helped to sell them. There was a brisk demand. At the end he gave me a blessed candle for myself and sixpence. I bought the morning newspaper, which cost a halfpenny, and turned for home. On the road near the chapel I met a little boy. I knew him, but just to let him know, I asked him who he was. He was a Protestant, the son of a church sexton

who every Sunday rang the Protestant church bell which had a
sound like a cracked pot, we used to say.

The lad didn't give me a suitable reply, so I began to use
third-degree. He ran in to his father crying: 'Daddy, Daddy, I'm
choked.' I didn't try to choke him. I was frightened and ran for
it. I had got a start of a few hundred yards when, looking round,
I saw the church sexton taking as it were the range. He hitched
up his pants and came hot-foot after me. I ran. All the people I
met stared at me wondering what mischief I had done. I wasn't
thinking. I was merely running. Behind me my pursuer was
gaining ground. He was within fifty yards now. I met a man
going with his horses to plough, and Mr Sexton shouted:

'Stop him, stop him, he choked my son.'

The ploughman looked upon this act of mine as a recommen-
dation. 'I'll not stop him,' he roared, 'but I'll stop you. You
Orange dog.'

And he did hold him up sufficiently long to let me get a fresh
start.

He came again, like a bear robbed of her whelps. Fifty yards
behind.

> Anigh draws the chase
> With unperturbed pace.

I met a half-wit. Willie shouted out: 'Stop him.' He was wiser
now. 'Who is he?' he asked.

'That's young Kavanagh,' the half-wit replied. I was vexed,
yet had I but known it I was saved.

My pursuer ceased running now that he knew who I was. He
walked towards my home. I crossed the hills and hid among the
whins for a while. When, as I thought, the storm had blown over
I went down the worn, green face of the hills and home. I was
shocked. The church sexton was standing on our kitchen floor
quoting bits out of the Bible. My parents were showing great
deference to him. Tom Hales, a journeyman shoemaker who
hailed from Belfast, was hopping with religious rage on his seat
and hammering away at his last like a mad man.

'Will you come here at once, you bla'guard?' my mother

whined affectedly. 'Will you come here and tell us what you done?'

The sexton cross-examined me.

'Did you meet my Bob at our gate?'

'I didn't pass your gate,' I said, 'I came across the hills.'

'Eight, thou shalt tell no lie,' he texted. 'In our religion the first thing we're taught is to tell the truth.'

He got no satisfaction out of his race and I got no beating. There were some, and the journeyman cobbler was one, who said I should get a medal for my deed.

'I never took you to be the man you are,' Tom Hales said, 'you stood up for religion as good as any Belfast Catholic ever did.'

On the Thursday evening preceding the first Friday of each month two girls, a boy and myself, left school a half-hour early. We were carrying out a religious practice known as making the Nine Fridays. The saint who initiated this devotion was promised by Christ Himself that whoever made the Nine Fridays should not die unrepentant. That was a very big promise. But it wasn't the promise of death-bed grace that attracted us. What drew us was the fact that we got out of school a half-hour early to go to Confession. I made the Nine Fridays without a break for at least five years. It has given me great confidence.

When we got out on the road the first people we saw were the two women in long navy-blue cloaks. They were also making the Nine Fridays. Inseparable companions were these two women. They walked with long, striding steps shoulder to shoulder near the water-table where macadam was carpeted with soft dust. They looked like twins, though they were not related. They conversed in low, slow, devotional whispers. Nobody knew what they were saying, though I often heard the neighbours say:

'That pair of oul' hesps! Talkin' about their neighbours they are and nothin' else.'

'Indeed yer right, it's not for holiness they're goin', the greatest pair of voteens from here to Timbuktu.'

This was cruel comment, yet at that time we were inclined to agree with it.

We passed them at the same place every time. Their heads would be bowing up and down slowly, keeping time with their talk.

Further on the road we came up with another pair of older women. The first pair was unmarried and childless, these had their families reared and were enjoying the consolations of the Church and the pleasant gossip of the roads. They had emptied the purse of the world and were now, as they deserved to, sampling the good things of Heaven. When we arrived at the turning for my home my three companions waited while I hid my school-bag in the nettles beside the railway gate-house.

All of us lived along the road to the chapel – up long lanes the two girls; Larry, the boy, was only a short distance off the main road. Instead of hiding his bag he ran to his home with it.

Among the others who were making the Fridays were Mary O'Hare, who had a by-child, Rose Hanlon, who was married five years and had no children, John Moran who suffered from deafness, and many more who were afflicted in some way.

It wouldn't be fair to say that there wasn't a lot of genuine piety among the chapel-going crowd; but the good people aren't picturesque enough to imprint themselves on a young boy's memory. I have little memory for anything save the quaint and the bizarre.

Out of all our Nine Fridays I have only one thrilling experience to tell.

Not far from the school, as we were heading for the chapel, we came upon a man sitting on the grass margin eating beans. His trousers were torn and it looked as though he had fallen through a thorn hedge. He was a stout round-headed man of forty or so.

'Would ye have e'er a pin about ye?' he inquired.

We gave him several pins with which he fixed his immodest trousers. Then he rose and accompanied us along the road. He gave us beans and explained how he had fallen into McGeogh's garden.

When Larry left us to run home with his school-bag, the man with the torn trousers did . . .

I suppose he only earned a year in gaol. We didn't tell of the affair to any stranger.

When Larry came back I told him.

We made a great laugh about the business.

I remembered it, and that proves the rightness of the people's saying:

'The bad thing is aisy remembered.'

On our way to the chapel I remember one of the girls said:

'Should we tell it to the priest?'

'Oh, not at all,' the other girl said.

It wasn't an uncommon thing for people to confess everybody's sins save their own. 'I tell me little troubles to the priest,' they would say.

And that often meant telling how the neighbours were carrying on.

It wasn't right to eavesdrop at the confessional, but sometimes we couldn't help it. Father Tom was old and deaf, and on the eve of First Fridays the chapel would be full of solemn silence.

'Any other sin?' Father Tom asked.

A woman whispered something.

'Speak out,' Father Tom said.

'I'm heartily scalded of the Logans, Father,' we heard. 'That young flipe of theirs is abusin' me night, noon, and mornin'.'

'Anything else?'

'The Kennedy's goats are for ever trespassin' in our cabbage garden. I'm nearly losin' me temper with them.'

'And now for your penance,' the priest said. 'Say the Litany of the Saints twice a day for a fortnight.'

I was shocked. Such a penance was cruel. I had almost a mind to leave my place beside the confessional. Father Tom gave these long, hard penances to keep penitents away from his box. But in this case the punishment fitted the sins very well.

When we four schoolchildren got out of the chapel we compared notes.

'What penance did you get?'

'One Our Father and three Hail Marys.'

'Oh, ye must have toul' him nothin'.'

'I toul' him too much.'

'I got two litanies to say.'

'Oh, Holy Smoke, ye must have murdered someone to get such a dose.'

Outside the chapel a priest was walking up and down taking the air after the atmosphere of sin in the confession box. Over in the graveyard were a few men and women searching among the nettles for the graves of their relations. There was a goat standing on its hind legs scooping the bark off a yew tree.

The old women came out from the chapel one by one and waited at the door for their own particular companions. They looked at peace. They said:

'Father Pat's a grand gentleman.'

'Ye couldn't bate him.'

'I saw Peter Harvey there.'

'Thank God. He was a long while from his duty.'

On Friday morning we were excused late arrival in school. We had been to Holy Communion. Miss Cassidy kept the Roll open for us. She said: 'I'll expect you to be very good to-day. You have Our Lord in your souls.'

We in return tried to look our holiest.

By the grace of God the experience of sexual perversion passed us by as an idle wind.

Through the filter of innocence no tainted waters pass. But I remembered.

4 Feasts and Feasts

For weeks before Easter we looked forward to the feast – not the religious Feast, spelled with a capital, but the picnic out in the fields under some tree which we called 'the feast'. Sometimes we made a collection among ourselves and parents for the purchase of bread and tea and sugar and jam, sometimes our parents supplied all the viands but more often left us to our own devices.

Easter was approaching and the prospects of a feast for us were growing duller and dimmer. Neither my companions nor myself had a penny or the chance of getting one. So we set our wits to work. When Barney the Bottle could make a livelihood solely by collecting old bottles, surely, we decided, we could make as much as would give us a good feast of tea, bread, and jam. Easter Sunday was the day when everybody gorged himself with boiled eggs. Our parents always supplied the eggs – not without a grumble.

We started gathering bottles – porter bottles and whisky bottles; neither wine or medicine bottles were saleable, for what reason I don't know. Collecting bottles was considered the lowest form of meanness – worse in fact than accepting the Poor Law Relief or ordinary begging. But what did we care?

Coming home from school we searched along the banks of drains and in quarries where thirsty men often worked. We were very successful. One evening I found a round dozen porter bottles stuck down by the railway paling. They must have been a long time there, grass and twining herbs made them appear almost part of nature. Inside the green glass was covered with dead snails and red worms. I was very proud of my find, I expected at least a halfpenny each for the bottles. There were three other boys bunching with me, and when Holy Week arrived we brought all our bottles together and found that we had four dozen and a half.

John Gorman was a few years older than I and a good deal

39

cuter. I never hoped to reach his standard of intelligence, and I hated him on that account. He had washed his bottles *en masse* by putting them in a sack and dipping them up and down in a well.

'Go in to yer oul' one,' he said to me, 'and get a basket: it will look more like the thing to have the bottles in a basket.'

The 'oul' one' was what some children called their mother, and the 'oul' fella' was their father.

I didn't want to let my parents know I was engaged in a Barney the Bottle business.

'They'll do rightly in a bag,' I said.

'We'll be makin' little of our stuff if we haven't a basket,' he said. 'Go on in and get a good egg-basket.'

'The egg-basket is full,' I said.

'Well, take a fowl basket.'

I consented, and stole out with a large hamper that had two handles. We laid the bottles in it carefully and proceeded to MacNello's pub in Inniskeen. It was very heavy, a half-hundredweight or more, and we were well tired when we landed our cargo at MacNello's door.

John Gorman wouldn't come in. 'You go in and make the dale,' he said, 'your people dale in this shop and our don't.'

My lips were watering at the thought of the feast, so I buried my pride and dragged the basket of bottles after me into the shop.

'What the devil has young Kavanagh in the basket?' John Duffy, the head clerk said to me, and by way of an aside to the other customers.

'Bottles,' I said in a shamed way.

'Bottles,' he repeated, 'and musha what are yer doin' with a basket of bottles?'

'My father sent me with them,' I said.

'Well, yer the two ends of a liar,' he declared, 'but in any case we'll take a look at them. How many have ye got?'

'Four dozen and a half,' I replied, 'and all good bottles.'

'The bottles are all right,' he admitted. 'We'll give ye thruppence a dozen for them.'

'Thruppence a dozen!' I gasped.

'That's what we're givin' for oul' bottles,' he said, 'and only yez are customers here we wouldn't buy them good or bad.'

I was always good at arithmetic, as Miss Cassidy agreed, and I wasn't long doing the sum, four dozen and a half bottles at threepence a dozen – one shilling and a penny halfpenny. The feast that my imagination had spread under a huge elm now dwindled to a plain loaf of bread and tea. I was done for. Outside John Gorman was waiting. Once or twice he peeped in.

'How did ye fare?' was the first question he popped when I came out. He looked into the basket and then at me.

'Arrah damn its skin,' he cried, 'why did ye forget the jam and the currant-bread?'

'Damn to your skin,' I returned, 'how did ye expect a fella to get jam and currant-bread and everythin' for one and a penny ha'penny?'

'One and three ha'pence,' he said with a puzzled air, 'surely to the good God ye got more nor that for the bottles?'

'That's all I got,' I said.

'They codded ye up to yer two eyes,' he jeered, 'they saw ye comin'. Yer the worst market man I ever met.'

That was the kind of John Gorman. Although I knew that nobody else could have made a better bargain under the circumstances, yet confronted by his gibes, I felt mean and stupid. The Gormans always had the knack of appearing right every time and of making the other fellow appear culpable even in his most innocent innocence.

We had our feast after all with jam and syrup, three kinds of currant-bread and three kinds of eggs.

Mrs Gorman supplied the eggs, goose egg, hen eggs, and green duck eggs. We held our feast on the top of Gorman's hill, under an old white thorn. We made our own fire and boiled our kettle over it; we hung the kettle by a wire from a sour-looking limb of the white thorn. There were seven of us at the feast, including the two dogs. The goose egg took fifteen minutes to boil – or we thought it should, owing to its bigness. When it was ready to be eaten we were already full and finished. The dogs were going around sampling the leavings. We wondered what to do with the goose egg.

'We'll hide it under a stone,' one of the girls suggested, 'and we'll not look at it till next year.'

This was done, and whatever happened to the egg we never found out. The next Easter, when we lifted the stone, there was no trace of the egg. We wondered long over the mystery of the missing egg, and never blamed the crows or the rats who might be having Easter feasts in their own hunted world and could not collect porter bottles to sell at threepence a dozen.

Easter Sunday was somebody's birthday, and somebody's mother gave us a halfpenny each. After the feast we went in a body to the huckter's shop to buy what is now called rock, but which we knew as jib. There was no jib in the shop, and instead we bought three boxes of matches. Coming home, we struck the matches on stones in bundles of twenty. That we knew was either a mortal sin or a crime. We swore secrecy. We crooked together our little fingers and swore: 'Finger in finger and never draw back and if I do may my hand be cut off to-morrow morning.'

Then we went home, locked in our oaths.

On summer evenings, when school was over, with the two Gorman lads who were about my age, six or seven perhaps, I played. Dark cryptic games sometimes.

One of our principal pastimes consisted in catching bees as they sipped the honey from the tiny blue forget-me-nots and dandelions which grew on the slope of the railway. We were cruel. We killed them and then we held a wake, had pipes and tobacco, and whisky. We held a funeral and buried the deceased bees, matchbox coffined, in pyramids of dust in the lane way.

We gave them a Pharaoh glory. But there was one notorious iconoclast in the district who, driving each evening in his cart, made it his business to draw the cart-wheel through our pyramidic grandeur. We had no answer, he knew it and laughed. He reckoned without the strategic genius of John Gorman.

'Leave Charlie to me,' he said knowingly.

My strategic genius rolled a huge boulder of stone on to the middle of the road, and over it raised a pyramid of dust. It was by far the finest memorial we had ever seen.

We saw Charles coming in his cart, singing, he could only sing to the accompaniment of a rattling cart. We hid behind the fence and waited.

Charles leaned over the side-board, one eye shut, taking aim with the wheel; he wanted to cut the heap of dust exactly in the centre.

'Oh, damn to their skins,' he roared as the cart jolted, jolted, jolted, and turned, horse and all, over on its side. He fell into a heap of nettles, but it was our laughter stung him worst.

John Gorman was a naturalist in his fashion. One evening in April or May he climbed a beech tree where was a wood-pigeon's nest with eggs in it. As he climbed down very gingerly I noticed that one of his pockets was full.

'What are you up to?' I asked.

'Never you mind,' he said, 'but I'll tell you what you're to do. You don't let the wood-pigeons near the nest or tree till I come back.'

He ran off towards his home while I sat under the tree keeping my eye skinned for the homing wood-pigeons. They did come, but I shooed them off every time till my companion arrived. He had pigeons' eggs in his cap.

'I'm after boiling them,' he said, 'and now we'll put the eggs back in the nest and see what'll happen.'

He did so.

The hen pigeon came and sat on the eggs and the cock looked on, now and then tooting a tune that made the cuckoos envious. He nor his wife did not suspect the impending tragedy. We kept the nest under close observation, or at least my companion did; every evening after school he watched it, and if I wasn't there, kept me in touch with events.

'She's sitting on them still,' he informed me four weeks later. John never tired watching the pigeon on the boiled eggs.

At the end of another month he again told me that the pigeon was still hatching in hope.

For three or four months the pigeon sat on the eggs, we could only see her beak over the brim of the nest. Then one day came and we saw no beak.

'I'll go up and investigate,' John said. He went up. As he

propped himself between the forked branches near the nest he shouted down:

'Be cripes, do you know what?'

'What happened?' I shouted up.

'There's what happened,' he said as he pitched the wood-pigeon's nest right at my feet.

The pigeon was dead, and the boiled eggs fell on the soft, tufted grass and were unbroken.

'She hatched till she died,' John said. 'Did you ever hear of better?'

'I never did,' I agreed.

5 Within the Charmed Circle

We were sitting around the fire one winter's evening when the latch of the door was lifted and a head all wrapped in bandages appeared in the lamplight.

'Come inside,' we called, and a man came in.

'I was lookin' for Harry McElroy's,' he explained.

'I was just thinkin' as much,' my mother said. 'On yer head ye have it, God bless it.'

'On me head it is,' he agreed.

The man had erysipelas, popularly known as 'the rose'. Any person named McElroy was supposed to be able to cure the disease by touching the afflicted part. Harry McElroy being the only one of the name willing to make the cure – it was considered unlucky – had a practice large enough to fill any doctor with envy. As his house lay along the Mucker Road we had many callers inquiring the way. Some of these people came twenty miles.

Our present visitor had come a long way on foot and being tired, we bade him sit down. There were some other visitors in the house, and the arrival of this other naturally turned the conversation on cures and charms and such-like.

'No matter what they tell ye, no doctor can cure the rose,' one said.

'Indeed they cannot,' all acquiesced.

'I remember a fella once tryin' his hand out with a doctor,' one of the journeymen shoemakers said, dropping his boot – he could never work and talk at the same time.

'And he got cured?' somebody else said with contempt.

'Oh, he got cured in the right oul' style,' said the shoemaker, 'he wore the suit of dale boards when the doctor was finished with him.'

'Of course,' my mother said, 'the doctors know right well they can't cure the rose.'

'To be sure they know it,' a customer said, 'but they wouldn't give in.'

'Some of them agree to the cure,' my father said, 'there was oul' Doctor McKenna and he always sent for Harry whenever he got a case like that.'

'The divil thank him,' the journeyman shoemaker said, picking up the boot which he had been stitching. 'The divil himself thank him,' he repeated, spitting out.

'Does Harry take anything?' the man with the bandaged head inquired cautiously.

'He's not too hard to dale with,' my mother told him.

'About how much would he be expectin'?'

'Anythin' from half a crown up,' he was told.

'I'm better be goin',' he said, rising from his chair.

My mother accompanied him to the door and directed him to Harry's house.

'The second house on yer right with the gable facin' the road – ye can't miss it. God sind ye good luck.'

'Thank ye, thank ye,' he said, moving off.

When he had gone we fell to discussing all the diseases doctors couldn't cure, and all the complaints of cattle which baffled the veterinary surgeons.

'See the harmless stye on the eye, and if he hadn't the cure made it would stick to you for ever.'

'Aye, and if the cure wasn't made in the moon that the stye came in, the bleddy little nuisance would keep comin' back till that moon came again.'

'There's the water-beetle, and nobody but a Cassidy has the cure of it.'

The water-beetle was an insect which, if taken by a cow-beast in a drink, caused it to swell up.

'I remember,' my father began, 'how our cow took sick and swelled up like a barrel. I knew none of the Cassidys would give in to making the cure, so one morning I stole round Cassidy's house and found a piece of rag which I burned under the cow's nose.'

'That was as good a way as any,' someone interjected with deep satisfaction. 'The baste got well, I'll warrant?'

'She did,' my father agreed, 'but the funny part of the story was – the bit of rag I burned wasn't belongin' to a Cassidy at all, it was a leg of the servant-boy's trousers.'

All heads bowed, humiliated. Nobody liked the end of the story, it was heretical.

'Well, what do ye think of Father Pat?' father was asked.

'I believe he has power,' he said.

'Ye believe it! Are ye not sure of it?' the journeyman said, dropping his boot again and staring at father very hard.

'I've only hearsay to go on,' father said.

'Hearsay,' the journeyman said, reaching away from his bench as though striving to reach the land of certain certainty. 'What about Biddy Brady's Katie, eh, what about her?'

'What about her yerself?' my father asked.

The journeyman was disgusted and withdrew from the distant land of the Druids to Christian Mucker. He lifted his boot and commenced hammering away like mad.

'Keep yer hair on, Tom,' he was advised.

'There's some people,' he growled, 'not mentionin' names, and they believe nothin', no more religion in them than in a dog.'

There sat in our kitchen a man whose name was Larry Tom; he was waiting while his boot was being repaired.

'Shadow on the wall, nothing on the floor,' I remember him saying. The phrase gave me a good ghostly thrill.

'Shadow on the wall, nothing on the floor,' my mother repeated. 'And is it a fact, Larry,' she went on, 'that yer getting trouble from something?'

'Too true,' he admitted, 'it's the Sonny to be sure.'

'Devil another,' my father said.

'And is he coming to ye since the day he done away with himself?' my mother asked.

'Since the day he put the noose on his own neck I didn't get a night's rest. Shadow on the wall, nothing on the floor.'

'Ah, maybe it's only some of the lads playing a trick on ye,' my mother suggested.

Larry eyed my mother like an old Moslem priest might survey a Christian infidel.

'Play-actin',' he sneered, 'lads to play-act on Larry, and me with a double-barrelled gun stuck in the thatch, as everybody knows. I'd like to see the man would play-act on Larry. Shadow on the wall, nothing on the floor, how does that come in?'

'Oh, it's the Sonny sure enough,' my mother had to admit.

My father had never any doubts as to the authenticity of the ghost; he had great faith.

'I offered any three men that would sit up with me and face the Sonny a pint of whisky apiece. But would they do it? And some of them that would give the eye in their head for a glass of whisky. Last night we were sitting on the settle-bed facing the open door when the shadow flattened itself on the wall at our backs. And the walls shook till you'd imagine they'd come down on top of us.'

We listened in wonder and I shivered as much as the walls.

'Ye should get Father Pat,' my mother suggested.

'That thought struck me too,' Larry said. Larry put on his boot and, as he was leaving, he was wished all sorts of success in his struggle with Sonny's ghost.

Everyone that entered our house that day talked about the poor Sonny coming back. To all of them my father repeated Larry's eerie phrase: 'Shadow on the wall, nothing on the floor.' I heard how the Sonny had been arrested for drunkenness and, in the struggle with the police, had lashed out with his boot and broken the serjeant's leg. He escaped himself without a mark or a flaw and made straight home and hung himself by the neck till he was half dead, and then hung on to the rope till he lost the wind. All the details were discussed.

'It takes a six-foot drop to break a Christian's neck,' one man said with an air of authority.

'And how many feet did *he* get?'

'He jumped from the top of a bag of oats,' the authoritative voice said, 'and to make a bad job worse, the bag slipped sideways, and he only more or less slithered down.'

'The poor fellar,' we gasped all round. The only thing that was worrying us all was would Father Pat take on to shift the Sonny.

'For if he takes on,' we agreed, 'he wouldn't be bested by a poor creature like the Sonny.'

'Ah, but *will* Father Pat take on?'

It was the winter of the year. At eight o'clock the ghost became due. At a quarter to eight on a certain evening Father Pat entered Larry's kitchen and sat on the seat of the settle-bed facing the door, which was left open. He was armed with nothing more holy than his umbrella and a smile on his face that was set at damnation-point.

'Leave him to me in the Name of God,' he said when he came, and all the household gladly took the hint and retired to the back-benches near the hob. There were a few well-wishers of Larry's to witness the ghost's overthrow, and now and then they bestowed on his reverence that look of the protected usually reserved for policemen.

Eight to the minute, Father Pat had looked at his watch as much as to say: 'If he's late I'll cut him a quarter.'

The ghost wasn't much after his time. Shortly after eight the gable-end of the house quaked. Father Pat rose to his feet. Shadow on the wall, nothing on the floor.

The priest's umbrella swung around like a flail as he shouted: 'Go to hell and be damned to you.' And the shadow vanished into that place that is all shade and no shadow, or so everyone agreed. In any case the Sonny never troubled Larry from that day out. Father Pat's stock soared on the spiritual Wall Street.

'Oh, he's a powerful gentleman.'

'Not an inch better than any of the rest of the priests if they'd do it.'

'Sure, they can all do it if they like.'

Strange how the lies get about, the little seeds of heresy which bud and blossom even among angels. One heretic declared that he knew the man was acting the ghost. 'Sure, everybody knows it,' he said, and added, 'I can give yous this much to know that Paddy Connell is not the better of the fret he got when he was confronted by Father Pat. He never imagined that the priest would actually come to lay the ghost.'

'Are you tryin' to tell us that Paddy Connell was the ghost?' a man of faith asked.

'Paddy was the ghost without a doubt.'

'Yer the two ends of a liar,' the man of faith declared. 'Yer

49

tryin' to belittle Father Pat. And it's a skamer like you would
cry the loudest for the holy gentleman if ye were sick or sore.'

'It was Paddy Connell all the same,' the heretic repeated.

'Get out to hell, ye infernal liar. I wouldn't believe ye unless
ye said God was good.'

6 Pilgrimage

On the eve of the feast of the Assumption, the fifteenth of
August, there was a tradition of thunderstorms and heavy rain.
To have started cutting the harvest before the Feast was a great
mark. Sometimes when there was an early harvest the last straw
would be in stooks by that day. It was a great Feast in our part
of Ireland, greater even than St Patrick's Day. On this particular
year the harvest was early, so early indeed that we had our patch
of oats cut just as the thunderstorm, true to tradition, came on.
Paddy Corbett was swishing the scythe through the last few
perches and keeping a sharp look-out towards the west.

'Twill be a bad evening for the Well,' he said. ''Twill indeed,'
the man who was binding agreed, 'and I wouldn't miss the Well
for anythin'. I haven't missed it these twenty years.' Then to me
he said: 'Were you ever at Lady Well?'

'I never was,' I answered, 'and I'd like to go.'

'Well, you can come with us,' Corbett said, 'we're taking the
horse and cart.'

Lady Well, about fifteen miles distant, was a place of pilgrimage for the people of Monaghan and Cavan and Louth. It was
one of the many holy wells of Ireland. Every year all the neighbours around me went there and carried home with them bottles
of its sacred waters. These waters were used in times of sickness
whether of human or beast. Some folk went barefoot and many
went wearing in their boots the traditional pea or pebble of
self-torture.

We had just reached our house when the thunderstorm broke.
Paddy Corbett, though a man of much physical courage, was
afraid of lightning and ghosts. He crouched in a corner of our
kitchen, praying: 'O Holy Mother of God, protect us.' My
father kept working away at the boots right in front of the window, a dangerous place. I looked out watching the beautiful
shapes and colours of the electrified elements.

'That was anchor lightning that time,' I said.

'Christ of Almighty, d'ye hear that fella?' Corbett exclaimed from his safe place behind the dresser.

'Fork,' I cried exultantly.

'Holy Mary, save us from the bloody fool that is tempting God,' cried Corbett.

I continued naming the lightning flashes as they signed themselves in radiant letters in the darkened page of sky, and each time Corbett groaned.

At the bottom of our garden the limb of a tall poplar crashed.

'The house is split in two,' Corbett shouted.

'You're a woeful coward,' my father said to him.

'It's right to fear God,' my mother said.

It was a fast-moving storm; in half an hour it had gone by and we could listen with some suavity to the far-away thunder shouting about the Hills of Down.

Corbett was somewhat ashamed now, he actually denied that he had prayed.

'The lightning's nothing at all,' he said.

Neither my parents agreed with this opinion.

'I'll go and get the horse and cart,' he said, 'and Paddy can be ready to meet us on the big road. Maybe you'd come too, Mrs Kavanagh,' he added.

'I will and welcome,' she said.

The horse-cart was filled with people, three seat-boards which seated three fat women, the driver, two children, and myself. I was sitting in the bottom of the cart on a basketful of eatables. One of the fat women suggested that there wasn't sufficient room on the seat-board. Beside me was a pile of bottles of all shapes, sizes, and colours.

'Are yez all right?' Corbett asked.

'All right, drive on in the Name of God.'

The horse moved off. We were going on pilgrimage. The light that came after the storm didn't delay long and it was quite dark by the time we had reached the main Dundalk road.

'Let's go the Bohar Bhee,' someone suggested. The Bohar Bhee means the yellow road. It was the pilgrim's road that twisted by quiet fields away from the clever villages that laughed at ancient holiness.

We went the Bohar Bhee. Paddy Corbett lit the candle in his lantern. There were big houses along the Bohar Bhee. Through the heavy leaf-dripping trees we could see lights like brown stars in the windows of mansions. Paddy Corbett kept informing us of who lived here and there and everywhere.

'I'd like to be at the Well before it rises,' one of the women said.

'We'll make it handy,' Paddy said.

'Did you ever see the Well rising?' I asked the woman whose large knees were stamping themselves in the small of my back.

She laughed softly. 'Tut, tut,' she said, 'don't ye know right well I saw it risin'. What makes ye ask such a question?'

I was a doubting Thomas. Nobody among our load ever doubted miracles, on whatever feeble evidence founded.

We passed many pilgrims, some of whom were barefoot, and some whose limping gait told of the pea in the boot. A fellow passed on a bicycle.

'I don't know what the world's comin' to,' one of our passengers said, referring to the cyclist; bicycles were rare then.

In about three hours we arrived at Lady Well. The road in the vicinity was like a rowdy bazaar-ground. There was singing, not of hymns, but of comic songs that had nothing to do with piety. There were beggars of all breeds.

Paddy Corbett tied up his horse, and the tail-board being pulled out we all got down.

'Thank God,' the women gasped together, as they stretched their cramped limbs.

The field of the Well belonged to the Protestant Rector, and to get to the Well there was no 'right of way'. The Rector was a bit of a bigot and everybody else as well at the time, for that matter. He locked the gate and to reach the Well it was necessary to climb over a brambly hedge. Each briar wound inflicted on a woman's face or leg meant a curse for the Rector.

We got over without much serious loss of blood and walked down the slope to the place where the Well was. All the vicinity of the Well was packed with pilgrims. Like the mediaeval pilgrims very probably; some were going round on their bare knees making the stations, some others were doing a bit of courting under the pilgrim cloak. There was a rowdy element, too, pegging clods at the prayers and shouting. A few knots of men were arguing politics. I overheard two fellows making a deal over a horse.

'Here, I'll divide that pound.'

'I won't divide a ha'penny.'

'Ye'll have luck in my money.'

'And ye'll have luck in my horse.'

There was a general push towards the Well. I edged my way after Corbett, who could shove like a Rugby forward, right to the brim of the Well.

The Well was roofed with galvanized iron and leading down to its mystic waters were seven or eight stone steps. On the top step squatted an old woman who looked as if she had stepped out of one of Hans Andersen's stories. She had a face on her like an old wizened turnip. Beside her was a collection of bottles.

Paddy Corbett saw me watching her and said:

'Mind yerself, that's Bullah Wullah's mother.'

She was known by this name. The Well overflowed, it was supposed, at midnight and Bullah Wullah's mother secured the first pure draught which she afterwards sold at a penny a bottle. It was close to midnight and excitement was high among the pilgrims waiting for the waters to move.

At the height of the tensity some tough fellow at the back, with the instinct of a true Irishman, hit the galvanized roof of the Well a blow of a stone. This event released the taut strings for a while.

'The wather is comin' up,' Bullah Wullah's mother sang out. She was busily filling her bottles. Through a hole in the lower roof a few boys were letting down on cords bottles to be filled. Sometimes the bottle struck against the sides of the Well and only the neck came back.

'Bad luck to yer awkward paws,' one of the bottle-danglers cursed, 'only for you that bottle wouldn't get cracked.'

There were no priests or monks or any official religious there. The priests didn't like the Well and tried to discourage the pilgrimages. They said it was a pagan well from which the old Fianians drank in the savage heroic days. The peasant folk didn't mind the priests. They believed that Saint Bridget washed her feet in it, and not Finn MacCoole.

I got a bottle of water and Paddy Corbett grabbed a bucket from someone's hand and filled as much as would drink a team of horses. The bucket splashed all round as we pushed our way out of the crowd to where my mother and the other women were waiting.

'Did you see the Well rise?' the woman I had doubt-queried in the cart asked.

'To be sure I saw it rising,' I said. 'But it was in Paddy Corbett's bucket.'

We groped our way by the cart-lantern light towards a quiet part of the fence along the road. The hamper of eatables was brought. Paddy Corbett carried it. There is something good in the basket, my empty stomach thought. I got a big mistake for what was in the basket was boiled potatoes.

'Lash in,' the waitress said.

'Lash in to what?' said Paddy Corbett. 'Lash in to cowld praties? Be damned to that for a story.'

'They're nice new praties,' the waitress said, 'and the divil cook yez betther. Troth it's yez at to be glad of thim.'

Hunger isn't very epicurean or finicky and we were hungry. We attacked the new potatoes and Paddy Corbett, to shock the women, washed them down with a draught of the holy well.

The women crossed themselves.

'The Lord save us,' they said.

We returned to the horse and cart. The horse was an old stager that didn't mind being left alone. During our absence he lunched on a bundle of hay that stuck out of a donkey cart. Hard times had sharpened the poor beast's wits and he managed to keep out hunger if fodder was anywhere in the vicinity.

We returned home. The stars lit us all the way and the bright stubbles of the corn-fields looked like quiet lakes laugh-dimpled with dark stooks.

My mother and myself were tired when we entered our house. She made us tea and God knows we needed it. We were so fagged out that we forgot all about the water from Lady Well.

We had been on pilgrimage anyway. It was four o'clock in the morning and we were weary in body and mind, but in soul perhaps fresh as rain-green grass.

Our Lady was a real lady and human, she was not displeased, I knew, because some who pilgrimed in Her name were doubters and some cynics and a lot of vulgar sightseers. She is kind and no doubt she enjoyed the comic twists in the pageant round Lady Well.

7 The War

I was lying in bed upstairs one evening when I heard a great commotion outside our gate. I heard a man cry: 'Good-bye, and God be with ye, for we may never return.'

I looked out of the window and saw a neighbour-man marching with a military air down the road. On his shoulder he carried a long gun. He had been bidding good-bye to my mother. When mother entered the house she said to father:

'Carson's army is comin' to Carrick and oul' Owney is off to fight him.'

'All nonsense,' father said. He didn't even drop his boot.

'Carson will fight,' the journeyman said, 'but so will we.'

Some weeks later there was another commotion in our house. I knew it must have had a real cause because father had left his bench and was talking excitedly to a crowd of men in the kitchen. He was telling them of Germany and Austria and Serbia. They were listening with their mouths open. Father must have been rather excited or he would not talk to people who listened with their mouths.

'The Germans will bate the world,' one of the listeners said.

'There'll be a price for our stuff,' another said.

It was August, nineteen hundred and fourteen.

As I stood by our road gate some time later a man passing shouted to me: 'Home Rule is shelved.'

Father bought the newspaper every day. I heard him read the headings.

'Belgian Field Army falls back.' I was very thrilled.

Father went to MacNello's shop and ordered a ton of flour. The manager hadn't the flour in stock, but he accepted the order and payment. Ten pounds was the price. It was two weeks before the shopkeeper could deliver the flour and the price in the meantime had gone up five pounds per ton. The shopkeeper was vexed and wanted father to pay the extra money. Father laughed

57

at him and said: 'I'd be delighted if you'd bring me to court till I'd make a show of you.'

Father also rushed out to Carrick and purchased large stores of leather and cobbler's wants. He bought a bag of spriggs which lasted till the War was over. These spriggs were made in Belgium. Neither love nor money would purchase their equal during those years – a fact which father impressed on his customers. The price of farm produce soared. Everybody was in great good humour. They had money in every pocket. Nobody in that district joined the army. All hopes were centred in a long war and no one was disappointed.

Men who couldn't read bought the papers and scanned the pictures. One man reading the pictures upside down saw a warship wrong side up.

'A ship sunk,' he told everybody that asked him for the latest news.

Children were now kept more regularly at school so as to be able to read the news of loud war and louder market. At school we all studied the map of Europe. Names like Kitchener and Von Kluck were household words in Mucker.

Every Sunday coming home from Mass I heard all around me:

'It's a great war for the farmer. Cattle up four pounds a head.'

'The German's a good soldier. Up the German.'

A month or two later mother took me with her to the egg and butter market in Dundalk. She tried to get me free on the train, but the ticket-checker stopped me and made my mother pay half-fare for me.

The soldiers stationed in Dundalk barracks were leaving for France that day. As the cavalry rode past the Market Square all the back-street women cheered and wept.

'God bless ye,' they cried, 'and may ye win the war.'

Many extreme Irish patriots were deeply moved and some of them joined in the cheering.

A military band played in the square that evening. They were recruiting. The band played 'The Boys of Wexford.' I saw a woman crying and a crowd around her striving to pacify her.

'Paddy listed,' she cried. 'Paddy listed. He was drunk with the music.'

'God help her,' my mother said.

Coming home on the train all the talk was about the man that listed.

The start of the war coincided more or less with the passing of the journeymen shoemakers. Their visits were now divided by long intervals. The pulse of their world was beating irregularly, to beat for the last time when one of the brotherhood, Jem Fagan, walked out our door. Jem was a small fellow with large brown eyes that burned like a pair of live coals. Father used to say that the devil was standing on his hind-legs in Jem, but on this last occasion that devil was tame and meek and forlorn. Jem was near the end of his tether. The workhouse was gaping to receive his body and spirit. His last visit was pathetic. The old fire was gone out of his soul and his big eyes were dim. Father gave him a few shillings and mother offered him a meal. He talked very little, he who once could keep talk with a congregation. He used to tell stories in which he would lose himself. One time, with breakfast before him, he began a tale and completely forgot to eat. I looked at Jem as one looks at something that might belong to another world and time. I looked at him as Saint Patrick must have looked at Ossian when that great Fenian returned from Tirnanogue.

Jem wouldn't stay. He sat for a short while on the bench where he once worked. He loosed out his cobbler's kit and spread the tools beside him. He was having dreams. He rose and went out. Mother saw him out and I followed. 'Where are ye headin' for?' mother asked. I didn't catch his reply. It was something touched with affected bravery. When we looked at the bench where he sat we found that he had left behind him, a remembrance of the good days of journeymen shoemakers, his cobbler's hammer and a crooked awl.

The coming of the war coincided also with the passing of another colourful tribe of beggars.

In the district where I lived there once flourished a beggary richly coloured and full of ironic pride. As I recall their fantastic ways and their quaint nicknames I realise what a lot of poetry has been crushed under the wheels of prosperity. They were not penny-in-the-gutter beggars, but real romantic people of the roads.

Biddy Dundee, Barney the Bottle, Paddy the Bread, Mary Ann the Plantain. These nicknames were not put on by common vulgarians. Those old folk of the roads were living records of a poetry-living people. They all came to our house, not to beg but to sell the potatoes and meal which they had collected among the farmers.

Biddy Dundee never came to our house save at night-time. As a result I only saw her by lamplight when she appeared to me romantic as Padraic Colum's *Old Woman of the Roads*. She was a tall, loose-limbed woman of about sixty years, with a nimble mind and a fluent tongue. I remember Biddy standing in the lamplight on our kitchen floor and heard her sing:

> 'You'll take the high road
> And I'll take the low road
> But I'll be in Sco-ot-land afore ye.
> For me and my true-love
> Will never meet again
> By the bonnie bonnie banks of Loch Lomond.'

Barney the Bottle hailed from Crossmaglen. He didn't carry a bag on his back, he pushed an old perambulator in which he collected bottles and jam-pots. Barney the Bottle pushed his delivery van close to the water-table. There was no fast traffic on the roads then. All tramps walk by the water-table, it is kinder to their feet.

Paddy the Bread was a blind man. He often surprised us children when we put out our tongue at him and made faces.

'Hau, ye long-tongued article,' he would shout, 'yer face is ugly enough as it is without you makin' it worse.'

Mary Ann the Plantain was another beggar with a rhythmic nickname. She talked to herself and was usually threatening with her stick invisible tormentors. 'Grabbers, grabbers, the divil will have the whole ship-load of ye yet,' she would say.

Rocksavage was a big farm of three hundred acres. It lay among the small farms. It was the headquarters of a once-great estate. The house in which the two lady-owners of Rocksavage lived was known among the older folk as the Big House. During my knowledge the Big House was in a poor condition. It was rich in memories of the days of fast race-horses. On the dilapidated walls of the horse-stables in Rocksavage were scrawled the names of race-horses famous in their time.

'Ah, Master Kildare was the horse,' I heard, and father told me of the time when Rocksavage was truly a Big House. When the race-horses galloped around the fields ridden by jockeys from the Curragh.

And I heard of that great day for Ireland at the Races of Carrick. There was a 'Gentleman's' Race. The Plunkets of Rocksavage were 'gentlemen'.

A non-gentleman named Gartlan was mounted on a Rocksavage horse. Plunket, the owner, felt a little off form perhaps.

'Get down off that horse,' one of the other riders said to Gartlan. 'This is a gentleman's race and you're no gentleman.'

Bashford was the fellow's name. He was an Orangeman and didn't like the Plunkets of Rocksavage who were Catholics.

Gartlan dismounted and Plunket got up in his place. From the saddle he addressed the crowd.

'There's a gentleman riding now and not a damned Orangeman in Ireland can order him down.' The crowd cheered.

'Men of South Monaghan,' Plunket went on, 'don't lay your bets till my horse goes over the third fence.'

It was a great race. Plunket's horse was heavily backed. Bashford staked his large estate and all his money on his own horse. The Rocksavage horse won. Bashford left the course a beggar. A subscription list had to be opened to keep him from the workhouse. That was a day to remember, and the people did remember.

During the Great War Rocksavage farm was let in con-acre[1] on the eleven months' system. The letting was a godsend to the neighbourhood. Small farmers who before had only one old horse or a jennet now kept a pair of horses.

The letting was held in December. There would be a barrel of porter for the customers. The porter and the soaring prices of farm-produce combined to set the bidders merry.

I went with father to the letting. It was a bitterly cold day. In the cobbled yard behind the Big House a large crowd were gathered. The porter was being handed round in tin porringers

1. Con-acre: land let to farmers by the year.

by a hunchback. There weren't enough porringers. I saw one old man with a bucketful of frothy porter on his head. Tinkers, chimney-sweeps, professional porter-drinkers, they were all there. The auctioneer was waiting in the Big House till the porter would have time to work. Father had come to take an acre for potatoes. The auctioneer came out at last. He was a big, fat man with a glass eye. He mounted the stone steps of an old loft. He cracked a few dry jokes to test the temper of his audience. The laugh-replies were satisfactory. The porter was beginning to barm in bellies.

All the bidding was done by a nod of the head. There was an old fellow who suffered from head-shakes. The auctioneer accepted this fellow's reflex-action as an authentic bid. Everybody laughed.

When all the land in the vicinity of the Big House had been let, we trailed through the muddy fields. Puddles of yellow water filled the cattle tracks. There was only the ghost of the sun low in the sky. I shivered.

The auctioneer stood on a knoll in a stubble field. Those men who were hungriest for land gathered in close. Only one woman was among the crowd. There was no chivalry. She had to out-bid the field.

The stubble-field was put up for potatoes or turnips. Father bid fifteen pounds an acre. There was a lull. I thought the crowd were giving him a chance. I was mistaken. A near-neighbour nodded his head.

Sixteen pounds bid, seventeen, eighteen, twenty, twenty-five.

Father was the highest bidder. He took one acre. If his rival had been the highest he would have taken the whole field, he was buying for profit and not out of necessity.

I worked in all the fields of Rocksavage and developed a home-lover's sentiment for them. I knew every corner of those fields, and every well and stream.

Some of the fields possessed aristocratic names such as the Sundial, but others, like Eden Bawn, which means 'the bright face', told of the days when there was poetry in the land.

Rocksavage filled a great place in our lives. Before the War there were thousands of beautiful trees on the farm. Close to

our school these trees leaned over the wall and dropped us nuts –
monkey-nuts for making toy-pipes, horse-chestnuts of which we
made whistles and hazel-nuts which we ate.

Then came the timber-hunger and the trees began to fall.

> 'O what will we do for timber
> The last of the woods are down?'

No wonder the old Gaelic poet, lamenting the destruction of the
woods of Kilcash, sang so sadly.

Rocksavage trees were sold by auction. The man who bought
one cut down five as there was nobody to stop him. Father
didn't buy any of the trees. There were no young, strong men
in our house to help. There was no love for beauty. We were
barbarians just emerged from the Penal days. The hunger had
killed our poetry and we were mere animals grabbing at the
leavings of the dogs of war. Money was pouring in every front
door and pouring out the back door. Our house had no back
door.

At school we wrote compositions on the War. I got a home
exercise to write. Father wrote it for me – 'On Submarine War-
fare'. A very profound essay, it quite flabbergasted Miss Cassidy.

On the classroom wall was hung a map of Europe, coloured
red for the Allied nations, green for the Germans, and white for
the neutral nations.

An inspector came in one day. He examined us on our war-
knowledge. I knew every general on both sides. The inspector
said I should be a colonel. Miss Cassidy was very pleased.

The money was coming into our house in a steady stream.
Our hens were good layers – Black Minorcas and Brown Leg-
horns. Our parents paid more attention to the fowls than they
paid to us children. The hens were laying golden eggs.

Father and a constable of the Royal Irish Constabulary joined
in sending to Kent, in England, for a pair of prize cocks. The
constable was a fanatical hen-fancier. The pair of prize cocks
arrived at the Inniskeen railway station. Through the crate father
and the constable surveyed the birds. One of the cocks was a
real prize bird, a fellow with a fine curving tail and a rose-red
comb. The second bird looked like a starved chicken that had

been out in the rain. His comb was pale, and his tail-plumes would not be decorative in a woman's hat.

The constable suggested drawing lots and father agreed. Father won and the constable had to take the poor scraggy bird. Even though father won he declared that that would be the last time he'd have anything to do with a pig-in-a-poke business.

During the War money grew on the tops of the bushes. Blackberries were five shillings a stone. Rocksavage farm was the home of briars, rich fruit-bearing briars ignored by all the money-grubbers. Very few people ate blackberries, the one man who did we thought a bit touched on that account. Myself and two sisters were sent out each morning with cans and porringers.

'Go out and push your tenants,' our mother told us.'Whoever has the most in a dinner-time will get something.'

Very few children were gathering the berries, it was considered a mean business and there was a lot of pride among the people. So we had nearly all the berries to ourselves. We could each of us pick two stones per day and more if we chanced upon a real good spot. Before setting out we arranged our different routes.

One day I had the fox-covert plantation; it was on top of a high hill looking across to Cavan and Meath. Up here the blackberries grew in wonderful abundance, good ones the size of big plums. I filled my can full to the brim in a short time. I was raking in the money. All I had to do was pull the berries off in fistfuls.

Harvest men were working in the same field and when I had my can filled I went down among the golden sheaves and the sunny music of the reaping machine. My bare legs were raw with briar-scratches, and the stubbles when I sat down stung me. My hands were blue with berry-dye and my face as well – we used to stain our faces with the first blackberry.

Blackberrying was a great way of seeing the secrecies of the good earth, the rabbit-holes and the fox-dens that seemed to open into a fairyland, and the strange untrodden places in briary corners where a child could explore.

Rocksavage was a fine place for a dream-wanderer. There was no caretaker, or at least, no one to trim the hedges and whins where the fairy folk hide. The whins on the Forth Hill grew ten feet high, and in between them were magical countries where cowslips and banshees' thimbles grew. The banshee's thimble was a wild foxglove. I once put the thimbles on my fingers and was told that the Banshee would call for me before a year.

We lived long and happy days in that blackberry time. The world that was Rocksavage was boundless and uncharted as the broad places of the imagination. Time had no say in that place, a day could be as long as a dream. We were in the Beginning, before common men had driven the fairies underground.

On top of the Forth Hill was the Forth with its three royal rings and its cave in the middle. The cave I often heard ran to join another Forth five miles away. No one had ever been able to get the end of it till Ned Gilligan backed into it with a flash-lamp and declared when he came out that it was only ten or twelve feet long. I would have been disappointed but I didn't believe him, I knew there must be a secret door which the flash-light of science couldn't find, a door which led far away, far away.

We had ways of adding to the weight of our blackberries, we added water or sand. I thought of the people who would be using bramble jam and swore I'd never taste bramble jam the longest day I'd be alive.

Once we met a crowd of blackberry gatherers advancing towards our preserves. We advised them to go to another place where we said there were a terrible lot of blackberries and crab-apples. This crowd were also gathering crab-apples which were ten shillings a stone. The crab-apple business was a chancy one, like digging for gold, you might come upon a tree and make a small fortune, but the chance was greatest that you'd have all your walk for nothing. We wanted these people to chase the elusive crabs so that we might have the certain blackberries for ourselves. Selfish, of course! They turned at our advice and we were glad. I can still remember that it took ten porringers full to fill a can.

'How are you off?' I could often hear my sisters call to one another.

'Oh bad, only the bottom of the porringer covered.'

'I have three porringers full.'

'Give me a lock, you'll make a show of us.' We would shake

up the berries in our cans on our way home so as to make them look fuller. I once saw a man giving oats to a strange horse, he twirled a small quantity round in the bucket so that the grain stood high round the edge. So did we with the blackberries. We put the berries in a forty-gallon barrel which when full had a few buckets of water added to ... make the fruit more juicy, I suppose.

8 At the Shrine of Luck

'No matter, Pat, I'll come back to the gamble,' the servant boy's last words were as he left our district.

The gambling craze was in my blood, too. For years I spent every Sunday from Mass time till dark watching the spinning coins.

All over the country it was the same – toss schools at every cross-road.

'I'm goin' to the gamble,' I'd tell my mother.

'Well here's sixpence,' she'd say, and spit on it for luck, 'I don't know how it is that you always lose.'

I explained to her that it all depended on luck, and that as luck was supposed only to turn every seven hours, a man with a bare sixpence was liable to get broke in the meantime. Sixpence was all I got.

Down to the nearest gamble in a feverish hurry. A large crowd were gathered in a circle on the centre of the road.

A fellow had the halfpennies placed on the tosser and was waiting for some argument to subside before he spun the coins.

'A penny ye harp them,' I said.

'Take yer penny home and frame it,' the tossing-man replied. He was dealing in big money and had no use for a petty financier like me.

The coins were tossed, every pair of eyes turned up and followed the coins to the road. One halfpenny rolled on to the grass-margin.

'Hi! don't disturb the grass,' the tossing-man cried. 'Yez I'll turn the ha'penny.'

'I never saw such a scattery oul' tosser,' another man said.

On the centre of the road one man stood guard over the bets while the others searched for the missing halfpenny.

'Here she is,' a fellow sang out as he lifted the coin with gingerly fingers, 'here she is and I didn't turn her.'

There was a good sum of money on the road for it was the flush years.

Lads like myself often went to the toss-school with a sixpence or perhaps only a penny, and sometimes these small coins bred a large family for us. There were many rows and heated arguments over disputed bets. Two-headed halfpennies were in use also; the two-headed coin was made by filing down the tail-side of the two halfpennies and soldering them together. Such a coin put Luck on the dole.

It was a beautiful day in the summer of perhaps nineteen-sixteen. Beauty, beauty was everywhere but it was money we were after. How many precious hours did I squander, my eyes looking no higher than the toss of a pair of red halfpennies.

'A tanner ye tail them.'

'Done with ye.'

'Here's another.'

'Here's its brother.'

That was poetry I listened to and myself recited.

'Lift yer boot off that shillin',' I heard a man shout.

'Who's standin' on a shillin'?' the other demanded to know.

'You are.'

'Yer a stinkin' God-damn liar.'

Then the row began. I edged out from the crowd for the temperature there was too high. A man received a punch in the mouth, and retaliated by hitting the gravel. The gamble broke up. The scattered money-spinners sat on the side of the road. Talk was vague and far away; the row had brought back the dreamer that each man really was.

'That's a hell of a fine day.'

'Ye have yer share of it.'

'Look at the crows,' I said entering into the argument. I remember those crows, they were flying at an altitude higher than I had ever seen crows fly.

We all looked up and wondered perhaps that our eyes were made to see so high.

A hundred yards down the road a well-dressed man dismounted from his bicycle and lit a cigarette. As he rode past one of the fellows in our crowd got up and snatched the cigarette from the man's lips. The cyclist rode on, he was a pacifist, and the other fellow enjoyed the cigarette.

This joke restored our balance. Another famous gambler came up on his bicycle and, dismounting, surveyed us all.

'Yez look like men were after seein' a ghost,' he said. 'Why aren't yez tossin'?'

'You rowl a pair,' he was told.

He searched in his trousers pocket and produced a handful of silver and copper. He picked out two halfpennies.

'Who'll give me a George for this oul' Victoria ha'penny?' he asked.

Slowly the gamble began to gather momentum.

'I was starved for a gamble,' the new man said.

I went home and had my tea.

'Ye lost as usual?' my mother said. As usual she was right. No matter how well I did the detective-story *sang-froid* she could tell if my pocket was empty.

'I'm in the way of makin' money,' I said. 'My luck was just ready to change when I got broke.'

I managed to forage out a penny from a pocket in the house wardrobe – five nails stuck in the wall was the wardrobe. When I returned to the toss-pit, there were many new faces among the crowd and old MacGeogh was there with his greyhound Spot.

'Here, young fella,' he said to me, 'I'll bet ye a penny he harps the ha'pennies.'

'Done with ye,' I said. 'I'll be a sport.'

The coins fell two heads and two heads again and again till I had a shilling won. I was right about my luck changing.

'Ye'll rob me,' MacGeogh said.

'Sure yer rotten with money,' I said, 'ye won't miss it.'

He laughed; he liked people to say he had plenty of money: he wasn't a poor-mouth. Luck is a king and Luck is a beggar.

I saw one of the strongest gamblers get broke.

'Lend us a half-dollar,' he asked a fellow.

'Honest to Christ, Joe, I can't, I'm ridin' on the rims myself.'

'Well, give us a bob.'

'I'd give it and welcome, only that I'm just now gettin' into a run of luck, and that might change it.'

'Aw, it's all right, Peter,' the disappointed one said. 'I'll see ye for this some other day.'

The light was beginning to fail. It was decided to toss two shillings, they would show up better on the road.

'Get a stump of a candle,' a man suggested.

'Here,' another said, 'if you fellas would stand out a bit we could see somethin'.'

'That's right, stand out and let the light in.'

'Yez may do as I say, get a stump of a candle.' This speaker called me aside. 'Run up to yer house and get us a stump of a candle, good man.'

I wasn't thanked when I produced the candle.

'Get down on yer knees, chaps, and we'll have the candle here in the middle.'

They stood the lighted candle on the road and knelt around on one knee, all save the tossing-man, who knelt on both knees.

The moon rose above Cassidy's hills and a wisp of a summer night's hair turned to silver.

'If the beggar of a moon had to get up in time we could have done without the candle.'

'Yer all right as ye are,' the men who were winning said. 'Man, but it's a grand evenin'.' The men who were losing didn't appreciate the beauty of the evening.

A pair of lovers strolled past, and another and another pair. I was broke by this time and was free to observe the innocent things. My perception was very acute when I got broke beyond hope. I can remember the scents that blew across the road. Hedgerow incense for the shrine of luck. I saw the candle-lit faces of the gamblers and knew that there was something in the sight memorable and romantic. Luck had a lighted candle on his altar; from my bedroom window as I undressed I could see the steady light and hear the voices of the devotees.

'Heads a tanner.'

'Done with ye.'

'Don't be down-hearted, Jemmy, luck changes every seven years.'

I fell asleep, and dreamt perchance of Luck the King.

9 Relations

One Sunday morning Oul' Quinn arrived on a visit to us. When we came home from Mass the donkey cart was heeled up in our yard and the black ass was grazing in the meadow.

'Oul' Quinn is down at yez,' a lad passing our gate remarked to me.

'I believe so,' I said.

My maternal grandfather, Pat Quinn, whom we knew as Oul' Quinn, lived near Ardee, ten Irish miles away. He came but seldom to our house as he had a large contempt for father, who was a small man. Oul' Quinn hated small men, not that he was a giant himself. He had a big voice and a pair of small black eyes deeply sunken in his head. He had worked in England and saved a good deal of money, with part of which he bought a small farm. His son, Uncle Jemmy, worked the farm and also did some cobbling: he had served his time with my father before I was born.

Inside our kitchen the old man was sitting, talking in that rasping voice of his about the kind of beef tea the landladies used to give him in Leeds.

'She tried to skim the top of it,' he said, 'but I soon showed her.'

Oul' Quinn liked me because I had big bones, a big voice and could eat fat bacon. He liked a person who could eat fat bacon. He didn't like delicate people and fell out with one of his sons because he had married for love a puny girl. He was an unconscious disciple of Nietzsche. I must have been eleven years old at that time.

He looked me up and down. He searched in his trousers pocket. 'Come here,' he said to me. I thought he was going to give me at least a half-crown. Instead he handed me a black penny. I took it. I could speculate the penny in the toss school and perhaps it would breed.

'Did you cut any turf yet?' father asked.

'I did not,' he replied, 'and that's what brought me here.'

He was looking for me to come and wheel turf.

'Tomorrow mornin', if all goes well, we'll be startin',' he said. 'Will ye come?' he asked me.

'To be sure I'll come,' I said.

The next morning I started off for Oul' Quinn's place. I went on foot. Even then bicycles were something of a luxury. Only two of father's customers came on bicycles and on these two machines I learned to ride.

I was content to walk. I hadn't developed a speed complex. It was a morning in May and there was a slight frost on the grass. As I passed Meegan's house, Mrs Meegan was standing in the doorway.

'Musha, where are ye goin' at this hour of the mornin'?' she asked. That was her way of being inquisitive without being blunt. At any hour of the day she would have asked the same question.

'A little bit of journey,' I said.

'Hope there's nothin' wrong,' she said.

'Damn to the thing,' I assured her.

Further on the road I passed MacEntaggart's house. Old Mac, as he was called, was an ex-schoolmaster. He taught in the same school that I had attended. He was dismissed for drink. My father spent one day at MacEntaggart's school and thought one day too long. Old Mac was a rough schoolmaster. He was one of the most inquisitive men you could know.

'Good morning, young man,' he addressed me.

'Good morning,' I returned.

'Lovely morning,' he said.

'Not too bad,' I agreed.

'How's your father and your mother?'

'They're very well.'

'Have you many pigs?'

'Twelve,' I lied.

'Ahem, ahem,' he coughed. 'Did you see John MacCaffrey as you came along?'

'Damn to the sight or sight.'

'Where are you going?'

'To a turf bog.'

'Who are you going to work for?'

'Oul' Quinn.'

'Can you spell Antitrinitarians?'

'I must be moving,' I explained.

I moved off and though I didn't look back I could feel his schoolmaster-quizzical eyes on the small of my back like indigestion.

As I walked along the road I was working out a solution for an algebraic problem in my mind. Mental arithmetic was my strong suit. I knew nothing of algebraic symbols. I worked on hypothesis. It was my habit before setting out on a long journey to select a difficult equation from an arithmetic book I had. I could hold twenty or thirty digits in my mind. At that time I believed that the greatest problem ever propounded in figures wouldn't have baffled me. Miss Cassidy was right – I was good at arithmetic.

When I had travelled a few miles I was in the country of turf fires. I like the smell of turf-smoke. This was also the country of goats and donkeys. In my own district the goat and donkey were passing out; they were too spiritual animals for a people who had begun to take their gospel from the daily newspapers.

The houses I passed had not been repaired or remodelled for a hundred years. The people who lived here were come-day-and-go-day God-send-Sunday folk. Every half-door had a woman leaning over it. The menfolk were going to the turf-bogs with their sleans on their shoulders. I was used to slow, contented workmen, but these were slower than anything near home. They were intelligent as Chinese in a philosophic way and were well up on foreign affairs. One of them to whom I spoke asked me what I thought of what he called 'the Pope's peace proposal'.

'The Pope couldn't settle a sparrow-fight,' I said.

'My God!' he said sadly.

These people weren't too particular about morals. There were six pubs in the parish and the illegitimate children equalled the others.

I arrived at Oul' Quinn's place without mishap. My uncle had already gone to the bog. Oul' Quinn was sitting by the fire attending to a pot of cabbage.

'Good man,' he roared as I entered. 'Jemmy is in the bog.'

I looked in the pot. The cabbages were boiled to jelly and he kept stirring it with a pot-stick. A big lump of bacon turned awkwardly to the touch of the pot-stick. The turf-fire was as good as a range: there were three cooking places on the hearth. On one side of the pot of cabbage a cake was baking, on the other flank the teapot sat among the red ashes. It was a big teapot. My grandfather made tea sufficient for the whole day in one fill of the teapot. First thing in the morning he filled the teapot. He liked strong tea and this stuff ought to satisfy anybody.

'Fill yerself out a mug of tay,' he said, 'and take a pair of them eggs off the dresser.'

I did that.

The bread I ate was made from white flour but had been baked so long that it was brown. I never tasted sweeter bread and I said so. Grandfather laughed. 'That's none of yer raw bread,' he said, 'with a stripe in the middle.'

We sat a while talking. He praised England.

'The people in this country never get their fill to ate.'

'You're a Tory,' I said.

'I'm a Tory,' he laughed, 'a good oul' Tory.'

'Time I was heading for the bog,' I said.

'Time enough,' he replied. 'Go out and catch the ass and harness him; the winkers is up there on the thalidge.'

The thalidge was a sort of semi-loft made from rough planks laid across the side walls in the lower end of the kitchen. With the aid of a chair I climbed on to the loft. Between the thalidge and the thatched roof was quite dark and rich with ancient smells. It was an interesting place where one might expect to find an old pike or a Fenian gun. I crept over the planks on my belly.

'What are ye doin' up there?' the old man shouted. 'Get the winkers and come down.'

I came down from that museum that never had known a curator. The ass was grazing in the meadow through which flowed the River Dee, a lazy, sedge-bordered stream. It was a stallion ass. He was feeling gamey on this day for it was the courting season for asses. I got the winkers over one ear but over the other I couldn't. He took the bit with a wild snap. He wasn't a very kindly animal.

Grandfather helped to yoke the ass to the cart. We put dinner for two in a basket, and the door was locked. The dog was called and came bounding from his den in a clump of turf.

'That's a brave dog,' I remarked.

'He'd be nothin' to me if he wasn't,' Oul' Quinn replied. 'He's a good fightin' dog. Come here, Jack,' he called to the dog: the dog came up with his tail between his legs as he seemed to sense something unusual about me.

'There never was a Monaghan dog like that.' Grandfather lived in County Louth and was proud of his birthplace. When he praised the dogs he praised the county. It was the same way at home. Also, when you praised the dog you praised the master. In our country every man loved his own dog and despised all others.

'Is Jack paid for?' I queried Oul' Quinn.

'Why would anybody pay for a dog?' he returned. We were referring to dog-licence duty. 'Ye know,' he went on, 'a policeman can tell the smell of a dog not paid for at a half-mile, but Jack here can smell a policeman at a mile range.'

I looked at Jack with suitable admiration. He was 'trotting' after the cart: the donkey was being a little too lively so we needed to hold to our seat with eyes front.

'I never paid for a dog in me life,' Oul' Quinn declared. 'I had a dog one time and whenever a policeman came into the parish the dog went off and hid among the sedge at the river. The policeman came to the house. "Quinn," he says, "ye have a dog that's not paid for on yer establishment." "Yer a damn liar," I says. I could see the dog's snout peepin' from the sedge and takin' the measure of things. Not till the policeman was clear of the parish did me brave dog come out from his hide.'

A dirty-looking bull-terrier came out from a house and looked at Jack. Jack ran under the cart in fear. Oul' Quinn got down.

'Come out here and fight yer man,' he said to Jack. Jack crept or slunk away through the legs of the ass.

Grandfather Quinn waved his stick and roared after the dog. 'Wait till I get me hands on ye, ye low mane cur, there's not a drop of me blood in yer body.'

He never mentioned dogs to me after that day.

Uncle Jemmy and a fellow nicknamed The Clip were working hard in the middle of the bog. There were many others working on the bog but taking it easier than my uncle, who was a very greedy man for the world. My uncle and The Clip were stripping the foasy top sod off the bank and dropping it into the bog-hole beside the bank. Uncle was a fool-wise man with a big nose and though only about thirty, his hair was as grey as a badger. People said I was the dead spit of him.

'Ye have every move of Jemmy,' they said. 'Big nose, big voice – and yer a cod.' That's exactly what they said.

'What the blue blazes kept yez,' Uncle shouted. 'Yer welcome there,' he said to me after a pause. Then he introduced me to The Clip. 'This is me sister's son.'

'Good man,' The Clip said.

During that day and the next I wheeled turf from the place where it was cut to the spread ground. The bog was a lively place and time passed quickly. I worked in my bare feet and the soft oily turf made a new man of my feet.

On the second morning Uncle Jemmy was up at what I guessed must have been an unearthly hour. He called me. I rose and hadn't my usual appetite. The sun wasn't up when we started for the bog.

'You're a slave-driver,' I told my uncle.

'Never you mind, never you mind,' was all he said.

We worked for two or three hours at the turf before anybody put in an appearance on the bog. Jemmy – I never attached the prefix Uncle to his name – Jemmy was determined to take all he could out of me and I didn't grudge him his task. I was just as determined to take life easy. He tried to rush me and I sat down. Then I crossed over to another bank and dangling my legs over the brow of a bog-hole talked with the boys and girls.

'Yer uncle is a desperate hard man,' I was told.

'He'll be rich or damn poor,' another said.

'A good steady boy,' was Jemmy's own description of himself.

He was for ever boasting of the fine girls he could get.

'I could have her hands-down,' he said of the finest woman in the parish, 'she'd jump at the chance.'

'Of course you could have her,' his neighbours said, putting the fool further.

'Hands-down,' he always added.

A man who cannot find happiness and content in a turf-bog is a bad case. A turf-bog is a history of the world from the time of Noah. The name of the bog in which I worked was Anamarron.

The third day was wet so Jemmy sat in cobbling boots. As he hammered the iron rivets into the leather he would say: 'Yer father couldn't do it as fast as that.' Often he struck the rivet sideways and the flying missiles rattled on the dresser plates.

'Dangerous to be safe here,' a neighbour who had come in remarked to me. Jemmy eyed him but his sternity rotted to foolishness in his stare.

'Worse than war,' I said.

Jemmy wasn't a bad cobbler, though he hadn't the tricks of the trade; it is the tricks of any trade that have the tradition in them. Without the little touches of roguery a cobbler is only a plain pedestrian thinker who can never scale the heights where fairies of every craft dwell. The journeymen shoemakers had taught my father the secrets; father made sure to show them to me. Before I could put a tip on a boot I knew how to disguise a flaw in an upper, I knew how to give the impression to a boot that one would think it welted when it was only pegged. I knew a clever way of putting a bristle on the waxed end.

Jemmy didn't know any of these things. He was just a plain prose cobbler, or as he himself would say 'a good steady boy'.

The journeymen shoemakers were the wandering poets of cobbler-land who carried the light of the craft into the humdrum shops of Ireland.

'Ye ought to get a woman in here,' the stranger said to Jemmy.

'Woman,' Jemmy sneered, 'I wouldn't have the half of them in me way.' He was dreadfully afraid of getting a bad wife who would scatter his share. His father wanted to see him married as did also my own father and mother. I remembered father trying to fix a match for him with a returned American who was reputed to have a lot of money. The negotiations broke down on a financial issue. There were no hysterical tears and a violent, passionate sundering. Before Jemmy went to the rendezvous which was at the house of the girl's cousin, he came to our house for final instructions.

'Don't put yer woman in yer purse,' mother advised. 'Why it would pay a man to put a shift on a good girl than get a good-for-nothing with hundreds.'

Father was less idealistic.

'If she has the money let you see it or the proof of it,' he said.

'Be ghost,' Jemmy said, 'she'll have to show the dockets.' He paced our kitchen floor with his hands clasped behind his back. 'Aw, she'll have to show the dockets.'

It turned out that the girl had spirit sufficient to tell him to get out.

As we sat during this wet day we talked about this girl and that, and women-memories crowded out the smell of turf and fat-bacon.

The next day we didn't go to the bog either; there was a fair in Ardee and my uncle had a scraggy calf for sale. I helped drive the calf.

'How much for the scuttery calf?' the lowest grades of dealing-men asked us as we stood on the fair green.

Jemmy took their remarks ill. 'Galong, ye bleddy kid-buyer,' he told one.

'It looks like it never got its fill,' another dealer remarked of the calf, which was shivering on an elevation where we had put it to make the beast look bigger.

'Well,' said Jemmy, 'if it didn't get its fill that's not my fault; there was plenty for it to eat if it would eat it.'

He couldn't have said a worse thing. Dealers know that thinness due to hunger was curable, but a scraggy beast that would not eat was a gonner and a donner. Most of the cattle in this fair were thin for it was the May fair and the grass was scarce. We didn't sell.

Oul' Quinn arrived in town in his ass-cart. He took us into an eating-house and ordered a plate of steak and onions for each of us. 'Eat now till ye bust yer navels,' he shouted. I thought his remark most indelicate, yet the market-women laughed heartily. I began then to realise that women are cruder, more of the earth, than men, and that vulgar sentimentality pleases them. I began to learn still later that my poetic idealism was sentiment suffering from religious mania, and that the old men and women were the realists.

Oul' Quinn was the only one I ever knew who thought he should never die. He was over eighty years at the time. He said that only wastrels die and people who couldn't eat fat-bacon.

10 Fairyland

Though the fairies had many strongholds in south Monaghan only once did I stumble into Fairyland. It was an Irish ass – that wisest of beasts – that led me out of it.

My mother wanted to visit a friend who lived beyond the Hill of Mullacrew. We got the loan of an ass and cart and one fine Sunday morning in summer set off. I was driving, and on the wrong side of the seat-board, too. Every time I lifted the stick to beat the ass I tilted my mother's hat. She said I was a bad driver. I should have sat on the right-hand side so as to give my whip-hand free play. The ass knew I was an amateur and took full advantage of it. I suppose he laughed.

'You'll destroy my good hat,' my mother said.

'That saves my poor back,' was probably what the ass was thinking.

We progressed fairly well on the outward journey. The road was dry. There was a fresh breeze blowing in from the Irish Sea. We met people going to Mass. Once or twice the ass shied at scraps of wind-blown newspaper. My mother gripped the side-board.

We arrived and saw my mother's friend. At the end of our stay it began to rain. We looked up at the sky and decided that the shower would blow off. The ass brayed. The rain held off till we were a mile on our way home and then it came down. Luckily we had a winnowing sheet in the cart. The winnowing sheet was for putting over the cart to shade it from the sun – the sun would loosen the shoeing on the wheels; it served as a rain-proof now. It was pouring when we passed over the Hill of Mullacrew. I saw the old fair-green through the holes in the winnowing sheet.

The ass made poor progress over the muddied roads.

The Hill of Mullacrew was a bald common without a tree or land-mark on its crown. A flock of wild scraggy goats were carrying out manœuvres on the Hill.

Around the Hill's base there stood half a dozen houses and the relics of oul' dacency in the form of two public houses.

Outside one of the pubs we saw a man moping in the rain.

'Did ye see any bobbies?' he asked us. We said we didn't.

This man was on guard while the non-bona-fides quenched their Sunday thirst.

The roads around Mullacrew were a tangled skein; they were laid down by random and led everywhere and nowhere. My mother knew these roads well and we managed to pick our way till we came to the town of Louth. The town of Louth had seen better days. At one time all roads led there. One crooked street comprised the town.

All roads surely led to it and as far as we could make out none led from it. My mother knew the town well; she had lived there for a year and normally would have been a good guide through the maze of roads.

We encouraged the ass to take the most likely road. He grumbled a little. When we had gone down the road a half-mile or so my mother noticed it strange. It was still pouring rain. My mother inquired of a man standing on his doorway if we were on the right road for Inniskeen.

'Aw me poor woman,' he said, 'this road leads to the Mill o' Louth.'

He directed us to go back.

'The first turn on yer right after ye pass Watty Gernon's,' he said.

We turned the ass round. My mother knew Watty Gernon's house. We found a turning and took that way. The ass didn't seem too pleased. When we had gone a a bit that road we came to a locked gate: the road was a cul-de-sac. Back again we went. We came to a blacksmith's forge. Around the anvil were a crowd of young men playing cards. We inquired the way to the town of Louth. My mother said to the men that if she got back to Louth she would be able to find the right road. The men in the forge were not of one mind.

'The best thing to do, woman,' one said, 'is to turn to yer left at Duffy's Cross.'

'No, that's an out-of-the-way road,' another contradicted. 'Go straight the way yer goin' and take the second turn to yer left.'

Several others gave this opinion, and surely this multitude of counsellors darkened wisdom. We travelled on. In about half an hour we came to the forge again: the blacksmith was standing in the door.

'In the Name of God are ye here again?' he said.

'Indeed we are,' my mother said.

All that evening we drove around the wet roads. The poor ass was tired and as heart-broken as ourselves.

At one point the road was flooded; the ass refused to ford it and we were compelled to turn back.

'If we could only get back to Louth I'd be able to find the road,' my mother kept saying. But we couldn't get back to Louth.

We were in Fairyland, and it was a wet day.

Everything seemed strange. The folk we saw were not ordinary mortals.

I suggested letting the ass go what way he liked. I had often heard of people gone astray following the instinct in the shape of an ass after human reason had failed.

My mother agreed. There was nothing else for it. We gave the ass his head. I let the reins slack and the ass with his head bowed plodded along we knew not in what direction.

'This is Ballykelly,' my mother exclaimed shortly afterwards.

We were relieved. We were in our own familiar country.

When we got home father and all the household were watching at the gate.

'We had our eyes out on pot-sticks,' they said. 'Where were ye?'

'In Fairyland,' I answered.

Some days later I told the story to John Cassidy.

'Why didn't ye turn yer coats?' he said.

When old George heard the tale he felt like Saint Thomas when that Doubter who didn't doubt (Dostoyevsky was right, Saint Thomas believed all along) put his fingers into the wounds of Our Lord.

'Paddy,' George stared at me, 'ye were with the Wee Fellas.'

'Only for the ass we'd never escape,' I said.

'Indeed you would not,' he supported, 'sure the ass is a blessed animal.'

11 The Well-learned Scholar

I was in the sixth class. We were sitting at the back desk in the schoolroom. This was the place of the play-boys. Before us were our copies, dirty and blotted. We were supposed to be writing an essay. Some of us had only the heading down.

Country Life and Town Life.

We weren't interested in contrasts of that kind. We were inscribing with pen-knives our names or initials on the edge of the desk.

P. Kav, John Cassidy, Tom Brennan.

Long after I had left school I looked and saw our desire for immortality cut on that same desk. Our names wore well.

'Give us the lind of yer knife,' one asked.

'Wait till I finish my own name,' I said. He snatched the knife away.

Up in the front of the room Miss Cassidy was giving a gruelling to the fifth class. She was in bad humour. A girl beside me had her hand raised: 'Please, miss, Johnnie Duffy is sayin' bad talk, please, miss, please, miss.' Miss Cassidy didn't notice and the girl had to lower her hand.

From the classroom on our left a girl's voice came through to us. She was reading a poem.

> 'I walked entranced
> Through a land of morn,
> The sun with wondrous excess of light
> Shone down and glanced
> O'er fields of corn
> And lustrous gardens aleft and right.
> Even in the clime
> Of resplendent Spain
> Beams no such sun upon a land
> But 'twas the time
> We were in the reign
> Of Cahal Mor of the Wine Red Hand.

Anon stood nigh
By my side a man
Of princely aspect and port sublime,
Him queried I:
O my lord and khan
What clime is this and what golden time?'

Then the teacher said:

'That will do. Get out your geography books.'

Listening to Mangan's poem I was rapt to that golden time
in which poets are born. I felt as though I were in the presence
of a magician, and I was; there was witchery in some of Mangan's
poetry, it wasn't normal verse. Mangan's poem as read by that
girl awoke in me for the first time those feelings that are beyond
the reach of reason.

We had Tom Moore for the singing lesson each day so that I
have never been able to read Moore without putting an air –
generally the tune the old cow died on – to his words. I was
ashamed once when someone heard me singing *Let Erin Remember*, it was like being caught praying.

I liked the speed of Sir Walter Scott's *Lady of the Lake*, and I
remember how one day when coming from the Fair I inflicted
most of it on a ploughman.

Thomas Campbell occupied a high place in my esteem:

Our bugles sang truce for the night-cloud had lowered
And sentinel stars set their watch in the sky
And thousands had sunk to the ground over-powered,
The weary to sleep and the wounded to die.

Strangely enough, Milton, whom I never liked afterwards,
awoke a response with his

Haste thee nymph and bring with thee
Health and youthful jollity.

I knew Tennyson's *Brook* from its source among the coot and
hern till it poured itself into the brimming river. Some extra-
smart pupil pointed out that the brook mightn't run during a
dry summer. For his contradiction of the poet he got three slaps,
which he richly deserved.

In the realms of prose I remember from school two short pieces, Henry Grattan on William Pitt: 'The Secretary stood alone, modern degeneracy had not reached him, but aloof and uncompromising his object was England.' I do not know what followed nor do I know what followed Macaulay's descriptive rhetorical opening except that Warren Hastings was the subject who had 'a high and intellectual forehead, a brow pensive but not gloomy, a face pale and worn'. I used to day-dream myself to fit that description.

Not a word was in our school-books about the new poets and writers who were bringing about a renaissance in Irish letters. I think there weren't any living writers represented in our readers. This may have inspired the question a man once asked me.

'How is it,' he said, 'that there's no poets goin' now?'

Three things I remember from my school-days, three things of joy which have not been entirely futile. The first is the hymn *Hail, Queen of Heaven*, the second that girl's reading of Mangan's poem, and the third the things Miss Cassidy said to me on her last day in school.

She sat facing me and held my hands. Her face was green and haggard, she was dying of cancer of the stomach. A few weeks before this day one of her pupils had been sent to a high school.

'Oh, Patrick,' she said with all the pathos and sympathy of a sick woman, 'if *you* could get to high school you'd leave them all far behind.' She spoke her heart to mine for a half-hour. I cannot remember the actual words she said. She spoke brokenly, appealingly, wistfully. She believed in me.

I was not deeply moved at the time, but I had an instinctive feeling that in the chinks between her cracked speech there was the intuitive wisdom of a woman.

Miss Cassidy cried leaving the school, and no wonder, she had taught in it for forty years.

I left school when I was twelve years old. There came as substitute for Miss Cassidy, who was living in hope, a young girl. She was a nice girl out of college. She had a soft voice and told innocent stories to us. We weren't used to soft, innocent words. Some of the boys got unruly and did what they liked. There was singing, shouting, cursing, and quarrelling in the school. I was tame, for I had fallen in love with the new teacher. It was a pure unbodied passion. I wished then to be older as I now wish to be younger.

Unlike many of my later women this girl returned my love with interest. Cupid had nothing in the world to do with these arrows of life. Once as I sat with my nose within striking distance of a composition on the density of water, she stopped behind my desk and ran her fingers through my hair. The pulse of my soul – not my mere heart – missed a beat. I wanted to do something heroic to prove my love. I dreamt of her – and in her presence was enveloped in warm, suffocating shyness.

> In the clear dawn, before the east was red,
> Before the rose had torn her veil in two,
> A nightingale through Hafiz' garden flew,
> Stayed but to fill its song with tears, and fled.

One day the lad next to me at school drew his pen across my copy. Normally I shouldn't have minded, for my copies were never too clean. I usually averaged six fair-sized blots to the page. I hit the fellow. He hit back on the double. Before a minute we were into each other like devils. We fought through the desks. We punched, kicked, and called each other names.

The new teacher was standing trembling in a corner of the room. The other teacher was standing in the classroom doorway, not too much upset.

All the boys and girls were standing on the desks cheering and laughing. Most of the boys cheered my opponent. The girls were with me. Perhaps they knew by instinct that I was fighting for love. I don't know what my opponent was battling for. Perhaps he too was suffering and inflicting suffering for an ideal no less pure than mine. I know it wasn't an ordinary scrap. Courage, beauty, love – we were fighting like the knights of medieval Europe.

'Good man, Paddy,' the girls cheered me.

'Lay into him, Joe,' the boys encouraged my opponent.

I made a terrific right swing. My opponent ducked and I struck the wall.

The girls gasped.

'Oh, such a whack!'

Blood was spouting from both our noses, which gave the fight more colour than the actual wounds deserved.

We fought round the map of England and past the map of Scotland. We fought into the hall-way. The assistant mistress very tactfully shut the door. With our audience cut off our heroic flames were without a fan, and soon flickered out. We began to see reason.

'What fools we are!' I said.

Joe agreed with me.

We sat together on the school-yard wall and dried the blood off our faces. Some of the children peeped out the windows. They thought we would finish the fight in one murderous last round. Instead they saw us staring dreamily out of bleary eyes towards the west. Over there where the cherries were beginning to redden on Rocksavage orchard wall.

'We'll go and see if they're ripe,' Joe suggested.

We rose and crossed the hay field towards the orchard. The perennial rye grass flowed like an easy tide on a summer sea. We talked of cherries and football matches. We jumped the drain from the hay-field into the potato-field which ran to the orchard wall. The potatoes were beginning to blossom. Three drills of Epicures were in full bloom, their beautiful white blossoms were lovelier than lilies.

'When Miss Cassidy comes back we'll get it,' Joe said.

'You may swear that,' I replied.

'The new teacher isn't a bad poor devil,' Joe said.

'She's all right,' I said.

We looked up at the cherries overhanging the high wall.

'They're not ripe,' Joe said.

He was right. Only on the very topmost branch was one red-ripe cherry, like a drop of blood shining in the sun. Sappho, the greatest poet of love, has said something about the fruit on the topmost bough. It might have been symbolic, that high cherry. A symbol of first love. Before night some wild bird would have picked it off.

'Don't stand there like a mope,' my companion said. 'Come away, the scholars will be goin' home soon.'

We walked away.

'Yer like a man was up all last night,' my companion remarked. 'What are ye dreamin' about?'

'About nothing,' I answered.

'Ye couldn't be dramin' about less,' he commented.

I never went back to school. I was ashamed. In my heart I yearned to return – to get more knowledge? – no, but for the sake of my first love.

I despised learning. 'What good is grammar to a man who has to work a spade and shovel?' I often heard people say. This propaganda influenced me at the time – between twelve and fourteen – when the tide in the affairs of most men is at the full. I missed the tide. But wasn't I an educated man? 'Sure, he went as far as Miss Cassidy could put him, and that's good enough for any man.'

One of the tunes my father used to play was called *The Well-Learned Scholar*. I don't remember if he played it on the evening I returned from school for the last time. If he didn't he should have. I was a learned man fit to go anywhere under the sun.

12 Michael

Michael helped me to make my soul. Off and on for four or five years from the time I left school I worked for him, weeding, thinning turnips, tying corn and so forth. In exchange he did our horse-work.

Michael was a free-and-easy type of man. He was aged around forty. He had a kindly, slippery face. He was a very strong man, though his knocking knees and drooping shoulders would lead you to think him a weakling. He had a wife and four children and his mother and father living with him, but this didn't cramp his style a bit. His house in the wilderness at the back of God-speed was a real hard case: its thatched roof was black-rotten, and the rain-stripes had yellowed every inch of the plaster on the walls inside.

Michael was fond of horse-racing and very fond of porter. Part of our daily talk consisted in debating the stomach capacities of various drinkers. I once suggested that a certain neighbour could let down a fair share of porter. Michael looked at me as a teacher would look at his best pupil who had shown great stupidity.

'I thought I had ye well larned,' he said. 'Sure that fella has no gut on him for porter. Man alive, I thought you knew more than that.'

'Well, Micky Flynn has a good let-down.'

'Middlin' fair: thirty pints hard-runnin' 'id butt him all the same.'

And so we discussed this intoxicating subject for hours.

We were thinning turnips on the top of the high hill. We worked up the hill on our knees, coming down we dragged along on our bottoms. It was a blazing day in mid-July. Michael was teaching me a song. I remember one verse and a half.

'The jury found me guilty and
The clerk, he wrote it down

> And Judge Bolton passed the sentence and
> Bound me for Charlestown.
> Oh ye'd pity me agéd father and
> Him standing be the bar,
> Likewise me agéd mother
> A-tearin' of her hair,
> A-tearin' of her grey silvery locks
> While the tears came rollin' down—
> Sayin': Son, dear son, what have ye done
> That yer bound for Charlestown?'

Michael was very anxious that I should have the words right for, as he said, 'it was well composed'.

The field in which we were working was a large one and did not belong to Michael. It was let in con-acre by the eleven months system, and Michael had taken an acre for turnips. On either side of our plot were other gangs of turnip-thinners. Sometimes we shouted to one another, and sometimes we exchanged visits. At the far side of the field we could see a pair of hungry crows pulling turnips up by the roots. At the roots of the turnips they often found grubs. If a crow found a grub at the root of the first few turnips, he continued pulling, and his friends would come too, and pull and pull till they had devastated a whole field.

Early in the morning was the time the crows liked to do this work. I watched a field of turnips for a fortnight once. From daylight at four o'clock in the morning till eight, when the regular labourers would arrive, I sat on the misty brown quilt of the turnip-field. I saw the world coming to life. I was intimate with the shy creatures of the earth. The rabbits were out nibbling the dewy grass, sometimes a ball-headed weasel would come out on the headland to take a view of the dawn-fields. A hawk dancing high above sleepy thrushes would be a thing to remember with tears. I knew which chimneys put up the first smoke. And the crows! They were brazen chancers of the first water! I pointed a stick at them – they paid not the least attention – they knew it wasn't a gun. I had to chase them from close range.

At the far side of the field in which Michael and I were working we could see the two bold crows pulling turnips for all they were worth. We didn't mind; the turnips weren't ours. We stopped working to watch the crows. Whenever they came to a strong-rooted turnip one crow pulled the other by the tail. You would almost hear them say 'all together'. I once saw three crows tug-o'-warring a big turnip up. They pulled systematically, turnip after turnip. Now and then one of them would upturn a clod or a stone.

'July is the hungry month,' Michael told me.

The owner of the turnips at which the pair of crows were working came into the field.

'Hooroo, damn yez,' he shouted, and clapped his hands. He looked mournfully at his turnips withering in the sun. Then he crossed the drills to us.

'Yez are a damn mane lousy pack,' he was saying. He meant us, we knew, not the crows.

'What's the bother?' Michael asked him.

'A lot ye care,' he replied. 'Did ye not see the crows pullin' me turnips?'

'Not a see or see we saw,' Michael said.

'Bad neighbours, bad neighbours,' he said slowly.

Neither Michael nor myself minded this dark opinion. Michael was like that, and he trained me likewise. We wouldn't flare up at an insult unless such a display of temper was going to show a profit. Michael was a true pacifist; he would run rather than fight. He was as yielding as a wet rope.

'What kind of turnips have ye over there?' he asked the bitter man after a few moments.

'They were doin' nicely only for the damn rascals of crows. I'll be robbed from house and home.'

We had to walk a half-mile to Michael's house for dinner. The dinner in Michael's house was always the same, though it wasn't the national dinner of potatoes and cabbage. Potatoes and butter was the meal. On this occasion the milk wasn't churned so we had either to churn or do without butter. The dash churn stood near the door because the weather was hot. Michael's wife poured three pan-crocks full of cream into it. She tightened down the lid with a crack of her fist's heel.

'Now in the name of God,' she said.

'I'll take the first brash,' Michael said.

Churning with a dash-churn is heavy work. I was tired when we had finished. Michael's wife took the lid off and looked into the churn. 'God bless it, but it's lovely,' she said.

She scooped up a plateful with her hand and mixed some salt through it. Twice or three times she put her buttery finger in her mouth to test the butter's saltiness.

'It's a little pale,' the old woman said.

'More like goat's butter,' Michael remarked.

The pot of potatoes was turned out on a creel. The old woman picked a few and put them among the red coals. She liked roasted potatoes.

I had a good appetite then. Potatoes and butter is a better dinner than you'd imagine. It never dawned on the cooks that this was anything but first-class fare.

The next day was held the Dundalk Races. I knew by Michael's giddiness that he intended going.

'We'll better put on a bit of a spurt,' he said that evening. 'I'd like to get the weight of these turnips thinned the day.'

He started to work in earnest then. He was a two-handed thinner. He would grab a turnip with one hand and with one sweep of the other take out all the surplus plants around it. One, two, one, two, he moved along the drill. The legs of his corduroy trousers rubbing together made a whistling sound. I followed at about five yards distance: I couldn't get closer than that, no matter how I tried. I was grabbing all around me and doing almost as much damage as the crows. I hung on, and when the day was ended I was no more than five yards behind.

Michael had three loads of oats for sale. It was bad, damp grain because he had gone on a drinking expedition towards the end of the harvest and the rainy weather came on. He took a sample of the oats to Dundalk. All he could get for it was twenty-seven shillings a barrel, though the price that day for fairly good grain was thirty-five shillings. As he walked about the streets he met a neighbour who had a load of good oats in the market.

'Give us a handful of your oats,' Michael said.

He got it, and welcome.

He put the good oats in a paper bag similar to the one containing his own damp stuff and entered the office of Gray, the corn-buyer. He showed the good sample to Gray. Gray took a handful of the grain and squeezed it through his fingers. It was dry as shot.

'What do you want for this?' Gray asked.

'Thirty-eight bob,' Michael said.

'There's no such price going,' Gray said.

'I'll take thirty-seven and a tanner.'

'Thirty-five if you like,' Gray said.

'Yer a dacent man,' Michael said, 'and I'll let ye have it at thirty-six.'

'Thirty-five if you like,' Gray repeated.

'I'll not let it go at that,' Michael said, and he took the sample from the corn-buyer's desk and made towards the door. At the door he turned and addressed Gray.

'Will ye give the thirty-six?'

'Thirty-five shillings is the top of my book,' Gray said.

'Well, thirty-five and a tanner.'

Gray made no reply to this.

'Ah, well,' Michael said as he moved towards the desk again, 'I'm as well let you have it as any other.' And he handed Gray the bag containing his own damp stuff.

Gray did not reopen the bag but just marked it and gave Michael his contract note. The principal legend on the note stated that all stuff delivered must be 'according to sample'.

I met Michael as he was coming home from the town. He was drunk, and saying to himself: 'According to sample, according to sample. Am I right or am I wrong?'

He asked me to drive one of the carts next day. He was going to ask my neighbour Owen to drive another. I was delighted to accept, for Owen was the gayest man in the county, and our trinity of carts would not be equalled by any in the town for fantasy, laughter, and wit. Neither Owen nor myself drank hard stuff. As we passed Hughes's pub Michael's horse stopped, from habit.

'Come in, chaps, for a lubricator,' Michael invited.

We declined the invitation. We sat on our loads outside the pub.

'Do ye know,' Owen said to me after a longish wait, 'if he asks us in again we'll not refuse, we'll drink port wine.'

'Right you be,' I said. And we followed Michael into all pubs during that day.

When the oats was being spilled in Gray's store the foreman was astonished. He lifted the grain in handfuls and let it run through his fingers. It ran badly.

'Who bought this stuff from you?' he asked Michael.

'A judge of good corn,' Michael replied.

The foreman looked at the sample and then at the bag of oats spilled on the floor.

'There must be some mistake,' he said. He sent up to the office for Gray, and Gray came. Gray looked from the sample to the spilled oats and from the spilled oats to Michael.

'A trickster,' he said under his breath.

'A what?' Michael flared up.

'Nothing,' Gray said. 'Empty the damned stuff.'

Owen and I trailed Michael in and out of every pub. For every pint of porter Michael drank we drank a glass of port wine each.

Coming home, I sat on the seat-board beside Owen and trailed my own horse at the tail-board. Michael drove alone in front. He was pretty tight. He was singing:

'For sake of health I took a walk one day at early dawn,
   I met a jolly gentleman as slow he walked along.
   The greatest conversation passed between himself and me
   When at last I got acquainted with the Turfman from Ardee.'

Owen was a religious man. He was illiterate, but very intelligent. He quoted the Scriptures like a theologian. His favourite quotation was:

'Where ever three people are gathered in
   My Name I'll be in the middle of them.'

'There's only two of us together,' I said. 'Do you think if we had Michael on this seat-board with us we'd have Christ?'

Owen wasn't a man for answering theological riddles. He was a true Irishman. He broke into his favourite song:

'O rise up, Willie Reilly, and come along with me,
   For I mean for to go with you and leave this countryee,

94

To leave my father's dwellin' place, his houses and free lands
And away goes Willie Reilly and his own dear Coleen Bawn.'

The rattle of a cart over rutted roads, or any roads, is the proper accompaniment for a ballad-singer. We were all at least half-drunk.

A late-autumn evening. As we rattled along, singing, there was no trace of melancholy in our gaiety like that melancholy which undertones the frenzied laughter of April. The last leaves were falling around us. We were glad. Nature in a green dress is a breaker of hearts: she promises romance and but seldom fulfils.

The lights were bright in the small windows. The great life of Ireland was beginning. We were dreaming of long nights around warm fires with good talk over cups of strong tea.

'That's the Great Bear over Meegan's hill,' Owen said, pointing with his arm.

'There will be frost to-night,' I said.

In the front cart Michael, having finished his song, broke into loud laughing speech.

'According to sample, am I right or am I wrong?'

'Yer right,' we replied through the frosty mist.

On one occasion when Michael was taking out his potatoes the races of Dundalk occurred. He had five or six young boys and girls helping at the work.

As I was going home on the evening prior to the races Michael took me aside.

'I'll be away to-morrow,' he said, 'and remember you're the boss when the boss is not at home.'

I drank in this flattery and Michael proceeded to enlarge on my great powers.

'You're the kay of the work,' he said, 'remember that. You're the kay of the work.'

I promised to remember, and I did remember.

Next day I certainly made those under me work. I whipped them with scorpions as the servant put in charge of his equals has always done. They tried to use the strike weapon against me, but I broke them as any big capitalist would break a trade union. I expected Michael would have much praise for me next day.

He hardly noticed. I asked him what kind of luck he had had at the races. He pulled out of his pocket a handful of bookies' cards.

'That's not the sign of good luck,' he said, showing me the cards. 'I had a tip for Green Button and like a fool I didn't back it.'

He then left to forget his ill-luck in the local pub.

I was still the key of the work, but by now was a bit rusty.

Michael would allow me to do the most expert kind of farm-work. I was no more than fourteen years old when he tied a white sheet across my shoulders and bade me sow an acre of corn. He wasn't too particular, and neither was I. I scattered the seed in every direction. On the top of a knoll I stood and sowed round and round in a circle. The correct neighbouring farmers looked on and shook their heads. They hated to see a man doing such a sacred job as sowing corn without due respect and dignity. What surprised them later was that the corn I sowed came up more even than their own careful acres.

There was a deep respect among the people for the plough. In a quiet way it was an idol. To tamper with a plough was a dark sin.

'The unluckiest thing ye ever done,' I was told.

Michael was no idolater. The plough was to him just a piece of metal for tearing up the soil. He never deliberately left it facing north at night as most of the other ploughmen did.

He ploughed deep. 'Rip the soil,' was his motto. He didn't mind whether his furrows were straight or crooked or his centres level. There were humps and hollows in his ploughing. Men passing along the headland surveyed his work in critical sorrow. Michael was a bad example, they felt.

'Crooked bread makes a straight belly,' Michael would tell them.

They told him he would lose half his seed in the holes between the 'scrapes'. Michael laughed at them.

'If ye don't put beef on the land ye'll have no corn.'

There was a saying among the people that good luck is better than early rising. Michael had good luck. He was also rather clever, and there was some method in his careless methods. He told me all the mysteries of life – all the things that are mysteries to most young boys. There was sweetness and light in his teaching of sex. He was not cruel or vulgar. He was a good judge of a horse; he never had a bad or ungainly beast about his place. And he wasn't secretive about his knowledge like other horsey men whose mystification is only a veil over ignorance.

'It doesn't take a very smart fella to know a sound horse,' he said.

'The Mulla fellows wouldn't say that,' I said.

'The Mulla fellas wouldn't know a horse from an ass,' he said. 'Ye know more than the Mulla fellas yerself.'

The Mulla fellows were famous – chiefly among themselves – for horse-judging; they talked twisty codes like the dealers from Cross.

One night Michael came into our kitchen: he was drunk. He spoke into my father's face.

'I know nothing,' he said. 'I know nothing.'

The tone of his voice suggested proud ignorance rather than humble knowledge.

My father was no flatterer. He said to Michael:

'If you were telling lies all your life you're telling the truth now. You do know nothing.'

Michael was abashed. He produced a half-pint of whisky and proceeded to draw the cork by means of a crooked awl.

He is dead these number of years. I am sorry he is. He was a weak-kneed man, he side-stepped trouble when he could. He would have made a poor soldier. But he was my friend. He told me hard facts in soft words. He was kind. At his funeral the priest preached a fine panegyric over him. He was a near-saint, the priest said. I was glad. I had been soul-apprenticed to a saint.

13 The Drover

'Did ye throw a drop of holy water on yerself?' mother called from her bed as I lifted the latch to go out.

'I did,' I said.

'Well, God send ye good luck, and remember, if there's any runnin' to be done, let someone else do it.'

The time was five o'clock on a July morning. I was going to the fair that day as a drover. The previous evening Pat the Hack had come to our house and asked my parents if they would let me go with him to the fair.

'He'll go, and welcome, Pat,' they said.

'Dacent people,' Pat said.

So here was I now on a beautiful morning in July setting out for Pat's house.

The sun was high up, there was a sultry heat in the air. A heavy dew still sparkled on the shadowed grass. Hay, new-mown, filled my nostrils with a perfume worth millions if it could be bottled.

I had an ash-plant – a drover without an ash-plant is like a soldier without a gun. Now and then I took a swing at an elevated pebble and sent it flying like a golf ball.

I crossed a grass-field taking a short-cut to Pat's place. The long grass was dry and fibrous as flax. A number of snails were heading for the shade of stone ditches after having drunk in the elixir of life, the dew. I came out on to the road again. I met a man driving a springing cow slowly before him.

'Good mornin' and good luck,' I salute.

'Thank ye, thank ye,' he returns. 'Isn't it a glorious mornin'?'

'A holy terror,' I say.

I turned down the narrow lane that led to Pat's small fields and house. It was a dark lane that for a long time had not known the sharp discipline of a briar-hook. Trellised with wild-woodbine and roofed on places with wild roses, through which the songs and light of a high summer morning were strained. Baked and half-baked cakes of cow-dung lay at my feet. In this cool place the cattle found shelter during the day from the gadflies and all the tormentors that come with beauty and love. Even now one old cow was coming up the lane. Far away on the New Line Road I could hear the wild cry of home-sick cattle.

At the end of the road Pat the Hack's fields began. Three poplar poles lay across the gap, but the upper two poles were broken down by the fly-goaded beasts.

I could see Pat's house at the farther side of the field. He wasn't up, I guessed. I could hear the anxious impatient cackle of hens in the hen-house. The white paint-starved door of Pat's cabin gleamed in the sun. I rattled on the door. Inside a dog barked.

'Shut up, Tim,' I heard Pat growl. 'Who's there?' he called.

'It's me,' I answered.

'Me, me,' Pat mumbled, still only partly awake. I could hear him putting his hand on the side of the settle-bed and knew he was gathering his sleep-scattered wits.

'Are you not up yet?' I shouted.

'Ow is that yerself? Wait one moment till I pull on me trousers and I'll let ye in.'

'What are ye rootin' at up there at such an unnatural hour of the mornin'?' Pat's sister called from the room behind the fire-place.

'This is the fair of Carrick,' Pat reminded her. 'And yer better rise and make us a bite of breakfast.'

He drew the bolt of the kitchen door, and I entered.

'We'll be dog-late for the fair,' I said.

Pat looked at the dresser. 'It's not six yet,' he said. 'It's not six till the sun shines on the second of them blue plates.'

Pat the Hack was a patriarchal-looking man, his face was almost completely hidden in white whiskers. His favourite and only quotation was

'And Satan finds some mischief still
For idle hands to do.'

His sister, barefoot, was on her knees by the hearth. Pat sat on a stool and turned the wheel of the fan-bellows while his sister filled the kettle.

'Terrible warrin' in France and Flanders,' Pat said as we sat eating.

'Pat here is a terrible man for the papers,' his sister said. 'He gets the *Democrat* every week.'

'The Germans will bate the Alleys,' he remarked between spoonfuls of duck egg.

'Yer father is nearly as fond of the readin' as Pat here,' the sister suggested. 'I suppose he gets every week's *Democrat*?'

The *Democrat* was a local paper which specialized in Petty Session reports and County Council meetings.

'Have ye yer plant?' Pat asked me as we rose to go out.

'I have, and a good one,' I said.

'God speed yez,' the sister said as she sprinkled us with holy water. 'And mind now,' she added, 'if ye can't get a dacent penny for the heifer she's no fallen goods: we have plenty of grass.'

The heifer was wild-timid as a creature of the jungle; she didn't want to leave the field, and a tough job we had to get her out on to the main road. I walked in front, watching out for open gaps.

Ahead of us we could see cattle and a motor-load of jobbers pulled up.

'If we got in with them cattle,' Pat said, 'we wouldn't have much bother with the heifer.'

'What do ye think I should be askin' for her?' he queried after a while.

'Forty pounds,' I suggested.

'I'll not take less from any man.'

Cattle were coming up behind us. The cries of lonely beasts filled the air.

The heifer, when she sighted the cattle in front, started to gallop. 'Stop her, stop her,' Pat called to the men. She leaped to one side and, failing to get past, jumped the hedge. 'Damn to her soul, God forgive me, but she's after jumpin' into Johnnie Connor's garden,' Pat cried as we hurried up.

'How are we to get her out of that?' I asked. The garden was ten feet under the road-level. The heifer was walking vaguely about among the cabbages and onions, here and there snatching a wild bite of green cabbage.

We got her out on the road again. Her athletic feat had drawn the attention of the jobbers.

'What are ye askin' for the wee roan?' one jobber asked.

'Forty-five notes?'

The jobber gave the heifer a quick look over and walked away saying nothing.

'Here, Willie, ye'll give the dacent man a bid,' a fellow called after the jobber.

'Aw, he's altogether too wild, I couldn't look at him,' the jobber replied.

'Let him go,' Pat said. 'One jobber never made a fair.'

We met jobbers on foot, on bicycles, and in rattling old Fords.

Pat's roan heifer was a nice saleable beast. Nearly every jobber cast his eye on her.

'Who's sellin' the wee roan?'

'I am,' Pat replied.

'How much have ye on her?'

'Forty notes.'

'Ask me thirty and I'll be talkin' to ye.'

'*You* bid me thirty and *I'll* be talkin' to *you.*'

The jobber who had been leaning over the door of the old Ford now got out. He handled the heifer.

'She's a bit thin of herself.'

'If that baste got a month's good grass ye wouldn't know her,' Pat said.

Other men now gathered round and, before we were aware, the heifer had changed hands. We had still to drive her to the town, but there was a load taken off our minds.

Demand for all sorts of cattle was brisk, nearly every beast was bought and sold before we reached the town. We were very happy. What were we talking about? We were all poets, dreamers, and no man was old.

'Did ye spray yer praties yet?'

'No. Ho, ho, ho, don't let them cattle get down the Curraghmore Road ... No, I didn't spray yet.'

'Who won the match on Sunday?'

'A draw-game.'

'Mulligan wasn't playin'.'

'Ho, ho, don't let them cattle mix with ours, they'd rip other.'

I was listening half-consciously.

> And my thoughts on white ships
> And the King of Spain's daughter.

Pat the Hack was talking politics with a young thin-faced fellow who was pro-German and a Sinn Feiner. Pat was a supporter of the Allies and the Irish Party.

'Up Sinn Fein, good oul' Germany; England's gettin' her oats now and time to ate it.'

'Up the Irish Party,' Pat retaliated, 'and to hell with Germany.'

'For Christ's sake shut up about the oul' dirty Party, the dirty, slobberin' Irish Party.'

'Up the Party.'

'Why don't ye go out and fight for England?'

'Up the Party and down with Sinn Fein.'

'They sowld Ireland.'

'Too much to ate you fellas are getting,' Pat shouted, 'that's what has Ireland the way she is. And Satan finds some mischief still for idle hands to do.'

That clinched the argument as far as Pat was concerned: he turned away from the fire-eater and joined the conversation that was being woven from more homely material.

'Give me a fill of yer tobacco,' a fellow said.

The man who had the tobacco held up a small piece between his finger and thumb. 'If I took anythin' of that there would be none left,' he said.

'Christ of Almighty,' the first man lamented, 'but I'm starved for a smoke. I wish the bleddy war was over.'

'I know a fella can get all the tobacco he wants: Frank Dooley, he has a cousin workin' in Carroll's factory.'

The tobacco-starved one looked towards the giver of this information. 'I'll try Frank to-morrow,' he said. 'I'm smokin' dry tay-leaves this last month and the mouth is burned off me.'

Two boys on their way to school passed us on bicycles. 'Up

Sinn Fein!' they shouted and sang, 'Sinn Feiners, pro-Germans alive, alive O!' which was a parody on a popular song.

'There'll be a quare crash when this war is over,' a man said.

'There will that, whoever lives to see it.'

Everybody was happy that day and the non-smokers in paradise.

Pat's heifer walked quietly among the other cattle, but it was easy to see she only wanted an opening and back she would go. A load of squealing young pigs passing gave her her chance; she dashed between the cart and the fence and galloped, and – as the Americans would say – then some. Up and down like a see-saw her backbone moved.

'Stop her, stop her,' Pat the Hack called to the drovers coming up behind us. The drovers ho ho'd, but didn't put themselves out. One of them flung his ash-plant at the beast's head and still she galloped.

'Folly her, you,' Pat told me.

I watched the heifer disappear around a bend and thought of my mother's injunction: 'If there's any runnin' to be done, let somebody else do it.' I walked leisurely after the beast, hoping that she might get tired before I did.

A mile back I met a man with a young bull on a halter. 'Did ye see a roan heifer?' I said.

He saw her all right. 'She flew past like greased lightning,' he told me, 'and ye may take it at yer aise, for if ye were as light on yer foot as a Tyrone ragman ye wouldn't overtake her.'

'To hell with her, anyway,' I said as I moved off.

Pat the Hack went on to the town and got paid. In the evening the jobbers came and took the heifer back – she had gone straight home. The jobbers found little difficulty in driving her, they were experts in the use of the ash-plant.

The story of the heifer that came back is nearly symbolic of my life. I have failed many times to get my cattle to the fair. I got nothing for my trouble except joy – and joy cannot be minted to buy bread or cigarettes. But though the coin of joy isn't legal tender in the mundane shops of the world, it is in the lands of Imagination, and I to-day, jingling my purse of memory, know I am richer than Rockefeller or Henry Ford or the Rothschilds ever were.

14 Patriotism

There was a big political demonstration in the village. I was allowed to go. I got twopence for travelling expenses. I was the richest boy in our crowd. I lost the two pennies on the roulette-table which stood on the outskirts of the demonstrators' meeting.

It was a meeting of the Ancient Order of Hibernians. There were thirty bands in the procession, and as many banners. The music didn't impress me, but the banners were beautiful. Green silk and shining gold. All the constitutional saints of Ireland had their images painted on those banners. The time was nineteen hundred and seventeen. I crushed my way towards the brake on which the speakers sat. The Hibernian orators were florid men. Good actors, too, they knew how to coax a cheer or a laugh from a lazy crowd.

One speaker rose and made a dramatic gesture with his arms as he advanced to the front of the platform. I listened intently. He condemned Sinn Fein. He said it would end badly. 'Remember what your Cardinal said,' he shouted, 'Sinn Fein will end in red ruin, defeat, and utter collapse.' The crowd cheered.

Another speaker said: 'In a few weeks a bubble will have burst and John Dillon will be able to tell the Irish people what it was Arthur Griffith wanted of him nineteen years ago.'

The sense of his statement meant nothing to me, but his dramatic fervour hammer-drove the silly symphony into my mind.

Among the fruit stalls on the edge of the crowd my companions were having a good time. Biddy Murphy, a seller of oranges and Peggy's Leg, was raising her protesting voice above the oratory. Looking around I saw her gripping John Gorman by the collar of his coat.

'Ye whipped a stick of Peggy's Leg,' she said.

'Search me,' he was saying.

I joined my companions. Biddy Murphy was a true orator of old Ireland. She had a bad tongue, yet not an obscene tongue. Her language had spiritual riches deep in its guttural folds.

'Peggy's Leg and Nancy's Thigh and Mary Anne's Oul' Ankle. Come on, me lucky lads, one penny a stick.'

A constant stream of men flowed to and fro between the meeting-place and the pub. Leaving the pub, they shouted: 'Up the Hibernians, up them every time.'

' 'The Party was never stronger,' men were saying as we walked home.

'Never stronger, never stronger.'

A year later. Taking place a general election that was more than a mere election. It was the battle of youth and the New Ireland versus the old men and the old servitude.

Ford cars, side-cars, and cars of every description were flying the roads. Above them floated green flags, tricolours, and the Stars and Stripes. The Stars and Stripes was part of the Sinn Fein flag in those days: we all of us who were young thought that the United States would declare war on England in our cause. The American papers took our part and did perhaps more damage to England than guns could. The green flag was the flag of the Hibernians.

My father was a supporter of the old order, though in his heart were throbbings – the pulse-beat of a New Ireland.

I fought hard during those hectic and glorious days expounding all I knew of the Sinn Fein policy. The Hibernians told me I didn't count because I hadn't a vote.

It was evening on Polling Day, nineteen-eighteen. I went to the village where the polling was taking place in the school beside the river. On one side of the road outside the school-gate was a row of stout fellows with square-set, determined faces. They had sticks in their hands, thick ash-plants, and blackthorns with knobs on them as big as horse-chestnuts; they held the sticks by the wrong end for walking with, but by the right end for a fight. These men were the members of the local division of the Ancient Order of Hibernians. One of the men bore aloft a green silk banner – the pole being poised on his trousers-waist.

Saint Patrick looked down from that banner, poor Saint Colmchille on the other side had to be content with a view of Barney Duffy's potato field – he was exiled still.

On the school side of the road a younger and less savagely determined-looking body of men moved about with hurleys on their shoulders. These were the Sinn Feiners. Only one old man was on the Sinn Fein side as far as I remember -- old Mat Kearney, a man of close on eighty, with a white, woolly beard on his face. On the footpath stood one solitary policeman -- Sergeant MacCotter of the Royal Irish Constabulary -- the nonintervention committee of that time. Inside the school-gate was a small table around which were gathered four or five men deeply immersed in the mysterious depths of the Voters' List. They were saying to each other:

'Was Tom Hagan voted yet?'

'He was not, and neither was Jack Brennan.'

I knew both these men were dead, as I had attended their wakes.

'Was Mary Carroll voted yet?'

One of the men ran his finger down the list.

'Mary was voted all right,' he said.

'Well that itself,' they sighed, relieved.

The fellows at the table were the political wing of Sinn Fein and they were bringing supporters for the cause from the graveyard. Occasionally a Ford car would rattle up and the occupants come to the table.

'How are yez gettin' on here?'

'Not too bad, we've only twelve or fourteen to vote in.'

'We voted the register out in Blackstaff and Kennelly and Drumlusty.'

'Yez done well.'

On the road a great cheer goes up. 'Up Sinn Fein.' Cheer, cheer, cheer.

'And to hell with the Hibs.' Boo, boo, boo.

The square jaws of the men with the knobbed sticks set with a still more robust determination. A side-car driven by Joe McGuinness came up. On the side-car were two supporters of the Hibernian candidate. The square-jaws relaxed into a tiny smile. When these two supporters went in to record their votes a broad smile illuminated the table from which the dead men arose to support Sinn Fein.

'We voted them pair in first thing this mornin',' I heard said.

When that pair emerged from the school-house, to use the popular expression, they were fit to be tied.

They climbed up on the side-car and, as they were being driven away, one of them waved a green handkerchief and shouted: 'Up the Hibs, up the Hibs every time.'

After the closing of the booth the policeman vanished. The air was vibrant with revolutionary feeling. Down at the pub the noise of a scuffle sounded: a large flag of tasselled green which had waved before the public-house was torn down. Some of the men with the hurleys dashed towards the pub. The lads with the gnarled sticks and square jaws stood on the grass-margin as if paralysed. The ghost of pity awoke in me for them: it was the only ghost of that breed was in the vicinity of our polling booth in nineteen-eighteen. What were they waiting for? I wondered; had they as little sense as foolish, faithful Casabianca?

Saint Patrick never stirred, there wasn't a breeze to move his green robes. By the reflection of a torch – a lighted sod of turf on a stick – I saw the passive image of the saint. Colmchille kept his vow of exile and remained looking over Barney Duffy's field.

The Sinn Fein hurley men moved towards the centre of the road.

Zero hour. A Sinn Fein hot-head made a rush for the Hibernian banner. The battle was on and I was an eye-witness. I got standing on the bars of the school-gate and had as splendid a view as any war-correspondent could desire. Around their standard-bearer the stick-men rallied, the last defenders of Dan O'Connell's Ireland.

'Get goin', get goin',' I heard.

The Hibernians fought well, the blackthorn and ash-plants whistled through the dusk. The Sinn Feiners were in on the banner now and one of them had seized Saint Patrick by the leg, dragging his whole body out of shape: the pole of the banner dunted its bearer's solar-plexus and he dropped to the ground with a groan. That was the beginning of the end. The Hibernians fled in the direction of the pub. We all followed. I saw one of the fleeing Hibs get a foot and slap that sent him sprawling ten yards away. When he arose he was crying. I saw that two of his teeth were broken. He was a fine young lad. 'Oh, what'll I do at all?' he cried to me, 'what'll me mother say?'

As I was preparing words of sympathy a brute came up and struck the poor fellow a blow in the eye.

'You savage,' I said to the brute, 'did you never read Thomas Davis? "Freedom comes from God's right hand and needs a godly brain, and righteous men shall make our land a Nation once again."'

'That's the stuff to give them, that's the stuff to give them,' I could hear.

The Hibernians failed to reach the sanctuary of MacNello's pub, a further contingent of Sinn Feiners cut them off.

The banner of green silk was torn to shreds. I found Saint Patrick's leg and mitre on the road next day, and another patch of silk that must have been the face of Saint Colmchille.

It was a fine thing to be young during the years that followed. I joined the Sinn Fein Pipers' Band that was started. A musical ear was no qualification for that band, and, in fact, it seemed a drawback, for of the fifty who joined the band I was about the only one had an ear for music. The majority of the bandsmen didn't know one tune from another. Our parish was most unmusical, and the townland of my birth took the cake in this respect. As an instance of this I was one day lying at the back of the railway when I heard a fellow come whistling down the Mucker Road. That's John Woods, I said to myself, for he was whistling true notes. I was right, it was John. For two years we practised on the pipes. On Christmas morning we turned out. An army of cats in retreat couldn't have made a more forlorn noise. Every man played whatever tune he knew, and no two of us knew the same tune. But it was glorious all the same. Myself and another lad joined the I.R.A. when it was being organized in the parish; the next meeting we were told we were too young. That was a bitter disappointment to us.

I remember an evening in October when myself and this same

lad were standing along the road in the shadow of a large elm tree. Three men came marching up abreast.

'Halt! Who goes there?' we shouted.

'Hughes's millmen,' they answered promptly, and came to a perfect halt.

'What kept you out till this hour?' we asked.

They explained how they had been delayed setting up the threshing-mill in somebody's greasy haggard.

'Well, you may go ahead,' we said.

'Thank you.'

'Thank you.'

'Thank you.'

The three men repeated their gratitude in a row.

I learned a lot of patriotic songs: *The Old Fenian Gun*, *Who Fears to Speak of Easter Week*, and many another. Everybody was singing songs of war and glory, and having to listen to these songs was a great trial to a person with an ear for music.

In spite of all the loud glory and movement of those years I count them among the lost years of my life. I had just left school and was squandering the precious coin of life on the roulette-table of Ireland. There was no deep thought then, no profound spirituality; it was an emotional movement that left no dregs of beauty when the flood had passed.

15 The Hiring Fair

It was the summer of nineteen-twenty-one.

'I'm goin' to hire,' John Gorman said to me.

'You're a fool,' I said.

'You that's the fool,' he said, 'looka the wages that's goin' – twenty quid a half-year for any kind of man. Yer a poor soldier to stick around here when ye might be earnin' good money.'

I didn't fancy hiring with a farmer, that was as bad as jail.

'Why should I hire?' I said. 'I'm wanted at home and you're not.'

'Yer goin' to miss all the sport.'

I changed my decision as quickly as a football referee. 'Very well,' I said, 'I'll hire too.'

The next day was the hiring fair of Carrick. We started out on foot as it was only six miles and we expected to get a lift in some vehicle or other. It was a warm day; there was a blue haze in the air.

My companion had a bundle under his arm – a very big bundle. I never imagined he had so much extra clothes.

'Be the holies, John,' I said, 'you have a fine big bundle of shirts and things.'

'Shirts and things,' he repeated laughing. He handed me the bundle. 'Feel that,' he said.

'What's in it?' I asked wonderingly.

'Straw.'

'What's the idea?'

He eyed me with superior eyes.

'Don't ye know damned infernal well that no man might face the hire market without some soart o' bundle.'

We were standing on the white main road to Carrick with the bundle between us when a cart hove in sight. When it came up to us we boarded it over the tail-board without asking permission. The driver turned round.

'Eh, what's this,' he shouted. 'Get down, ye pair o' beggar's gets.'

We hopped down. He was armed with a heavy ash-plant.

'There's for you,' I said.

'We'll have to leg it,' John said. As we continued our advance on Carrick John told me all the ins and outs of the business. 'But,' he added, 'you're hopeless without a bundle.'

'Well, we'll get a bundle,' I said. 'Your bulky parcel was aisy got up.'

We went to a haggard in which the remains of straw ricks were going to dust in the sun and wind. My comrade supplied me with some of his wrapping paper and when we got on the road again I looked like an Irish emigrant making for Cobh. He looked at me with an air of satisfaction.

'Ye look more like the thing now,' he said.

'We ought to be on the heels of Carrick,' I said.

And so we were. The spire of the chapel appeared like a paling post on the top of a hill half a mile distant.

'Thanks be to God,' my comrade said, crossing his breast.

'Amen,' I answered in the same comic strain.

Carrick was a town of three streets and many nameless lanes. For her size she was a most industrious town.

Every inch was crowded when we arrived. The horse-fair, ass-fair, pig-fair, fowl market and hiring market were on this day. And not forgetting the second-hand clothes stalls which were an important item on the agenda.

We pushed and crushed our way through the loud throng of ass-dealers. They were a dark breed of men who wore mufflers and carried blackthorns and spoke an ancient language. They had merry ways, too; we had heard the ballad:

'It wasn't the men from Shercock
Or the men from Ballybay,
But the dalin' men from Crossmaglen
Put whisky in me tay.'

We saw and heard a deal in an ass. The animal's owner was a thin, harmless-looking woman, her son was holding the ass's halter. The ass-dealers liked harmless-looking people. The dealer

111

in this case was a square-headed young fellow, wearing on his face a stubborn stubble of about a month's duration. He had the woman's hand in one of his paws and his other open palm was poised.

'Here,' he shouted, 'ye'll take what I said.'

'I said nothin',' the woman replied meekly.

He turned upon her a countenance composed of scorn and threats.

'Are ye tryin' to pull out?' he asked, and he at the same moment seized the ass by the halter.

'Let go that baste,' the meek creature said with amazing firmness, 'or if you don't I'll knock the grin of ye. The ass is mine. If yer want to buy him straight and honest don't have any of yer hunker-slidin', for Mary Fallon is not the girl to stan' it.'

The ass-dealer calmed down.

'There's no one in the world tryin' to take the wee baste from ye. Here, houl yer hand.' He struck the woman's open palm a great smack. 'Thirty bob,' he said.

'In the name of the three gay fellas,' the woman said, like one who had heard an incredible tale of evil, 'in the name of the three gay fellas have ye no cuttin' up in ye to go bid me thirty bob for an ass that's worth five pounds.'

The dealer looked at her and she looked back with equal eloquence. A crowd had gathered, but we were in the front row.

'What's between yous?' another man butted in. He was told. He looked at the woman and patted her on the shoulder. 'This is a dacent woman I often had a dale with,' he said, 'and this is a dacent man that's buyin'.' He spread out his two hands and simultaneously seized the wrists of the buyer and seller. Their hands both waggled like the hands of paralytics; they wanted to show indifference.

'Listen to me, dacent people,' the middle-man said, wagging his head, 'yous will not break my word. Here let yous split the difference,' and he slapped the pair of paralysed palms to unity.

'I sowl chape,' I overheard the woman say to her son afterwards.

'Ah, well,' the son replied, 'I often heard da sayin' that ye were better be sarry for sellin' than sarry for not sellin'.'

'Mebby so, mebby so,' said the woman, as she and her son disappeared into the crowd.

'There'll be no hirin' till after twelve at laste,' my comrade advised, 'but in any case we would be better to be gettin' our places on the stan'.'

The 'stand' was that part of the sidewalk at the junction of Carrick's three streets where the hiring fair was held. Custom had sanctified or sanctioned it. On one side of the street the boys stood with their faces towards the workhouse, on the other side were the girls with their backs to the Bank of Ireland. 'You can be stiff with the bank to yer back,' was the favourite phrase among the girls. 'There's nothin' in front of us but the work-house,' was the phrase among the boys.

The Black and Tans, eight deep, were marching up and down the centre of Main Street. All the thimble-players, roulette-men, and tough guys from Hell to Ballyshannon were in the town that day, and they were right to come, for the money was flush in those days and flowed from no pockets more freely than from the pockets of the servant boys. Five-pound notes were common as dirt. Right beside me was a roulette-table on which I specu-lated three pennies without any return. There was an old servant boy losing pounds, shillings, and pence on the eight-to-one yellow. I thought it a shame. I believed the roulette-man had a brake-contrivance on the machine. I began to object in a sort of important manner, and if I did I wasn't the only bluffer in the town. The I.R.A. were acting the policemen at that time, and as every man with a stiff lip was suspected of being an I.R.A. man, no wonder the roulette-man was a trifle windy. Twice or thrice the roulette-man thought to stare me down.

'A damned shame this work,' I said out loud, 'and it can't go on.'

I repeated this for a few times, a few people looked at me with hero-worshipping eyes. I thought I heard some whispers.

'Yis, he's an I.R.A. man. He'll very likely lift the rogue of a roulette-man, and it would be the bleddy right thing, too.'

The roulette-man was a small fellow, but if small, his sight and hearing were good and his judgment of men profound. He looked me over in a knowing sort of way; he was taking my measure, I guessed, and though I wished to appear big, I felt small as a mouse. Quietly, tactfully – even as a smuggler bribing a customs officer – he ran his full down-turned fist around the backs of three or four people at the table. I knew he had money in his fist; I knew I was being tempted to take a bribe, and I welcomed the tempter. I took it quietly, and quickly lest he should withdraw his hand, and slipped out of the crowd, leaving my dignity and my social conscience behind. I counted the money – there were four shillings and sixpence in it, it bulked well, for it was nearly all copper. In about twenty minutes I saw the drunken servant-boy coming away from the table searching in his pockets with that feeling of futility which the certainty of knowing their emptiness is apt to give.

I found my comrade in the midst of a knot of farmers, he was like a beautiful girl surrounded by many eager suitors.

'I was in on him first,' one big-voiced, round-shouldered Meath farmer was saying.

'Yer a liar, sir,' another one declared.

'What does the lad himself say?' a third said, addressing John.

'The man that gives me the most money is the man,' John replied, with a fine market voice.

'Here, gossoon,' another addressed my comrade for the first time, 'what do ye say to twenty-two quid and five bob earnest?'

'I say nothin'.'

'Well here, ten bob. Are ye satisfied now itself?'

'The money's all right, but what kind of work would I have to do with you?'

'Not hard at all. Ye can milk, I suppose?'

'I can.'

'And feed pigs and calves?'

'Why not!'

'Well, gossoon, it won't kill ye the work I have for ye to do. Ye'll not have to rise any mornin' afore seven. Our house is one of the best for grub, take that from me.' And he continued eulogizing his kitchen for five minutes.

'Right ye are,' John said. 'It's a bargain.'

Another man came up and spoke to the fellow who had hired my comrade.

114

'Ye got a boy!' he said.

'Yis, I got a lump of a lad.'

'Well, do ye know,' the new man went on, 'I've searched the town and I couldn't get a boy for love or money.'

'There's a fella there, he's for hire,' said John, pointing to me.

The pair of farmers turned round suddenly and looked at me as if I were an avatar.

'Yer for hire?' said the new man.

'Er – er – well, yes, no, I am,' I stammered, as a day-dreamer will when awakened to prosaic reality.

'Are ye sure yer for hire?' the man who had hired John asked. 'We're not here to be codded.'

'I'm for hire,' I said.

'Ye don't look like a fella was,' the man who couldn't get a boy said.

'Look at his bundle,' John said.

And sure enough my bundle allayed all their fears; it was as imposing a portmanteau as ever went under a servant-boy's arm.

'Were ye ever hired afore?' my man asked.

'No,' I answered.

'Well, before I bid anything, can ye milk?'

'I can milk anything but a hen,' I said.

'Ha, ha, ha,' they laughed, but only like men to whom laughter caused pain.

'Ye can feed pigs?'

'Yes.'

'Mebby ye can plough?'

'I can surely,' I said. 'I was trained by Charlie Cassidy.'

'By who?'

'By Charlie Cassidy,' I repeated.

'By damn but,' he turned to his neighbour, 'this fella would suit me down to the groun'.'

'How much do ye want?'

'Five and twenty notes,' I said airily.

'Be the norther that's a dread. Here, I won't make little of ye, I'll bid ye twenty.'

'I'll take what I said.'

'Here,' the other farmer said, catching both our wrists just

115

like the fellow dividing the difference in the ass-deal did, 'here, yous will do what I say – tear that five-pound note that's atween yous.'

'I'll not do it,' my man said.

'Neither will I,' I added.

'Well then, there can be no dale,' the man who held our wrists said.

'Here then,' my man said desperately, 'I'll not go back of the dacent man's word.'

The clap of our palms meeting in solemn contract was much louder than the clap that clinched the ass-deal.

'Yous will all come in here to Higgins's and have somethin',' farmer number one said. We all trailed him willingly into the pub. Never two more contented-looking farmers entered a pub than these. They had secured two unbroken colts in an ass-fair.

We sat round a table in the snug.

'Mine's a pint, what's yours?' John's master queried as he fumbled for his purse.

'I'm very dry,' my master said. 'I'll have a pint, too.'

'And you chaps?' he turned to us.

'Lemonade.'

'Lemonade.'

John's master produced a purse that was a blackish calico rag – like a trousers pocket only much longer – it was worked by a draw-string which was sufficiently long to hang round his neck – it was known as the kiflog in that part of Ireland.

He had a great deal of notes. I calculated that that purse contained close on a hundred pounds if all the paper in it was legal tender.

When John's master had received his change he turned to John and said: 'Here's yer earnest money.'

'Be damn, but I nearly forgot,' my master said. And he put his hand in his pocket and gave me two half-crowns.

Then we got our instructions. The two farmers lived together near Ballytain and would be going home together in the same cart. They gave us their names and inquired ours. My master's name was Jack O'Brien and John's, Harry Cumiskey.

'Yous will meet us here outside this pub,' Harry Cumiskey

said. 'Let me see now, what time. It's a quarter to two now. Yous will meet us here at a quarter to five.'

'Right ye be,' we said, as we left them behind us in the snug and went out into the bizarre-coloured town.

I suggested having dinner. John didn't want any, he said, so I picked out a well-known eating-house.

The eating-house was full to the door, people were eating standing up with their backs to a large dresser. I was right: I had my chair with me, a good fat bundle.

One of the ass-dealers put his head in the door as the landlady was interrogating me on the condition of my digestion, the capacity of my stomach and the delicacy of my palate.

'A little bit o' mate, Mary,' the ass-dealer called out.

'All right, Joe, I'll be attendin' to ye in a minute,' the landlady replied.

'Oh, I'll have a little bit of mate too,' I said.

To the ass-dealer a little bit of mate meant a big lot of mate at a small price, so I afterwards found out. Some of the clients of Mary Dooley's eating-house were attending to themselves, going to cupboards for bread or to the pan for beef, or to the hob for the teapot.

Right before the fire sat an old man in his bare feet, he was attending to his sweat-scalded toes. The heat of the place was a sultry heat, a paradise for nothing but alligators; the steam from the pans and the mugs of tea and the red faces of the people combined with whatever sun was getting through the cobweb-curtained window to make me wish to go to the North Pole.

A great plateful of greasy water, in which floated a piece of steak resembling the old sole of a boot that was softening in bog-water, was placed before me. My table was the floor. The ass-dealer sat beside me on my bundle, I saw him feel with his fingers through the paper wrapping and then he looked at me.

'Yer in the hay-market, I see,' he said, with a huge black smile. He was a friendly sort in spite of his visage and was anxious to talk. He eyed my plate askant.

'That's a notorious great dinner,' he remarked. 'This is the best atin'-house I ever came across: you'd find nothin' to touch it in any part.'

117

I didn't protest.

Another ass-dealer came in and spoke to my neighbour. 'Did ye feed?' he said.

'No, not yet.'

'It's time: I've a few black asses and they're not as lively as they ought to be.'

'Well, I'll be out there in a few minutes and we'll give them a touch.'

'Do you feed your asses in the fair?' I inquired.

'We do,' he said, 'sure only for that they'd go to sleep on us.'

'Oats and hay you give them, I suppose?'

He laughed a great big ball of a laugh that burst through the screen of deadening heat and steam like a jet of cold water oozing from the Sahara.

'Is that the way it's with ye? Don't ye know how asses are fed?'

'Hay and oats or a bag of grass,' I suggested.

'Hay and oats be no good to asses,' he said. 'The stick is what they get when they begin to get drowsy. Why, man, if ye saw an ass after his feed he's as lively as a red-bellied bee in a June meadow. If ye come with me I'll show ye the asses a-feedin'.'

'I don't want to see it,' I said.

'Oh, very well then.'

His dinner then arrived, the dead spit of mine in every detail. He started eating, with his fingers pulling the steak asunder so, as I supposed, to give his teeth a chance.

'Man, that's grand beef,' he said a few times between mouthfuls. 'Mary,' he called, when he had finished. She held out her hand in a confidential way and he put money in it, looking at the landlady as much as to say: This is a little affair between ourselves, nobody will be any the wiser.

'How much is the charge?' I asked.

'Two shillings,' she said.

I paid and escaped into the comparative cool of the narrow, crowded streets.

By this time the marriageable girls were coming in and were paddocking their bicycles prior to going on parade. I observed them with the critical detachment of violent sexless adolescence.

They paraded in pairs mostly, but there were many singles out on their own. Although everybody understood the romantic nature of their business, the girls themselves wanted to convey the impression that they were in the town on hard matter-of-fact business of some urgency. Where the crowds were thick the girls pushed and rushed like as though rushing at the last moment for the train. Then where the streets were half-empty they slowed down and stood about so as to allow time in the boys' minds for new enthusiasms for beauty to mature. If the 'marrying men' were in the town the girls knew it, and God knows the 'marrying men' were a small minority, so small indeed that to find one would require luck and patient genius equal to the finding of a needle in the bundle of straw. The marrying men were usually hairy-faced farmers of around forty-five or fifty years of age. Their idea of romance consisted of stopping a girl in the street and asking her in for a treat.

'Come in here and take a trate from me,' I heard one fellow asking a pretty young thing. She went in with him. As they sat in the snug near the street-window I could hear their conversation. I eavesdropped on lovers, an ugly thing to do. But in this case the gods could hardly have been outraged at my conduct.

'What do ye think we should get for that horse of ours?' the pretty girl said.

'He's a good baste,' the man replied. 'What height would he be?'

'About sixteen two,' the girl said.

'A nice bit of a horse,' the man's voice came through the glass with priestly solemnity. 'He should be worth forty notes.'

'We had a couple of men in on him,' the contralto voice said. 'Tommy Malone wanted to make out that the horse wasn't right.'

'Do ye know, Biddy, Tommy would hardly know a horse from a cow. Have yous many pigs?'

'Only four stores, but the two sows are carryin' and are due in a week's time.'

This was the only part of the romantic *tête-à-tête* which veered towards the Censorship Board and I felt that it was time for me to be going.

There was a toss-pit going strong in White's yard. A lad on the outskirts of the ring was calling out:

'Heads another half-dollar, heads a half-dollar.'

'Done with you,' I said. I didn't put down my money and he looked at me inquisitively.

'It's a note I have,' I explained, and I clutched preciously at a scrap of newspaper that was in my fist.

'Two heads,' rang out and there was a great scramble for the bets.

'That's a half-dollar I'm in ye,' I was informed.

'Oh it's sure, you needn't be afraid,' I said.

'I'm not a bit afraid,' he said. I looked at his long spade-jaw and quite believed him.

I was trusting to luck to lift me out of debt into flush prosperity. I had no luck: heads every time. Then the man with whom I was transacting a credit business decided that he would take a toss. He fought his way to the centre of the ring and grabbed the tosser. He put down a pound.

'Is that all covered?' he asked. 'Does anyone want a bet?' Then he remembered me.

'I'm goin' a half-dollar with you.'

As a good race is better than a bad fight I slipped round the entrance to the yard and ran.

I heard afterwards that the fellow with the spade-jaw had headed the pennies a half-dozen times. Each time he tossed he would call to my ghost. 'That's ten bob I'm in ye, that's sixteen, a pound.'

When he had finished I understand that I was thirty shillings to the bad. I heard he was furious when he found me among the also rans.

As soon as I had run out of the yard I met the cart which was to bring me to Ballytrain. The two farmers were in it, and John Gorman facing the tail-board.

'We were lookin' the town for ye,' Jack O'Brien, my master said. 'What in the Name of God did ye do with yer bundle?' he asked, amazed.

Then I remembered that I had left it behind me in the eating-house.

'To blazes with it,' I said.
It was none of his concern.
'Jump up,' he said, and I got into the cart over the wheel.

16 Servant Boy

Jack O'Brien's house was a long slated one-storied building on the side of a rushy hill. The land around was poor but the wits of the people were sharper on that account. If a Meath man or even a Louth man were asked to live on land like this he would die from shock. The natives of Ballytrain and neighbourhood were very thrifty clean folks. Any young fellow with a fair good appetite would put out of sight the dinner that was put before a whole household. There was hardly a house in the parish that hadn't a priest in the family, I heard before I had rightly arrived, and then I remembered what Pete Rooney told me once. 'In every house where a priest was being made,' he said, 'the kitchen door would be locked at meal times.'

This aspect of priestly functioning didn't attract me. I always had a good appetite.

Jack O'Brien had an oldish sharp-boned sister living with him, he was never married. The sister's name was Maggy. She talked like one who had lived a while in society houses, and this was true. She was far too polite for a rank kitchen, I thought, and her kitchen was too orderly for hungry cats to hope.

I got supper better than I expected though nothing to brag about, then I was shown my bed. It was a structure composed entirely of rough boards in the corner of a loft; on one side of the bed stood a winnowing machine, and on the other side a small heap of fusty oats. The bed was canopied, or more correctly, had a loft, on top of which reposed sand riddles and corn sieves, old boots, and scraps of harness. 'Leave by a thing that you don't want for ten years and at the end of that period you may throw it away if it's not wanted.' Thus ran a wisecrack or adage or whatever it is among the people I knew. It was on the loft poised on the four posts of my bed that Jack O'Brien put the junk he might want before ten years.

He saw me viewing the over-weighted structure suspiciously. 'There's no danger o' that comin' down,' he assured me.

The night was warm; I slept on top of the bedclothes in my naked innocence. I slept very well considering how the big black dog-fleas were doing gymnastics. I was always rather lucky in regard to fleas, they never fancied my flesh. The flea is a creature of the imagination and my poetic temperament didn't include this form of ecstatic pain.

Morning, very early I guessed, the sun was just risen above the cool green hill-top rushes. I sat up in bed having slung a pillow across my head and then let it slip to the ideal position at the back of my neck. Home was never like this, I thought, I was free, as free as a bird or a squirrel or a fool's heart.

I stared towards the roof and began to catalogue the various antiquities that lay upon the collar-ties; there was a flail, white and moth-eaten, a scythe that belonged to the early nineteenth century, a pair of turf-creels, a calf-muzzle, and on a nail on the farthest wall hung the hide of a goat, horns, hooves, and all.

This is a great life, I mused, God knows what's to follow though. I never liked being very happy knowing surely that after light comes darkness. This idea has always terrified me: our home was so lucky and I was so lucky: there would come a crash.

Yet no crash ever came. There is not much drama in real life. The curtains of Reality are very weak.

I was happy during part of this morning in Ballytrain; I had moments innocent with revelation. I caught glimpses – through the impurities of glass – of that transfigured hill the dreams of poets and children climb. In those days I would not dream of mentioning anything rare and innocent in the market-place. I understood that there are things not to be mentioned under penalty of loss. Many years afterwards, when I was older and farther from angelhood, I told of that beatific wonder to clods and disillusioned lovers. I asked them if they didn't see something beyond the hills of Glassdrummond. They laughed and said I was mad.

And I saw no more. I had sinned. As I lay with my neck against that pillow I lived a long time.

The sun had gone up and was filtering through the slated

123

roof. Time to be getting up, I thought, and then I heard footsteps climbing the stone steps to the loft door.

Knock, knock, knock, on the loft door, and Jack's voice shouted in: 'Are ye sleeping, Paddy?'

'No, I'm getting up,' I said, and to prove my story no lie I jumped out on the floor and unbarred the door.

I said my prayers while putting on my clothes, it was the custom. Then my religious eye noticed that there was a holy-water bottle hanging by a boot-lace from the post of my bed. It was a half-pint whisky bottle, cobwebbed, dusted on the outside, and green-scummed on the inside. The water in the bottle was old and smelly but this didn't take away its holiness. I sprinkled a few drops on my face and went down the steps.

'The breakfast won't be ready for a while,' Jack said to me, 'so you'd be better go down to yon meadow and cut a sheaf of grass for the foal-mare.'

'Very well,' I said.

'Ye'll find the scythe hangin' in a boortree on the left-hand side of the gate.'

I brought back a sheaf of grass and deposited it at the mare's stable door. Then I went in for breakfast.

The breakfast was as generous as thrifty Ballytrain could allow: slices of coarse brown bread toasted on a pan of lard, tea that wouldn't damage anyone's nerves and as much salt as you could desire.

We sowed turnips that day; Jack had the drills opened for some days and he set me to shut them, a job I knew nothing about.

The mare was fidgety too for her foal, locked up in the stable. My father used to say that I had so much conceit I would take on to put a leg on a horse, and I felt as I started after the drill plough that my impudence was equal to anything. The soil was heavy, sticky, and lumpy, but luckily there were no rocks, else I should have crashed into sudden disgrace. I felt I was doing real well. When I returned to the headland from which I started my master was there. He was shaking his head with a sort of sadness or pity.

'Be damn but this is a holy dread,' he said. 'Why, man jewel alive, an infant child could make a better hand of it than that.'

'Is it not all right?' I queried.

'All right, aye,' he said contemptuously. 'I'm afraid I'll have to harrow down that drill, 'twould be a holy show in such an exposed part of the field.'

So it was that I fell from the dignity of ploughman to become a yardman, feeder of pigs and calves and a squarer of dung-hills. I got on very well for a few days; the kitchen wasn't the rankest, but it was a tolerable enough place. The worst feature was the constant nag of jobs waiting to be done, for ever and ever, it was a circle, and a vicious one at that, a wheel without a spoke of time missing.

My comrade John lived quite near. We met the first evening and exchanged notes.

'What kind of dump are ye in?' John asked.

'A sort of middlin',' I replied.

'Then it could be worse, but the place I'm in is the worst of the worst. I was polluted with fleas last night; there were millions of them and as big as spiders every mother's son of them.'

We knocked about the roads but there were few people to whom we could talk, nobody in that neighbourhood stopped work while there was a glimmer of light.

'They'll be rich or damn poor,' my companion said, using the old ready-made saying.

'Damn poor then, they'll be,' I said; 'the land wouldn't feed snipes.'

The funny thing was that the poorer the land the tidier the house, the more money in the bank and the better chance of a priest.

In our country nobody ever had more than a hundred in the bank – except, of course, the two publicans – and the only kind of priest any of our neighbours ever made was one for the Foreign Mission.

Around Ballytrain the only flourishing tree was the boor tree; there were some blackthorns and a stunted breed of whin. The fields were very small and shaped to draw the water. Every man was a dealing-man; if he didn't deal in crooked horses, he was a fowl-dealer or a dealer in the insurance business.

Oh, there was a brisk trade in the insurance of everything that could be burned or that could die.

We met a man who gave us the history and genealogy of the whole country-side. He himself had had, he told us, a two pounds ten a week insurance book. 'And,' as he explained, 'some low mane dog put a caveat in against me.' He wasn't afraid to give away the tricks of the trade, and explained to us the wickedness of insurance companies and how the people were too smart for them.

'Here's a good story I must tell you,' he said. 'Round about here every house is insured and last year there was a hell of a row because one man burned out of his turn. Ye see the way it was, it wouldn't look if every house were burned on the one week, so there was a union formed and it was arranged that I'd burn this week, and you the next, and you else the next, and so on till yer turn would come round again. This fella had a bill to pay – he was makin' two priests and that no joke – so he burned out of his turn. There was a hell of a row, and very nearly a lawsuit over it. The man maintained that he didn't burn out of his turn, but the union had the books and it was lucky for him he didn't contest it in the law court for he'd be bet blind.'

On the morning of my second day Jack came to the loft door a shade earlier than the first day and by the end of a week he had the sun beaten in the early rising contest.

'Paddy, get up.'

'What time is it?' I would ask.

'Time any dacent boy was up, that is if he manes to earn his breakfast.'

'It isn't six.'

'Paddy, get up. The clock is all right if yer goin' for a train, it wouldn't pay us to go be the clock.' I told John Gorman about it.

'I'm in the same boat,' he said, 'only that I don't rise till I feel like it. I have me boots beside the bed and every time I'm called I rattle the boots on the floor and say: "I'm gettin' up, I'm puttin' on me boots."'

The very next morning I heard the call just as the first thin music of dawn was peeping through the mist. I held my boots by a long lace, and rattled them on the floor. 'I'm puttin' on my boots,' I said. Then I lay back and went to sleep.

'Be damn, but this won't do at all,' I heard some time later. 'Are ye still lacin' yer boots?' I rattled the boots again. He was a dubious-minded man.

'These di does won't work here, Paddy,' he said. 'If yer goin' to rise, rise, and if yer not, get yer bundle before the hirin' season's over, I don't want to be left in the lurch.'

From that day till the day I left him a fortnight later relations between us were very strained. I could do nothing right in his eyes. I did actually break some implements: I broke the middle prong of a three-pronged fork, thereby rendering the implement useless except in a row.

'Aw, ye'll rob me,' he cried, as he looked at the skeleton graip. 'That's here this twenty year, and thicker men than you wrought with it, but it took you to make a job of it. The next thing ye'll break is the steel crow-bar.'

And then Maggy came out and surveyed the damage.

'The good graip, too,' she remarked.

'The good new graip indeed,' her brother said. 'If it was any of the others I wouldn't much mind, but that one is no more than twenty years on the dunghill.'

I was dismissed, but I had to put in my day.

'Go down,' he said, 'and weed the little lock o' praties that we left behind us yesterday.' I did so. I only pulled the top off the weeds as I was leaving that evening, and as I had finished early I went over to the field where John Gorman was weeding and told him how the ball had hopped.

'We'll be home together,' he said. 'You'd never guess what happened on Saturday night?'

'What?'

'When I came in late from the fields and had me supper et and was just givin' a shine to me Sunday boots, Judy, that's the mistress, put down beside me a dozen pairs of boots at laste. From Harry's number twelves down to the child's all in a row. I looked at the boots and I said nothin' and they looked at me and they said the same. I tell you me temper was risin'. To think I'd polish the boots for a pack of beggars like them. I took a fit

127

and kicked the boots through the kitchen and up on the table and dresser, I kicked the guts out of them. Judy went wild and was thinking about sendin' for the police and no police in the country. When Harry came he took it cool enough; he told me I might go, so I'll be with ye home.'

I was delighted. I was heartily tired of this thrifty land which had an abundance of nothing save rushes and priests.

John Gorman was full of an extraordinary curiosity. He wanted to know the ins and outs of every natural puzzle. As we tramped along together he was continually stopping and examining some strange flower or tree and asking: 'Now what name is on that? It isn't a cowslip and it isn't a primrose.'

I was impatient. To me home was the only real flower, which makes one wonder why it is always the home-lover who wanders.

An American girl, a relation who used to visit us, said to me once: 'I'll come back here in twenty years and you will be here.' I promised in my heart that I would not fulfil this prophecy. The twenty years are not up and I'm not at home.

My father and mother laughed when they saw me home.

'Sit down on the sate,' said my father, 'and learn the trade. It's never goin' to be a load.'

'And mebbe he'll think more of it now that he's seen the world,' my mother remarked.

I was always very pliable. I took my father's advice, though with reservations, and sat down to the cobbler's trade.

17 Serving My Time

While I was being initiated into the secret Guild of the Cobblers the Treaty was signed. Father read it from the paper. I was upstairs putting on my trousers at the time. I was mad, I was disappointed.

'It's betrayal,' I shouted down. 'Ireland has been let down by Griffith.'

And so it was betrayal of the rising generation that hadn't had a fight. I wanted a fight. I had missed the Black and Tan scrap and now it seemed we were in for the monotony of peace. I did very little cobbling those days. I was in bad humour.

'What do ye think of the Treaty?' people asked me.

'It's what Father Maguire says,' I told them, 'a rosy apple that's rotten at the core.'

Many other young fellows were of the same opinion as I was.

'Do you know, Jack,' I said to a neighbour one of those days, 'I'm standing in a place I never stood in before.'

'Where?'

'In the British Empire.'

'Do ye say that?'

'I do say it,' I said. 'Griffith and Collins took the bribe.'

There never was a worse apprentice to any trade than I was. No wonder, for with the country partitioned and a new generation robbed of its inheritance how could any young man be contented on a cobbler's bench?

People came in and said to my father: 'Damn, but ye have him on the sate at last,' referring to me.

'He doesn't care for it,' father said.

'Aw, he'll get outa that,' they reassured him.

I didn't hate cobbling, but I affected a hatred in which everybody believed save myself. I must have broken father's patience.

'It's no load to carry,' he advised me, 'and you might be glad of it yet.'

129

Whenever he tried to show me anything, before he had half-explained I would say: 'I know, I know,' and proceed doing it the wrong way.

'In ten years you won't know half as much as you know to-day,' he used to tell me. In spite of my deliberately willed resistance I did manage to make some progress. In spite, too, of my belligerent national spirit, before a few months I could peg an insole though I couldn't guarantee to make it waterproof. People wanted waterproof boots in that boggy place. 'Will it keep out the water?' they asked. Father would stand the boot in the pan of water which was used to soften stubborn leather. 'Put yer hand into that boot,' he said, 'and if ye find a drop of water I'll let ye have them for nothin'.' Of course the boot wouldn't soak in moisture unless there was suction, but the people forgot that.

The Civil War came and I managed to get in a bit of work for Ireland on the side. Some members of the I.R.A. operated in that area. I joined their evenings and got a kick out of it. We cut the telegraph wires every evening. First we cut a length of wire from the railway-paling, tied a stone to the end of the wire, flung it over the telegraph wires and pulled them down. It was much more dangerous than the Black and Tan fight. Three of our fellows took an old Ford car, it was called commandeering the car, and were put up against the wall of Dundalk Gaol and shot. The Black and Tans were gentlemen when compared with the Free Staters. My parents would have been annoyed had they suspected the cause of my nocturnal absences. My patriotic activities sharpened my zest for work, though not of course very sharp. Two hours at a stretch on the seat was all I could stick. Then I took a run round to John Caffrey's house. John lived close to us, usually all alone save when I or a taciturn fellow named Cooper paid him a visit. I was sitting in Caffrey's house one day when father called to the door.

'Have ye a man hired here?' he asked John Caffrey.

'I have not,' John said.

'I thought ye had. Come out here, ye lazy robber,' he called me.

During the years I sat on the apprentice seat the hurry of life was passing from my father. He was becoming mellow and rich with memories. He believed in ghosts. I made an agreement with him that after his death I would meet him if he could come back. Although when he was on his death-bed I cancelled my part of the contract (father was in a state of coma) I really believe that he did come back in spirit. Mortal eyes have never seen a ghost, only the eyes of the spirit can see, and I saw.

He told me that after her death his mother had spoken to him. I refused to believe and he was grieved.

'I wasn't drunk or dreaming,' he said.

'You only imagined it,' I said.

'Not imagination,' he said, with deep earnestness. 'My mother spoke to me after her death.'

There was hardly anything my father would have me believe in preference to this story. To so few has clear proof of immortal survival been given. He was a man of faith.

I believe now.

A cobbler's shop is a garden of philosophy. On wet days our house was filled with all the seers and savants of the neighbourhood. On the very wettest day would come MacGeogh to get a tip on his boot. MacGeogh was a tidy, well-preserved man of seventy: he had never married. Each time he came he retold for us the stories of his many law cases. And what he said to the judge.

' "Me lord, sir," says I to the Master of the Rolls, "I have no schoolin' but I can tell the truth." "Do ye know, MacGeogh," says the Master of the Rolls to me. "Do ye know, MacGeogh," says he, "ye ought to be in my place." '

'Didn't Connor beat you?' I said.

'Bate be damned,' MacGeogh growled. 'Do ye know me sweet fella, Connor didn't bate us, we bet ourselves.' He looked at the boot I was repairing. 'Rise me well on the outside of that brogue,' he said.

MacGeogh was a vain old man. He had hardly ever lost a lawsuit. His talk had quality which the written version of his stories lacks.

' "Where did ye get all the money, MacGeogh?" says his lordship to me. "Me lord, sir," says I, "I earned it with the

131

sweat of me back." "Yer a nailer, MacGeogh," says his lordship. "I dismiss the case against MacGeogh with full costs." Did ye put a good lift on the outside of that heel?'

'I'm making a first-class job of it,' I said. 'I'll put you straight on your feet.'

'As for Connor,' MacGeogh said, reverting to the lost lawsuit, 'we bet ourselves. Me own engineer tould the judge that I didn't lave an ample fence after me when I cut the march-ditch. Huh, himself and his ample. I wasn't much of a scholar but I knew what ample meant.'

Once a month father travelled to the town to buy a bag of leather. He pushed the full bag out the train window so that we had only a few yards to carry the heavy weight. It wasn't allowed, but the guard of the train wasn't too exact. We watched out our back window for the bag of leather to appear from the window of the train. Sometimes it burst and then there would be a wide scatterment of tips and sprigs and fresh herrings – father never came home without herrings.

My father had the habit of talking to himself, a habit I myself have got.

'Yer oul' fella is drunk,' a lad who was with me in father's company one day said.

'He's talking to a gentleman,' I said.

One evening four big men burst into our kitchen: they were out of breath and we thought something extraordinary must have happened.

'When was the Carrick railway made?' the first spokesman asked father.

'It was started in eighteen-eighty-three,' he said, 'and finished in eighty-seven.'

One of the men gave a loud guffaw and clapped his neighbour on the back. 'I won the bet, I won the bet,' he said. We had to wait for the commotion to subside before we were let out from our mystification. It was a public-house bet of a gallon of porter per man. The dispute had arisen in a nearby pub as to when the railway line had been made. 'We'll lave it to the Kavanagh,' they said. The fellow who won the bet had wagered that the other three were wrong. He himself didn't know when the line was made, but he wanted to be in the swim. The four men left as hurriedly as they came.

One summer's morning a man in his bare feet slipped into our kitchen; he came in so noiselessly that he was standing behind our benches before we knew. We were almost sure he was mad. We knew him, he was an ex-schoolmaster named Tom Fee. Very fond of his pint, his people hid his boots to prevent him getting anywhere. He was friendly with my father and had walked five miles to our house for aid and succour in his predicament.

Tom Fee could talk well. When we got over our first shock we listened to his grand discourse. On this morning he was expounding American politics. Democrats and Republicans and the future of the United States in general, I heard the whole story from Tom Fee. He had his gunther's chain under his arm, for he was a surveyor of land and each year measured out acres on Rocksavage farm. As he wasn't getting younger he would often as not guess the acres. Some people might get a few perches more than an acre if Tom's guess had been lubricated beforehand. I think Tom was one of the surveyors who took part in a survey of Ireland which was a cause of much amusement. When all the acres had been added up there wasn't enough room in Ireland for them. If Tom wasn't in that survey-comedy he told us about it.

Micky, an old quarryman, was sitting by our fire, talking to my mother while we were putting the finishing touches to a pair of new boots for him.

'Ye were married to a daughter of Keegan's?' my mother said, so as to show an intimate interest in a customer.

'I was,' Micky said.

'And musha how is she doin'?' Mother asked.

'She's dead,' Micky said.

'Well, may the Lord have mercy on her sowl,' Mother said. 'I was at school with her. It was a hard knock for ye, Micky.'

Micky nodded his head. 'Hard enough,' he agreed, 'but as the fella said, I got another.'

The pair of new boots we had made were heavy, suitable to a quarryman: there was a pound of hobnails in each boot.

'Will ye wear them home?' we asked.

'I will not,' he said. 'I'd like to keep them a while for Sunday dacency.'

While I was sitting on the seat one evening in the autumn of nineteen-twenty-two, a hand appeared at our back window. It was the signal. I hurried the job in hand to a finish and got up and went out.

Two men were outside waiting for me. One of them had a gun and the other a pair of wire-cutters.

'Anything important on?' I enquired.

'Goin' to hould up the eight o'clock train,' I was informed.

We cut the telegraph wires more from habit than out of tactical necessity. I was given a Colt automatic and put on sentry duty. The gate at the level-crossing was turned inward towards the line so that the red light was against the train. The gate didn't close across the line, it only reached to the ends of the sleepers.

As it was after eight o'clock now I deserted my post and joined the other men.

'What the hell is keepin' her?' they wondered.

'She'll come in her own sweet time,' I said.

Twenty minutes after eight we were becoming very impatient. Something must have happened, we thought.

'The curse of Hell on Duffy,' one of the men muttered.

'Perhaps he's takin' her home across the fields,' the other man suggested humorously.

Duffy was the driver of the train.

And just then we heard the puff-puff of the train. Sounded as though she were starting but it wasn't from the station. We waited on the railway slope close to the gate. The red light was against him, he was bound to stop. Yet he didn't, he made the engine do her fastest when he saw the red light. The train passed us at thirty-five miles an hour. We looked after her hungrily.

'What do ye think of that?'

'Why didn't ye blarge?' I was asked.

'I had no orders,' I said.

'Orders be damned.'

What had happened was this – the train had already been held up further down the line and a barrel of porter and several chests

of tea taken from it. I believe it was tobacco and cigarettes we
were after.

At a point along the line known as the Black Stick it was a
common thing whenever a housewife ran short of tea, flour, or
any other necessity of the kitchen, for her to call on her husband
to get the old gun – while she procured a red petticoat – and hold
up a train. It happened almost every day. The rails would be
soaped if necessary.

When trains failed to stop there was nothing for it but to fall
back on Conway's. Conway's house was robbed on an average
twice a month. It was one of the Big Houses. I was never in a
robbery save one, though at that time it was the normal business
of the country.

Later in the season I was out again, this time on more official
duty. Two houses of the most prominent Free Staters were to
be blown up as a reprisal for the shooting of the three men who
had commandeered the old Ford car. We blocked the road with
big stones, we cut the telegraph wires. While working the wire-
cutters the handles jammed my finger badly and that was all the
wounds I received in the cause of freedom. The bleeding finger
edged my nerves a bit. A lorry or motor-car – I didn't wait to
see which – appeared in the distance. 'The Staters,' I heard. Then
I ran. I ran across ploughed fields and through briars and over
ditches, I ran home without once looking back. First thing next
morning I went to see the ruins of the blown-up houses; they
stood intact: a humane man, a real I.R.A. man, had called off
the attack.

I didn't stick to the last, as the cobbler has been advised to
do. There was the farm to be attended to and the neighbours to
be repaid with my labour for horse-work. Father wished it so –
cobbling is a hard trade on a young man.

A customer of ours who believed in the old, glorious ideal of
Ireland refused to believe that the Civil War was real. 'It's only
a dodge,' he would say, 'it's only a dodge to fool England.'

Our townland – and indeed every townland – was divided and
there was much bitterness. It was in those days I acquired the
expensive smoking habit. I was usually worth a shilling a week
and this went up in smoke. For many years I never smoked in

the presence of my parents, so great was their power over me when I was in their presence. Out of it I let myself go. I also went to a dance or two then; from one of the dances I escorted a girl home for the first and last time. I didn't relish the job and had only taken it on to oblige a companion who had clicked the girl's sister. My wooing wasn't very passionate. I could think of nothing to say to the girl, who was ugly as sin, so I just whistled.

We didn't stay two minutes with them. I remember that as we trudged home in the small hours we knocked down the pier of a man's field-gate. We flashed a lamp through the bedroom window where the man slept alone. We got a crooked wire and putting it through a broken pane, dragged the bedclothes off the man. He didn't wake up. We thought it great fun as it was, but not for the frogs.

At another dance I witnessed a great battle for a girl. Not with lethal weapons was the battle fought, but with the deadlier weapons of calumny and googly eyes. The girl sat on my knee. She was very pretty. I could have had her if I hadn't had a faint heart. Even to this day I could curse myself for letting that girl go.

After a dance I would be in a bad humour for several days. I would do damage to many a good boot that not even the guile of an old craftsman could hide.

'My God,' father would exclaim, 'ye cut the upper right at the welt. Go out and dig between the cabbages.'

Among the cabbages I was little less awkward. I once broke the handle of a spade. I stuck the ends together. About two days later I saw father rush into the house.

'I'm after breakin' the spade,' he said.

'Sure what about it?' I soothed.

On a day when I was alone in the house a man came in and asked me if I could give him a bottle of leather-water. He had soft feet and the leather water was good for hardening them. He gave me sixpence and I told him to call again when he wanted a new supply. He did return, but wanted no more water. 'Made a new man of me feet,' he told me.

'I made it special for you,' I said.

We had a few bad days. It was mostly runners of yearly bills we had. Father would prefer one ready-money customer before five who ran bills.

Around on our floor, as was to be expected, would be a lot of rusty nails and rivets. My brother, who was a child of four then, got a prick of a rusty nail and his foot became septic. The neighbours looked at it and said:

'God bless it but ye ought to send for Harry McElroy, it surely is the rose.'

We were in some doubts but eventually sent for the doctor.

'I'd have Harry in if I was in your place, Mrs Kavanagh,' one woman said.

'We'll try the doctor first,' mother said.

Harry wasn't sent for after all, as my brother recovered. The people said: 'Ye were lucky got the doctor, but what if it had been the rose?'

As the second string to my fiddle I was sent to a farmer to serve my time to that trade. The farmer was a breeder of prize horses and it was considered a good place for me. On my first day with the farmer I fell from grace. I was leading a roan stallion out of his stall. Whether the stallion took a peculiar hatred of me or not I can't say but he began to kick. He kicked the heavy door of the stall to smithereens and the boss saw the disaster. I took a fit of laughing. The boss took the horse from me and said a lot of vicious nothings. It was a bad start. This farmer was very exact and clean and I was neither. My apprenticeship to Michael had been purely spiritual, and that kind of learning was little use when dealing with temperamental stallions and cross bulls.

'Ye should stick to the cobblin',' one of the servant boys advised me, 'it's a good trade.'

The worst feature of my master was his method of silent reproval: he never blamed with his tongue. One day at dinner I was twirling a mug around when it flew off, leaving the handle on my finger like a ring: master and mistress looked on and said nothing. I didn't stay with the farmer at night, I slept at home.

'Come in for yer breakfast,' they called me the first morning. I hesitated. I expected to get a second call: it was the custom of the country never to accept a first invitation. People would often invite one to tea or any meal and expect a refusal. Things were done differently here. I got only one call. I waited a fair while for the second and when it wasn't forthcoming my appetite disposed of custom.

I worked for this man during six or seven months. I might have learned something that would have been useful even to a poet had I been sensible. My whole object then was to put in my days as quickly as I could and as easily as I might and as a consequence the wisdom of a prize farmer lighted for me no beauty.

Spring time came round and I found myself getting very sick: my legs wouldn't keep up with my head. I stumbled and fell helpless. But in the meantime other things of more dramatic tensity had happened.

18 The Outlaws

The River Fane ran through our parish on its way to the Irish
Sea. It was a clear, swift-flowing stream. Anglers came long
journeys to dream and smoke tobacco on its banks. These anglers
said the Fane was as good a trout-stream as there was in Ireland.
I shouldn't say so – the trout in its waters took after the people
of Inniskeen in being hard to catch. Like the people, they knew
humbug, and were dubious-minded as a jealous husband.

We who lived near the Fane had no use for trout-angling: it
was too delicate, idealistic a sport for strong men of reality. But
the salmon that came up in November, we liked those fat fish.
In November the salmon came up to spawn. They would be
sleepy then, like good-thriving pigs.

'Will ye come to the river?' a fellow asked me on a particularly
dark evening in November.

I knew what he meant. A night's salmon-poaching with a gaff
and a carbide bicycle lamp.

I had never before been on the river. Salmon-gaffing was cruel
work. But it wasn't that. I thought it wasn't worth the risk. For
even though you might escape the water bailiff and the new Civic
Guards what good was it all if you got pneumonia? On this
occasion I did go. There's a great kick to be got out of risking
one's life if it's only for a spent-salmon.

There were four of us. We met at a place known as 'the splink'.
It was very dark. A sleety rain was spitting from the north.
There was not a star to be seen.

'A great night for the job,' one man said.

'Ye might swear that,' we replied. A dark night was the night
for gaffing salmon.

Between us we had two gaffs and two bicycle lamps. The gaffs
were spears with a barb, attached to the end of poles twelve or
fourteen feet long. I was a lamp-man.

'Keep yer eyes skinned,' was the order of the night.

I cast my lamp's light on the dark, troubled river. The fellow beside me with the gaff grew quietly excited.

'Do ye see yon fella?' he whispered. I saw nothing.

The gaff-man walked right into the river and shot his gaff at something.

'I got him,' he cried to me, 'he's as big as a calf.'

There was a terrible commotion in the water. The man with the gaff was being knocked about in every direction. The other gaff-man rushed to his assistance and prodded the waters with his gaff. He couldn't spear the salmon. That salmon fought hard for its life. For a full half-hour he leaped and dashed hither and thither. Once the man with the gaff was knocked in the river but he still held on. I was getting my poaching-sight. I caught a glimpse of the salmon at last. It was more beautiful than stained-glass, for that was what its body-colour reminded me of. Like very beautiful stained-glass in a dark chapel, when the sun shines through it. The sun on this occasion was my lamp of perdition.

The salmon was dragged out on to the bank. It was about thirty pounds' weight. From the water's edge to where the salmon lay the seed of the fish sparkled in the lamplight – the bright silver of life. One of our company rubbed his boot over the spawn until its shining beauty was mixed with the black clay.

'Better lave no clues,' he said.

We put the salmon in a sack. We walked into the river up to our waists. It was bitterly cold.

There was a sound near at hand of stones being disturbed from a ditch. We listened.

'Did any of yez hear anythin'?' one asked.

'For Christ's sake shut yer gab,' a vicious whisper answered him.

We covered our lamps with our caps and stood still.

Nothing happened. It wasn't the water-bailiffs or the police. Only some drunken man perhaps on his way home.

We waded up the river for a mile. The next salmon caught was to be mine. I was anxious to get that salmon. There is no humanitarianism among folk who live close to life. Townsfolk provide societies for the protection of animals because they are one remove from primitive life. We had no sympathy for the salmon any more than for the fat pigs which we slaughtered at our front doors.

The river deepened at this point, and roared between walls of rock. It was here the salmon loved to lie, on their way towards the spawning beds below Moyle's Corn Mill.

'I'm not goin' to get drowned for the sake of a salmon,' I heard a man say.

'Nor me either,' I said.

The other two men would stop at nothing.

'When yer out for the night be out for the night,' one of them said to us.

'Halt, halt.'

The voice split through the blackness from a clump of black-thorns on our right. We were trapped, I guessed. On our left-hand side the river ran twenty feet deep. A light was flashed on us, but we took the precaution of turning our backs to the clump of bushes.

'I know yez,' the bailiff said, 'I know ye, Paddy.'

There are a lot of Paddies in Ireland so his guess wasn't so brave after all.

'Mind ye don't shoot the bugger,' I heard one of our fellows say to another.

I thought it was only a bit of bluff. The next thing I heard was a revolver-shot. The water-bailiff dropped his lamp and put his hands over his head.

'Hook it outa this as quick as you can,' Paddy C., the man with the gun, said to the bailiff in a camouflaged voice. He did so.

'The rotten oul' cur,' the gunman said when he had gone.

'Well, we're better be hookin' it outa here, too.'

'You said it, the Guards will be down on us before half an hour.'

'Is it the Guards to lose a night's sleep to folly us! No damn fear.'

'They'd get half the fine, you know.'

That settled it. We waded our way towards the shallow part of the stream and climbed out by clutching at the whin-roots which stuck through the rocky bank like the toes of a tramp through a bad boot.

We had our salmon in a sack hidden under a heap of withered potato-stalks which had been dumped beside the river.

I was shivering with cold wetness. My three companions must have been iron men. They laughed and talked as though they were drinking porter at some gay bar.

'The Guards, the Guards.'

The words, spoken by the man in front, passed through us like an invigorating electric shock. Anything was better than this misery of black, wet coldness. Not that the Guards were terrible beings to encounter. We ran. At least, I ran. I ran quickly. I crossed the potato-field. The soft, heavy soil clung to my boots. I dashed into a potato-pit. Before I stopped to meditate I had put a prudent distance between me and the river.

Next day I encountered the fellow who had given me the invitation to the river. He was laughing when we met.

'What did ye do last night?' he asked, in a slightly ironic tone.

'What did I do?' I said.

'Ye ran.'

He waited to let the coward-awfulness of his statement enter deeply into my soul. When I was completely flat-humble, he deigned to tell me the sequel. I knew by his manner that I had missed something.

'We waited till the Guards came up. The sergeant was in it. George jerked behind a clump of whins and got behind the Guards. In less than a pair of minutes the pair of black hures were on the broad of their backs. We gave them a tarlin hammerin'.'

'We'll all be lifted,' I said.

'Divil a that,' he assured me. 'The Guards will be ashamed of their bleddy life to let on. But afraid of the worst keep yer mouth shut.'

I did that until now. I hope it is statute-barred. For though the individual policemen may forget, the Law – like an elephant – never does.

The eighth of December is a Catholic holiday. Since nineteen hundred and twenty-two I have kept it as an anniversary and a day of special devotion. On that day, nineteen twenty-two, my

career as a young gangster touched the high spot, fused and
went out.

'Will ye come out with the Mummers?' a fellow asked me.

'I wouldn't think twice of it if I knew the rhymes,' I said.

'Rhymes be hanged,' he said, 'ye know enough.'

There were about fifteen lads in our troupe of Mummers. I
had an insignificant role at the tail of the play. I wore an old
black bowler hat and had a cardboard false face.

We headed across the fields, jumping drains and scrambling
over hedges. We were well received by the people, hardly any
house barred its door against us. We carried a melodeon though
none of us could play the instrument. The old folk in the little
houses gave us a warm welcome: they looked upon the Mummers
as an old Irish custom, which it was not. The big houses looked
upon us as hooligans and it might be they were right. During
our travels a bottle of poteen made its appearance. One of our
characters, Oliver Cromwell, had the bottle on his head.

'Hell freeze ye,' Saint George cried, 'don't drink the cow dry,'
and he grabbed the bottle.

'Howld on there,' Oliver Cromwell shouted, 'I didn't get two
sups out of that bottle.'

'Don't drink it all,' another historical figure pleaded. 'What
about me that has me two feet in water?'

This fellow had missed his step when jumping a drain.

In one big house to which we forced our way we were met by
silence. A side of bacon hanging from the rafters dangled above
our heads. One of our fellows snatched the bacon from its hook
and we all dashed out.

We went up to a house in a bog village known as Sooty Row.
The door was slammed in our faces. The 'Doctor', part of our
cast, carried a huge wooden beetle which he had taken from a
tub of pigs'-mash in one of the houses. Bang! Bang! Crash! He
struck the closed door and smashed it to smithereens. Then we
all ran.

In another house we got eighteen pence and a warm welcome.
That should have satisfied us but it did not. A pile of griddle-
cakes stood on the table near the door, one on top of the other.
The bottom cake was a lovely fruit cake with cherries and raisins

sticking out its sides. As I went out the door I heard a noise and a commotion. I looked round and saw five or six cakes – like the wheels of turf-barrows – rolling about the floor: the fruit cake wasn't among them. One of our number dashed past me hugging that cake. The man of the house stood in the doorway and we heard him say, very politely: 'A meaner lot of young men I have never known.' The cake was devoured in a minute. I got very little, just a crust from which the donor had carefully picked the raisins and cherries.

By the roadside we sat down to count the money. There was a row.

'Yer keepin' some of it,' the purse-bearer was told. He got raging mad. 'There's the rotten money,' he said, as he scattered it on the road. One more instance of the truth of the saying: 'A narrow gathering gets a wide scattering.'

We split: it was more or less a political split. The Free Staters turned for home, the Republicans continued ahead.

There was a dance in a near-by hall. I didn't want to go as I was fagged out.

For my part the dance was a complete flop. I couldn't see a nice girl in the place.

'How is it no nice girls come here?' I queried a crooked fellow who sat beside me.

'They don't,' he said. 'A fella could see more nice women with the skilly corner of his eye in a chapel that he'd see in forty dance-halls.'

To one of my comrades I put the same query and he advised me to get a pair of specs.

'When are we comin' home?' I asked.

'Home!' he exclaimed. 'What the hell would take ye home? Home was never like this.'

After a while I noticed my comrades clustered together in a corner of the hall. They were talking in signs and whispers – a language I understood somewhat imperfectly. One of them held up his two forefingers on seeing my impatience.

'It's all right,' he said, 'ye'll be home with us.'

At five o'clock in the morning we left the dance and plodded slowly along the pitch-dark road. About a mile from the hall we came to a full stop.

'Come here,' one of the fellows called me aside. 'I suppose I may tell him,' he said to the others.

'Oh, why not?'

'We have a mind to raid King's pub,' he told me laughingly.

'For guns?' I said.

He laughed again. 'Come on, lads,' he said.

Outside Tommy Breen's forge the coulter was removed from the plough. We walked round the pub: it stood on an island in the centre of four roads. Nobody lived on the premises except the barman.

While the first door was being prised open I was put on sentry duty. None of us had a gun. I heard footsteps approaching in our direction.

'Halt that son of a bitch,' I was ordered by the man with the coulter.

'Halt!' I shouted. 'Hands up.'

The footsteps came closer and I discerned the figure of a tall man and apparently a curious man. I stuck out my forefinger and cried:

'If you come on another step I'll plug ye.'

'For Christ's sake, don't shoot!' one of the men at the door advised.

The man stopped, but not, I think, till he had a good view of me. He recognized me, too, in spite of the darkness, for a few years later he gave me a hint to that effect. We knew him, too, yet not well enough to take any risks.

The front door was open now.

Crash, crash, crash, the coulter came down on the cash register. Then it was devil take the hindmost and I was the hindmost. A splutter of coins rolled to the floor. As I was down on all fours trying to finger the money out of the darkness, some big foot crushed my greedy fingers. I only got three coins and all of them spurious. The bottom of a public-house till is the home of bad money.

Some of our men now went to the bar. Down from the shelves

145

the bottles of whisky were taken. Whisky indeed! It proved as spurious as the money in the till. Only coloured water on the shelves for show, all the good whisky was stored under the counter and remained safe.

Every man carried half a dozen bottles of the alleged whisky. I had a half-bottle of port wine which the others disdained to touch. I had also ten or twelve packets of cigarettes.

We came home by an out-of-the-way path across the hills. Now and then the pop of a cork sounded, followed by a splutter of disgust as some of the stale water was being sampled.

'Christ, another bottle of water.'

'Here's an honest-lookin' bottle. Let's try it.'

'Aw jay, such stuff, smell it.'

'Pooh, pooh, five years ould at laste.'

'We got nicely codded in troth.'

We were standing by the edge of a lake. As the bottles were being tasted and found grossly under proof, one by one they were flung into the calm waters.

'It was the best thing could happen,' one fellow said. 'Had it been real whisky we'd have been found paralytic drunk by somebody.'

We walked slowly and wearily. 'Keep yer mouth shut about this,' I was advised. He said he was only afraid of the captain of the I.R.A. who gave orders to shoot for loot.

We passed through a land of death. I walked the last part of my journey alone, my comrades had gone their different roads. I felt weak as water. Outside our door I removed my boots and clothes. I crept noiselessly to bed. My father was a light sleeper yet I did not awaken him.

A few days later the word spread that King's pub had been robbed. Raided was the word used, which put an entirely different complexion on the matter.

When it was mentioned in our house I thought I'd faint. I believe the whole country-side knew quite well who did the raid, but in those days robberies followed one another so quickly that nobody had time to dwell on the niceties that make up the peasant conscience.

That was the only 'stunt' of that nature in which I was a

participant. I should have mentioned earlier that 'stunt' was the word for doings like this.

On that Christmas Eve I stood outside Michael Magee's pub in Inniskeen. At the bar and also at the grocery counter there was a brisk business being transacted. Michael's customers, in keeping with the spirit of the times – if not the spirit of Christmas – had taken over the shop.

Two men were filling drink behind the bar, while Michael and his barman looked on. Every drop of liquor on the premises was consumed that night. I saw a man lead in a string of nine men. 'I'll stand the drinks,' he said.

'Ten glasses of whisky here,' he ordered. Of course he paid no money.

At the grocery counter boxes of Bovril and pounds of tea were being taken from the shelves. It was Christmas time.

We outside the door wouldn't dare to go in, though as they say: it wasn't our hearts would hinder us.

From the shadows along the road as we went home we heard men murmuring in sodden sleep: 'A merry Christmas to ye.'

'The same to you, and many of them,' we responded.

19 Fever

As I have already stated I collapsed with the prize-farmer. I was sick. Doctor Brown was sent for.

'He has typhoid fever.'

At the mention of the word fever some strangers who were in the house nearly fainted. The fever must have done some depredation on their people, I thought. However, the neighbours rescued themselves from the terror of the fever by refusing to believe in it. They gathered into the kitchen and talked.

'Aw God bless yer sowl, Misses Kavanagh! He has no more faver than I have faver.'

'Sure what does Doctor Brown know?'

'I'd have another doctor to see him,' some other visitor advised.

My mother and father were in a state of panic. I was glad at what the doctor said. I was sure I had consumption and the neighbours in the kitchen were dead sure it was consumption I had. According to peasant-statistics nearly everybody died of consumption: appendicitis, warts, boils, corns, and bunions were all manifestations of the white scourge.

After I had been removed in the ambulance to the hospital the consoling neighbours gathered in strength to our house. The head of the debate was a big red-haired fellow who had been in hospital for two months, his name was Pat.

'So ye think now, Pat, it's not the faver?'

'Naw, he has no faver. Where would he get it?'

'Is it a taken thing?'

'God forbid, he'd smit the whole country.'

My father had come to hospital with me, my mother sat listening to Job's comforters.

'Mebby, Misses Kavanagh, with the help of God and his blessed Mother he might get well.'

One neighbour-woman came in to make inquiries. She wanted to verify a rumour. As soon as she had it straight that I was bad she dashed across the hills to her brother with the news. It is only the bare truth to say that this pair was delighted. Their eyes said: Isn't it great? Isn't it great? 'He busted himself,' the brother said. The woman laughed. 'I must be going,' she said. There were other people who might not have heard of my illness yet and she wanted to get in the first telling.

I used to be fond of being the first with a tale, and on a few occasions practised a bit of self-denial by standing back.

The glory of the country is the leisure people have to mind everybody's business.

To be sick was a disgrace. People kept a case of sickness in the household quiet as long as they could. When it leaked out the people would say: 'Now, aren't they close? Aren't they dubious minded? They must have the devil's bad opinion of the neighbours.'

When anybody around fell sick it pleased us all. We whispered our profound medical wisdom.

'Would it be anything bad he has?'

'Yer not the first asked me that.'

'Anything bad', usually meant venereal diseases, and the sum of two questions as above was – It surely is something bad he has. Why should they be keeping it so close if it was only a pain in the head?

This secrecy regarding illness wasn't confined to human beings. If a cow or a horse was sick the neighbours only heard of it by stealth. You might see one of them peeping through a hole in the hedge, and hear the talk.

'Begod that cow doesn't look good, she'll not over it, whatever it is she has.'

If the cow died she would more than likely be buried during the night. The neighbours would miss the beast.

'What the divil happened to Brown's cow? Do ye think did they sell her?'

And it might be some woman would put the question directly to Brown's wife. 'Did yez sell yon bracket cow, Judy?'

'Oh, we did to be sure,' Judy Brown answers. 'The jobbers came round and when the price was good we thought we'd be as well let her go.'

149

'Well, in troth I heard she died on yez.'

'Deed aye! The bad story is the quickest goes round. How is Peter's chist?'

'Peter, thank God, is grand, not the laste catch on him now.'

'Isn't that the blessin'!'

When Judy Brown parted from her persecutor she went into the kitchen.

'Who was that ye had out there?' her man asks.

'Biddy Magee.'

'A bad-minded article.'

'She heard the cow died.'

'Well, let her hear away. The cow's gone now and all our bad luck be with her!'

'Amen.'

When I arrived in the Fever Hospital I was put to bed. Just before I lay down I became terror-stricken I was blind. I looked towards my father's voice and could see nothing. Vaguely, dimly shapes began to form for me again. I wasn't stone blind, I could see a little.

The priest was sent for. I didn't want to see him. I didn't want to die, and the priest's coming is the sign of death. I didn't want to confess. The sins of adolescence are horrible ghosts, the nightmare of the soul and the fathers of remorse.

I could see the lighted candle at my head, but I could not see the priest. I wanted to tell him one sin, yet could not; the words choked me. I was only partly conscious.

'Are you resigned to die if it's God's will?' I heard him say.

I was not resigned though I mumbled something to the effect that I was.

The priest looked down at me. I didn't see him but I sensed him. He looked at me with pity for he believed I was booked.

For three weeks I lay in a state of semi-consciousness aware of only the electric bulbs at night.

My father came in every day to see me. He walked if the train wasn't in. He was in a far worse condition of fever than I was. I understand I used to speak to him, but at the time I never saw or heard him. He was grief-stricken, pathetic. One day he brought my sister to the graveyard and pointed out a grave.

'There's where I'll be buried if Patrick dies,' he said.

Masses were said for me, prayers on top of prayers.

Someone came in one day and put a scapular and a medal round my neck.

I had no intention of dying either in a state of grace or a state of mortal sin. The assistant nurse was a merry old grey-haired woman who did the night duty. She slept in the ward and took my temperature and rubbed my back.

A laugh is the best tonic in the world. I have had three great laughs in my life. One of these laughs, the second, was caused by a joke of the night nurse in that Fever Hospital.

Curious how a joke, the best and most effective joke, passes with the moment it comes in. If I tell the little joke now it will appear dull, not even silly.

She told me about a pet pig that the matron was trying to rear in the hospital.

'I had to give him a drink every night at twelve and just now I looked into his box he was blue all over,' and she laughed and laughed. But if the nurse laughed I do not know what way to describe the fit of laughter I had. I laughed and laughed and laughed till in the end I was afraid I shouldn't be able to stop. I must have laughed for a half-hour. Every bone and vein and idea was shaken asunder. That laugh shook the fever and worried it as a cat killing a rat. The matron once inquired if I was feeling hungry. I was, and hunger was no name for it. I was now five weeks without a bit of solid food. Every night I dreamt of lovely currant and cherry cakes. There was another woman who had the fever, and she told me she always dreamt of a big pot of steaming boiled potatoes. That was her dream of good eating.

I wasn't getting on as well as was expected, to use the hospital jargon. The doctor came in each day. If he wasn't an expert physician he, at least, had delicate manners. He always whistled outside the door.

One day four gunmen visited me. They created a great impression on the nursing staff. Even the deaf-mute wardsmaid understood the glory that was Ireland. I rose a cubit in their imaginations.

'You're an I.R.A. man?' Doctor Brown said. I was an elemental man, hunger had purified me from all vanity, and I told the truth. I wasn't an official member of the I.R.A. Afterwards when the fullness of my stomach brought back my vain glory I was mad at myself for saying what I did. The stage was set for a hero and the worshippers were all ready to kneel.

The doctor said I might have some solid food, the breast of a chicken and chicken tea. How beautiful that chicken tasted! How much better is reality than dream!

I developed complications: a clot of blood in one of my veins.

The doctor examined me gravely and said it was the devil's bad luck.

'You won't be able to get up now a while,' he said.

I was furious. I felt as a prisoner must feel sometimes feel, that sense of being shut in.

'Get me my trousers,' I demanded of the matron.

'Not till the doctor gives leave.'

If I had the trousers hanging beside my bed I shouldn't have minded, but the fact that they were locked from me fed the madness in my brain with frustrated food.

'Get me my trousers,' I pleaded.

I never knew that a woman could rise to such a furious quietness. Were you ever in a hospital? The mind of a nurse is one of the queerest machines known to psychology. You dare not cross a nurse: to do so in the humblest way is asking for trouble.

'Give me my trousers, for God's sake.'

The woman's face rose out on all sides like a set of toy balloons. I thought she'd explode and I was right in my thinking, for if she didn't actually explode, she deflated. She became as pale as a lime-washed wall.

'Do you know, sir,' she said, 'if you want to create trouble here you'd better be going.'

I smiled. After such an emotional disturbance her words were weak, futile spears. I was on the back of the matron's book. She reported me to the doctor, and the doctor all but dropped me from his panel. He would give me a look to see if I was alive and walk out.

Word was sent home that I was giving trouble.

One night I asked the assistant nurse if she could get me my trousers.

'Trousers,' says she, 'how am I doing without trousers?'

I was a prisoner. The feeling of bondage wasn't hurrying my cure. It got a grip on me like a lunatic idea. I didn't go mad. Eventually my trousers came flying through the room to land on the white quilt of my bed. 'There's your trousers now.'

I got up, and tried to pull up my trousers by the usual method, but when I tried to stand on one leg I fell in a heap beside the bed. Am I drunk, I wondered? My head was dizzy and my legs were not the best of props: they were loose about the knees and badly needed a tightening up with flesh. Seven weeks in bed had turned me into a rattling fine skeleton. 'If ye had to see yerself in them days,' a fellow said to me later, 'ye wouldn't know yer own name. Yer two cheek-bones were standin' on yer face like a pair of knob-handles on a corpse, and yer eyes – God bless the mark! – were all on the outside of yer face, ye could see every inch of them save the bit that ties them at the back. 'Pon me safe soul, Paddy, I never expected to see ye out again.'

I managed to get into my trousers. I sat by the fire in the ward – a prisoner on parole. At the end of an hour I was glad to get to bed again.

One day I heard a great commotion. I inquired of the assistant nurse the cause. She told me this: 'The Dummy – bad luck to her nails – committed herself, so we dragged her to the coal-house and shut her in.'

'Poor thing,' I said – for I could feel pity for all prisoners now – 'that's a shame.'

'She's a devil,' the nurse told me, 'she bit me when we were taking her out, and the marks of her five nails are in my arm as well.'

The ward in which I lay had ten beds. None of these had any clothes on them, and this gave the room the appearance of a scrap-iron store, or perhaps something less, far less, satisfying.

There was a tall, black press in one corner in which were stored red blankets of a workhouse complex. Two large windows at the front looked out on a rookery.

It was now April, and every morning early the crows set up a commotion like the voice of Bedlam.

There were Free State soldiers in the town, and each morning at eight the reveille on the bugle called the warriors to a breakfast of rashers and eggs.

Once I was praying aloud, sitting up in bed, when the matron arrived home from Mass. She heard the murmur of my devotion and came in to me. 'Can you not pray a little lower?' she asked.

'I might annoy the other patients,' I gassed. I thought she would hit me. Instead, the deaf-mute had come up behind her and hit her a blow of a duster.

Same morning I heard again the shuffle of a prisoner being dragged to the coal-house.

There came an end to my time in the Fever Hospital.

I was told I could go, and, added the matron, 'I hope we'll never have as troublesome a patient ever again.'

I did not say good-bye. I was still and all feeling a bit sentimental. I looked back once or twice. I thought that the deaf-mute at least would wave me a farewell, but there was neither hand nor handkerchief a-waving.

On the evening of my arrival home all the neighbours came in to welcome me and shake my hand.

Wonderful, I thought, how the face of the country had changed in my absence. I expressed my wonder.

'For goodness sake,' one of my household said, 'don't make out as if you were after coming from America. Don't have the people laughing at you.'

It wasn't considered manly to feel any poetic emotion. If a scene was beautiful you didn't say so. A man in love with anything was daft. The day after my home-coming I visited my friend George. He put out his hand to grasp mine.

'Lave it there,' he said.

We talked about the fever. George knew a great deal about fevers.

'When did ye get a cool?' he asked. I didn't understand.

'I suppose,' he said, 'that ye didn't get a cool till three weeks.'

'Five weeks,' I said.

'Good God! ye were bad, poor fella. Aw, I saw the time the

faver was in Callan's and I don't want to see any more. I saw four coffins comin' out the door, and nobody to carry them to the bone-yard. The faver is a boyo,[1] Paddy.'

I walked about on two sticks. People stared at me. 'Poor fellow,' their silence said, 'he's goin' about on crutches.'

The parish priest met me on the road and queried me about my trouble – beyond the bounds of good manners, I thought.

The P.P. had a high opinion of his medical knowledge, while the people had a still higher.

'Sure, Father Mac knows as much as a doctor.' The answers to this would be: 'Aye, and a damn sight more. Ye needn't pass Father Mac.'

A character known as the Rover Macoy called around. He wouldn't come in, but spoke to me through the window. I made as though to go out to him, and he ran away, crying: 'Don't come near me, don't come near me! Two of me brothers died from the faver.'

I wasn't fit for hard work. What could I be put to that would suit me, my parents thought?

Even that refuge of all poor scholars and spoiled priests – the insurance business – was mentioned.

Beside me was the cobbler's seat, with the hammer standing on its head on the bench. I sat on the seat and lifting the hammer, called out: 'Gimme a hoult of an oul' boot.'

'Ye could do worse,' my father said. So I continued sitting on the cobbler's seat, and customers came in and out. For many months fever was the topic of conversation, but it died out at last, in the talk, and in my blood – which was more important.

1. Boyo: play-boy.

20 The Wedding

I was going to the fair of Carrick. I was accompanied by a neighbour-man whose daughter was getting married. He was very fidgety on this occasion. He was going to the town to meet his prospective son-in-law and he had in his breast-pocket half the fortune which was to be paid over on that day.

Before we had walked very far together he brought forth the roll of notes.

'Count them, Paddy,' he said, handing me the notes.

I fingered them heedlessly.

'There's a hundred and fifty in that wad,' he said. 'Meself and Judy made all that, and it wasn't by buyin' new hats and fiddle de fols that we made it.'

'Judy was a good woman,' I said.

'Yer own mother was a good savin' woman, and between ourselves I wasn't a bad wee man meself.'

I handed him back the money. 'You were a good man,' I said.

'Yer own father was a good wee man,' he reciprocated, 'no better goin'.'

He looked towards the hills, and his dreams awoke.

'When I came from Scotland thirty years ago,' he said, 'I hadn't what would jingle on a tombstone. As God is me judge it's true, when I came home from Scotland I hadn't as much money as would put earnest in a besom.'

He must have been poor. I knew the ballad.

> The Castleblaney besoms, the best that ever grew
> Were sold for two a penny on the Hill of Mullacrew.

He invited me to the wedding. There would be a dance.

'Next Wednesday, if all goes well,' he said, 'Mary will be gettin' buckled. She's gettin' the best place in the parish, twenty-five acres of the best of dry land facin' the sun.'

156

'She's a lucky girl,' I said.

'No luckier than she deserves,' he said, 'there's not the batin' of Mary in Ireland.'

I knew by his talk that he had some slight misgivings. Strong, fifty-year-old twenty-five-acre farmers are not caught in the net of romance. They often wriggle out at the last moment. I knew a man who walked out of the church on the morning of his wedding. He left a fine young girl behind him for the sake of ten pounds. Marrying off a family of daughters was an expensive item for a poor farmer. A hundred pounds was the smallest fortune – fifty pounds down before the marriage and the other half by the instalment system.

You could easily know a farmer who owed his son-in-law part of the fortune. The son-in-law would come and take away a load of potatoes or turnips, or in the red-summer a load of mangolds for the pigs. Or he would be sure to run short of seed corn in spring and be forced to call on his wife's father for a few barrels.

The man with whom I travelled to Carrick met his future son-in-law on arrival in the town. They entered a pub and sat in one of the snugs. They were joined by a couple of amateur lawyers.

The pub in which they sat was opposite the sucker-pig-market. I was in the pig-market. We wanted a few young pigs. My mother arrived by train.

The marriage-bargainers came out of the pub. My travelling companion looked a trifle pale. My mother ran up to him.

'Is it all settled?' she asked.

'It's all settled,' he sighed.

'Well, thank God,' mother said.

The wedding was a success. There were three motor-cars. After the breakfast they drove off on a tour. Generally those wedding-tours went no farther than Dundalk. A pub at the Lower End was the rendezvous of wedding-parties.

The dance was held in a corn-loft over the pigsty. I got there about seven o'clock. The farmer himself was fixing candles to jutting stones around the loft walls. There was a half-barrel of porter standing in a corner.

'We didn't "tap" that porter yet,' the man said. 'We'll wait till the weddeners come home.'

In the dwelling-house was a great stir. Young girls were rushing around – slicing bread, setting the tables, singing and laughing all at once. Around the fire sat a few old women talking in low, peaceful tones.

'Run out and see if ye can hear the weddeners comin',' I was asked.

I went out to the yard and listened.

'No sign of them yet,' I said.

'I hope nothin' happened to them,' one of the old women said.

The invited guests were now pouring in, and some uninvited guests, too, such as servant boys and the professional philanderers of the parish. The fiddler arrived with his fiddle stuck under his coat.

'Is she "tapped" yet?' was the first thing he said. He was referring to the half-barrel.

'Very soon now, Pat, very soon,' the farmer said.

The tables were set. There were several kinds of currant cakes, plum pudding, rice pudding, ham and jam sandwiches. My lips watered. I knew that we could not touch the groaning table until the wedding-party had got the first run. We would get the leavings.

The fiddler played a few melancholy airs. It was easy to see that he was thirsty. The woman of the house called him to the room. I heard the pop of a cork and the woman's voice: 'This is a special drop I kept on the quiet.' The fiddler coughed.

'As good a drop of whisky as I ever tasted. Where did ye get it?'

'Backhouse's,' she said, 'it's Punchenstown.'

The fiddler coughed again. 'No, no,' he said, 'it's too dacent ye are.'

'Arrah drink it off, Pat,' she said.

'Ah, well, here's luck to the newly-weds.'

'The same to you, Pat.'

'Mary's gettin' a good man,' the fiddler said. 'A good man surely, no better.'

'She's gettin' a good place, Pat,' the woman said, 'thirty-five acres of the best of dry land.'

'He has forty acres, woman dear,' the fiddler said. I heard the clink of glasses again.

'Here now, ye'll have another wee tint.'

'Yer a wonderful woman, Judy,'

Over the rarefied atmosphere of February there came to our ears the sound of wild cheering. We rushed out to the yard.

'The weddeners are comin', the weddeners are comin'.'

The three cars drove up the short laneway to the house of the bride's people. The wedding party were drunk. As they left the cars and approached us they were cracking very private jokes.

'That was a great yarn Micky toul to Molloy.'

'Aw sure ye may be talkin'.'

And they laughed loudly. Two of the men went behind the door of the horse-stable: they were using this place as a urinal.

The bride and bridegroom entered the house. They were welcomed. All of us shook hands with them and wished them a 'gradle of joy'. The best man was explaining how they had fared during the day.

'We went as far as Dundalk. Nothin' would do Micky but we'd have to go into the pub at the Lower End. Aw, we had a great day. We had a dance in the taproom of the pub. Went all round the country after that – to Annagassan and back by Ardee. Aw, we had a great day.'

Among the wedding-party there had been a melodeon but no melodeon-player. However, one of the boys pulled the music-box in and out and nobody minded the absence of harmony. They cheered above the noise of the melodeon on the outward journey, and, coming home, the tormentor of music was too drunk to be able to do any harm to a sensitive ear.

We went to the loft while the wedding-party was eating. The fiddler came too.

'Take yer partners for a set,' the fiddler said.

We were about twenty boys and there was only one girl. She was well danced. A feeling of poignancy undertoned our merriment.

'This would make a very good wake,' a philanderer said.

'Only the corpse is missin',' another said.

And the bride and bridegroom and all the relations and satellites came out. The bride and bridegroom sat together on a sack of corn which had been laid along the wall. The bridegroom was sixty years old if he was a day, the bride was around twenty-one.

'A great match she made,' all the bridegroom's friends said.

'A young wife is the ruination of an oul' man,' a fellow beside me remarked. That stirred my curiosity. 'Why?' I asked.

'She'll run the life outa him. Why, man, he won't be worth a second-hand chew of tobacco when he's after sleepin' a week with that one.'

The dance. We took our partners for an Irish dance. We tapped around the floor. Even the sixty-year-old bridegroom was trying to walk on the music.

After the dance we sat on our hunkers around the walls while the porter was handed round. The man of the house and his son distributed the frothy liquor in pint mugs. I didn't want to drink, porter is cold stuff.

'Come on, drink up,' they forced me, 'there's others waitin' for that mug.'

I drank.

'He wanted to be forced,' somebody said; 'shy, but willin', like a bride in bed,' he added.

We were invited to supper in relays. Within the kitchen everyone was talking beyond himself. Even the old women let themselves go and said the wildest and most ridiculous things. Romance was in the air.

'Who'll give meself a squeeze?' an old crone by the hob sang: 'I seen the day when the boys would give their eye for a hoult with Bessy.'

'What kind of a night are yez havin' out there?' the bride's mother inquired.

'A holy livin' terror,' we told her, 'never saw the batin' of it for a dance.'

She was pleased. 'I must go out there meself when we get the tables cleared off,' she said.

By far the best part of the dance was the supper. The porter-sharks said the best part was the half-barrel.

Some time after midnight the bride started to cry, and a few of the girls joined her.

'You are as well to sing sorrow as to cry it,' I used to hear people say. The maxim, or whatever it is, worked both ways, for here were people crying joy. The girl was really lonely. In normal times in a normal country her husband wouldn't get a young girl like her even if he had fifty acres of land. But in South Monaghan marriages were becoming a rare event. The girls were losing their smiling self-confidence and alluring *hauteur*.

The horse was put in the cart. It was four o'clock. The bride's furniture and clothes were put on the cart. This load was called the 'flitting'. An old woman, a relation of the bride, got up on the load, as was the custom.

'Who's goin' with the flittin'?' strangers inquired.

'Maggy Malone,' was the answer.

The dancers dispersed. There was weeping and wailing as the 'flitting' rattled off. Only Maggy Malone, perched on top amid tables and wardrobes, kept her equilibrium both physically and emotionally. One would imagine it was a funeral was starting off. The bride's mother and sisters cried and laughed by turns. The father watched the cart out of sight.

'There goes a hundred and fifty pounds,' was probably what he was thinking. And a further hundred and fifty to be raised and paid by the end of the year. He was beggared, and he knew it. All his hard savings gone to purchase a husband.

'Oh, God, what did I do on you at all,' I once heard a man say after God had sent him the third consecutive daughter. No wonder he was displeased with Providence: daughters were a fragile and expensive commodity.

21 Death and Burial

'He'll not pass one o'clock.'

There were two others and myself keeping Red Pat company in the kitchen. The old woman of the house looked up to Red Pat both figuratively and literally each time he returned from the room and reported.

'So ye think he won't live till mornin'?'

'Naw, he'll not pass one.'

We looked at the clock. It was then half-past eleven. The old woman put on the kettle.

'Yez are as well have a cup of tay,' she said.

While drinking the tea, Red Pat, mug in hand, went to the dying man's room.

'Well?'

'He'll get another change before he goes,' he said.

'He got a lot of changes,' we all more or less said.

'Aw, when the right change comes ye'll see.'

'I wouldn't know a thing about a dying person,' I said.

'I could tell to the minute,' Red Pat said.

'Could ye, Pat?'

The time of death is a good time when life has been lived fully. There was something pleasant to contemplate in the death of an old person.

An old man or woman going on a cruise to Eternity with baggage complete and passports in order. The people said: 'He got a lovely death, had the priest before he died. One of his own children to put the blessed candle in his hand. What more could anybody want?'

A dying person was well watched. Night after night relays of watchers stayed up in the dying person's house. To let a man or woman steal into the Shade unwatched was a disgrace.

'God Almighty, but aren't yez a fine lot to let the man die unknownst.'

162

I took part in some of these vigils. I was far from being a good hand at staying up. But there were in the country a large number of people who almost made a profession of the business. Any of these could judge to the minute when the dying would become the dead. Red Pat was one. One glimpse at the bed was enough.

From the dying man's room his loud breathing came through the open door to us. Sometimes it lowered and then rose again in a crescendo. With the exception of Red Pat we were all nervy and conscious of great stupidity. Red Pat was suave and assured.

A louder-than-usual snore from the room made us jump. 'What was that?'

Red Pat had the mug of tea on his head and was in no hurry. 'Don't mind that,' he said.

I should have explained that the dying man had been in a state of coma for four or five days.

Red Pat went to the room again and I followed. He stared at the flushed face on the pillow for several seconds. The dying man's mouth was half-open.

'What do you think?' I queried humbly.

'He might go in an hour and fornint that he might last a week,' Red Pat replied.

When this opinion was conveyed to the others in the kitchen they became a little down in the mouth. We didn't want the man to live another week. It was a slack period in the neighbourhood and a wake and funeral would be a break in the monotony. The talk among us was poor. The folk who knew how to make conversation were dead. Worse than that, the one who was most stupid, provided he kept his mouth shut, was counted the wisest and best. One of our company was such a man.

'A dacent unmeddlin' boy,' he was called.

The priests liked him, too, but I don't think they'd have fancied his company around a fire in winter.

There was no love lost between this man and me. Throughout the night his seldom talk was with the old woman – wife to the dying man. He spoke in a low monotone, he wore a long face like a man filled with forlorn piety. I caught some of his words and the old woman's replies.

'God grant . . . happy hour.'

'Amen.'

'. . . say the Rosary.'

'You'll say it, mebby.'

'I will.'

The breathing of the dying man stopped for a moment and started again.

Red Pat crept to the room door and peeped in. We all stood up.

'How is he?' the old woman asked.

'He got a change,' Red Pat said, 'but he's all right now.'

We returned to our seats. There was a silence, broken only by the brazen ticking of an alarm clock. The old woman got up and went to the dresser. She groped behind the second row of plates and fingered forth a pint bottle. Every heart quickened at the sight of the bottle.

'Micker,' she addressed the silent, stupid saint, 'here's a bottle of fresh holy water I got yesterday.' She gave Micker the bottle. He accepted it with proper devotion. The rest of us were disgusted.

Holy water to keep the devils away and not a drop of that holier water that coaxes angels to a death-bed.

Red Pat was getting cranky. I was sleepy and fed up. Wish the old fellow would die soon, I thought.

It was not yet one o'clock. Perhaps after all Red Pat's forecast of Death's coming would be proven right.

Red Pat, standing in the doorway of the room, beckoned us with his crooked finger. We stepped softly to the room and stood around the death-bed. The breathing of the dying man filled the whole house. His mouth was opened wide and his chest was heaving. I had never seen a person dying before.

Micker, filling his cupped hand from the holy-water bottle, sprinkled around the bedside. Every devil in Hell, I often heard, comes around the dying man's bed trying to capture the soul. That is the time one's guardian angel has his work cut out for him.

> Angel of God, my guardian dear,
> To whom His love commits me here,

> Ever this day be at my side
> To light and guard, to rule and guide.

That verse is not mine, though it is bad enough to be anyone's. I remember it from the catechism at school.

The devils cannot stand holy water. Micker sprinkled every inch of the bed-clothes till they were almost like quilts after a shower.

Red Pat had his eyes fixed on the dying man.

'Should we say the Rosary?' the old woman asked him.

Red Pat didn't want to give a false alarm. He wasn't going to give orders for the Rosary, and maybe the man to recover for a week. That happened once. It was circulated freely that twenty times the Rosary and the Litany for a Soul Departing had been recited over a certain man and that two sixpenny blessed candles had been burned out before the passing soul had been escorted safely across the Border.

Behind me was the old woman with the blessed candle in her hand. The box of matches was on a table beside the bed. Suddenly Red Pat dropped on his knees. We all did likewise. We looked towards Micker, expecting him to start the Rosary. Micker turned to me.

'You say it,' he said, 'I forgot me beads.'

I said the Rosary. I had no beads so I counted the Hail Marys on my fingers. Just as I was beginning the Second Mystery the man died. The old woman put the lighted blessed candle between his fingers and held the hand shut.

'Yer a great hand at the Rosary,' Red Pat said as we got up off our knees.

'He is that,' Micker said.

The old woman ran to the kitchen and stopped the clock. The clock was always stopped at the moment of the man's death. The people at the wake would only need to look at the alarm on the mantelpiece to know. The stopped clock also showed that the dead person didn't die unknown to the watchers.

This old woman wasn't a bit sorry for her husband. She was a hard, practical woman, otherwise I cannot account for it.

A prayer-book was put under the dead man's chin to close his mouth.

We gave word to the near neighbours. At four o'clock on a November morning I went through the townland and called in the windows of the little houses.

'Oul' Mick is after snuffin' it.'

'Well, may the Lord ha' mercy on his sowl.'

They arrived shortly afterwards. As each man and woman came in they shook hands with the old woman and repeated the stock phrase:

'Am sarry for yer trouble.'

'Don't I know that?' the old woman replied to all.

The man had died at a quarter-past one. It was decided to have only one night's wake on him, seeing he died so early. They said it would only be putting unnecessary expense on the old woman, and she hadn't much spares.

Mr O'Hara was the undertaker. Two relations of the dead man went bail for the old woman.

The wake wasn't worth talking about. A few old men and women came and stayed just an hour or so. For once the old woman showed signs of emotion.

'Sure, it's not lavin' so soon ye are?' she mournfully said to the people.

Red Pat was there. He would stay up and so would Johnnie of the Parables. I was much too tired. The funeral had been arranged to take place at two o'clock on the morrow.

Now and then a man would come to the door of the wake-house and hand in a half-crown. This money was offerings to be paid on the dead man.

'I won't be able to come to the funeral,' they said, and all had excuses to show. There was a fair or an auction, or some such engagement.

The old woman didn't mind. Nobody would mind whether one attended a funeral or not so long as one paid offerings. At one time there was no standard figure for offerings, but during my time a half-crown was the standard. Of course you could pay five pounds if you liked. It was told how the half-crown standard for offerings came to be.

There was an old priest in the parish at one time when people came to funerals and paid odd amounts like eighteen-pence and one and nine. This priest worked on the people's pride. When the first few men went to the table and put down their shillings and odd coppers, the priest would call out:

'Patrick Morgan, half a crown; Peter Meigan, half a crown; John Callan, half a crown,' and so on.

The folk in the chapel would nudge one another and say: 'Paddy Morgan gave half a crown.' Nobody was going to let Paddy Morgan get the better of him. Every man at that funeral gave a half-crown.

The old man of whom I have been telling had a poor funeral. It wasn't typical of what we could do in that direction. There were only three traps in the procession and a mere handful of people on foot. As I walked after the hearse I thought of all the grand funerals I had attended. It was I was usually sent from our house to funerals. In my pocket I had a half-crown for offerings. I had no other money. Cigarettes kept my pockets free from cash.

When the coffin had been placed on trestles before the high altar of the chapel the priest came out from the sacristy. He scanned the seats and knew that little money was to be expected on this corpse. He read over the coffin and sprinkled it with holy water. Then he went to the little table which had been placed inside the altar railings.

The undertaker went to the table and put down five shillings.

'Mister O'Hara, five shillings,' the priest called out.

Mister O'Hara stood by the table to help the priest identify the strangers, if any. If there had been any near relations of the dead man one of them would stand at the table also.

We filed up to the table.

'Joe Green, half a crown.'

'Larry Fealy, half a crown.'

'Peter Woods, half a crown.'

Back in our seats we watched the priest and the undertaker count the money. We talked among ourselves and speculated as to the total offerings.

'There'll be five pounds.'

'I'll say six.'

'Four-ten would be nearer the mark.'

The priest cleared his throat.

'The offerings have amounted to five pounds ten. I wish to thank you sincerely, and I ask your prayers for the deceased man.'

That was all. Panegyrics were no longer allowed in the diocese. At one time the length and eloquence of the sermon over the dead was governed by the size of the offerings.

I remember a funeral which I attended at which the offerings amounted to forty-five pounds. The priest preached a panegyric an hour in length. He praised the dead man's virtue. He traced his descent from the Earls of Tyrconnell, although the world and its wife knew that the man's father had been a journeyman tailor from God knows where.

Twice I helped to dig graves. This was a most delightful job. A graveyard is a good history-book and family album combined. There were no professional grave-diggers in our parish. Three or four well-wishers made the grave. It took at least one bottle of whisky to make a grave. The bottle lay on the brim of the grave. Each man, before he took a turn at the spade, first had a long swig out of the bottle.

'I wouldn't go down in a grave without at laste one glass,' I was advised once, as we were digging in the graveyard.

'Why?' I queried.

But the man only shook his head sagely as he handed me the bottle.

I must have attended a hundred wakes and half that many funerals. I remember the time when wakes were wakes, before whisky got too dear. When I first began to go to wakes they were colourful ceremonies. I remember hearing the old wife of a dead man screaming around his bed:

'James, James, what did ye do on me? Och, och, but ye were the good man to me, James. What did ye do on me at all at all? Och, och, och.'

The arrival of continental Catholicism finally disposed of the druidic culture. Saint Patrick loved the Druids for their poetry and learning, and incorporated in his Christianity the rich colours and the mystical depths of the older faith.

So the wakes passed out, and we all began to wear long faces.

22 George

I was fond of visiting the neighbours' houses. Nobody was ever so busy that he couldn't give you a 'while of his crack'.

Once a week at least I visited old George. George was a cripple, a once-savage man who had mellowed into a teller of fairy-tales. He believed in the fairies. He was poor. Once I was sitting in his kitchen listening to his wonder-tales. I put leading questions sometimes when George was in bad humour.

'What do you think of Dromore?'

'Aw, Dromore is a gentle place,' he said. 'The Banshee ... Josie, Josie,' George called his daughter, 'put out that cat and don't have him atin' the blessed stirabout.' The big black and white cat was trying to lift the lid off the stirabout pot.

'It'll not do Jamsie a bit a harm,' his daughter said.

George looked from his daughter to me with a mournful look. 'In my youthful days,' he said, 'the children would do as they were bid. Now the youths that's going have no care, no consarn for the oul' folk.'

The cat, Jamsie, was at the pot again. 'Oh, ye tarlin villain,' George cried, and he flung a piece of coal at the cat.

George lived on a five-acre farm. He talked big.

'Five-and-thirty years ago I was in the Fair of Mullingar in the County Wicklow,' he would begin. He was weak on geography. 'I had a three-year-oul' horse there.'

'Don't be makin' a cod of yerself,' his daughter said.

'Aw, ye tarlin faggot,' he screamed. He had a hot temper.

'Paddy,' he addressed me, 'no one in God's world knows what I have to put up with.' His daughter had gone out, and when she returned George asked: 'Did she lay yet?'

'No, she's houldin' to it still.'

'Did ye look under the marley hen?'

The daughter put on an edge. 'Don't ye know as well as I do,' she cried, 'that the marley hen is lookin' hatch.'

'Ye don't smoke the tobacco, nor yer da anayther,' George said to me.

'An odd pipeful,' I said.

'Yer lucky can do without it,' he said. 'I didn't get a pull of a pipe since yesterday afore dinner. If that hen would lay we'd have the makings of a dozen eggs for the shop and Katie could get me an ounce. Tenpence an ounce – and it's daylight robbery. Go out again,' he spoke to his daughter, 'and have another look.'

'No, I'll do no such thing,' she said. 'Liftin' the hen be the tail will put her from layin' altogether.'

'Very well then,' George sighed resignedly.

Then from the hen-house there came the heart-gladdening cackle of a hen. George brightened up. He looked as happy as turnips in July after rain.

'Thanks be to the Almighty,' he said. He took his blackened clay pipe from the hole in the hob and looked into the bowl.

'There's just one wee smoke in it,' he said, 'just one wee smoke, and if I had to smoke that and had no more I'd be in a bad way: it stood between me and the divil.'

He lit up, and his memories danced in the rings of tobacco smoke.

'Aw, Paddy,' he began, 'in my youthful days times weren't like they are now. I worked for Charlie Kenny at sevenpence a day. From six o'clock in the mornin' till seven in the evenin': the youths that's going now couldn't stand that.'

'You were a tight hardy fella, I heard people to say,' I said.

'Who was sayin' that?' he asked.

Nobody ever said it, but I wanted to give my praise a background.

'Yer own da was a tight wee fella,' he said. 'He reared and schooled a big family of yez be his trade. A great wee man was the Kavanagh.'

His daughter was on her way to the huckter's shop.

As he puffed at his pipe I could see the fairies peering out like angels in a tom-boy mood.

'Aw, Paddy,' he said, 'this part of Ireland is a gentle spot. It isn't right to be trampin' the fields at nightfall except on good business. The Wee Fellas be about.'

The cat was staring up at old George. 'Get outa me sight,' he told the cat. He didn't like to see a cat staring him.

'The cat's a quare article,' he said. 'I'd be afraid he'd start to talk to me.'

'Your grandmother walked to Dublin in a day,' I said. The story of her walking powers was still current coin of conversation among the old folk.

'She did that,' he said, 'and back the same day. She had a letter for Charlie Kenny. But that was nothin' to her walkin' to the town of Monaghan every day when me grand-uncle was in gaol for a little trifle.'

I had heard the story before, but I expressed suitable wonder. George told me.

'Me grand-uncle was in Monaghan gaol for a debt of eleven shillings. Me granny brought him his dinner of champ [1] every day. Twenty-one and a half Irish miles to Monaghan, she'd have the champ warm enough to melt the butter. Sure, the youths that's goin' now are. . . '

Just then his daughter arrived with the tobacco. He surveyed the plug with a knowing eye.

'A bad ounce,' he said. 'I don't like to see the rider on an ounce.'

The plug of tobacco had been cut light-weight off the coil and a slip of tobacco was stuck on with a rivet. This was the rider. He stuck the tobacco in his greasy waistcoat pocket. 'Aw well, we'll have to be doin' with it,' he said.

We could see from George's window all the people passing on the County Road. George had wonderful sight for a man of seventy. A woman passed.

'Oul' Betty goin' for her pension,' George said. A man passed. 'Pat the Wrastler,' George stated. 'Did I ever tell ye how he came to wear that name?' he asked.

'About a thousand times,' the daughter butted in.

'You shut yer big mouth,' her father said.

'I never heard a word about that,' I said.

'Aw sure, nobody gives in to anythin' now,' he began. 'The youths that's goin' now know more than the oul' people. Pat was goin' home late one evenin' in the month of June. When he

[1] Champ: a dish made from mashed potatoes.

171

came to the dark part of the road at Rocksavage Avenue he chanced to look through the trees. The Moon was shinin' on the grass. The Wee Fellas were kickin' a football. "Come out here," says the captain to Pat. Pat went out. Every time he tried to folly the ball he got a riser that sent him on his mouth and nose a perch away. And mind ye, Pat was no aisy man to throw. So when Pat was lavin' the captain of the Wee Fellas called him to one side and says he to Pat: "Pat, the longest day ye live no man will be able to down ye." And not a man or men could ever down Pat from that day to this.'

'Such rubbish,' the daughter said.

Old George gave her a wild stare. 'Aw, the youths that's goin' now are a quare pack.'

He became silent for a while. Then he asked: 'Are ye on the sate these days?' He meant was I at the cobbling trade.

'An odd day,' I said.

'Stick to the sate,' he advised me, 'yer da made a good livin' from his trade. Can ye cut out yet?'

'Don't ye know right well he can cut out a pair of boots,' the daughter said. 'What d'ye think he is?'

'Who's talkin' to you?' the father said. 'Have ye yer pigs near ready for the hammer?'

'We're killing next week.'

'Yer mother is a great feeder of the pig,' he said. 'A notorious great woman is Biddy.'

A whirl-blast danced outside, lifting stray straws from the street. George took off his greasy soot-black cap. 'The day is Wednesday, God speed them,' he said. The whirlwind was to old George the fairies travelling across country.

George believed in all the old things – ghosts, fairies, horses, scythes, sickles, and flails, and he hated the modern equivalents of these things. 'They have the country destroyed,' he said, 'things are goin' too fast.' And then he said, with a touch of suspicion: 'Did ye see Johnnie lately?'

Johnnie was a near neighbour of ours.

'I saw him this very day,' I said.

George bowed his head till his shaggy beard was all crumpled against his waistcoat.

'Johnnie is a boyo,' he said when he looked up. George didn't like our neighbour Johnnie of the Parables. Johnnie had a dry, logical humour, which squeezed to suffocation George's fairies and ghosts. Johnnie often told me stories that reflected on the comical side of George's face.

'Aw, Paddy, Johnnie is a boyo.'

In the middle of two of George's three fields there grew lone bushes, huge thorn trees, thirty feet high. Although he was poor as a hawk and was often scarce of fire, George never even dreamt of cutting these bushes. One dark night a fellow climbed up one of the trees and flashed an electric torch about. George, from his window, saw and was confirmed in his faith.

The year his wife died a limb had broken from one of the lone bushes. George shook his head and prepared for the worst.

'I hear there's a ridge of oats missed in Meigan's field,' I said to George.

'Is that the truth?' he questioned solemnly.

'It's missed, all right,' the daughter corroborated truthfully. A missed ridge of corn or drill of potatoes was an ill-omen.

'I wonder which of them is goin' to die?' he said. 'Dacent unmeddlin' people – I'd be long sarry and a week sick to see them in trouble.'

'The ridge is missed, at any rate,' I said.

'Well, that's enough,' George said. 'It's the surest sign of a death in a family.'

We were still discussing the missed ridge when Caraher arrived. Caraher was the only beggar-man we had. He wasn't a common beggar, but a sort of gentleman collector of potatoes. He remembered his once-upon-a-time respectability and it seemed a heavier load than his bag. He was dull as respectable people usually are. When he was drunk he sang:

> 'Show me the Scotsman that won't love the thistle,
> Show me the Englishman that won't love the rose,
> But show me the true-born son of oul' Ireland
> That won't love the place where the shamrock grows.'

He was sober on this occasion, so he uttered his sober statement: 'Howld yer horses still, for God loves the childre.'

The Green Fool

I left for home. When I got there mother and a neighbour-man were leaning over the piggery wall examining the pigs.

'Where were ye?' she said.

'Over in old George's,' I answered.

23 Life and Death

'That's a good pig there,' the neighbour was saying to my mother as he laid his stick across the pig's back.

'Indeed he's only middlin',' mother said. She left the praising of our stock to the neighbours. 'Go on in there,' she told me, 'and drive out that other pig.'

'Man alive, that'a a notorious great pig,' the man said, 'eighteen stones if he's an ounce.'

'He's not eighteen, nor the colour of it,' mother said.

'I wish ye luck of them, anyhow,' he said, as he walked away, 'they're four as good pigs as I ever seen.'

Mother smiled.

'But sure, ye feed a terror,' he added as he shut our road gate after him.

Pig-fattening was an important part of Mucker's economy. The townland was well named – the place of the pigs. We kept four; any time we tried five one would die. Our near-neighbour, Owen, had pork in nearly every market. Another neighbour used to have the same set of pigs for as long as two years. This was a great crow down on these people. During the summer people who had pigs and were short of pigs' food did what was known as 'letting the pigs run round the summer'. This meant turning the swine loose in some lea-field or waste place and letting them survive what way they could. Not one pick of food would those pigs get during two months except, perhaps, now and then a gratuitous mangold that would be flung over the fence to them. There would be a fierce battle for such gifts like a crowd of boys scrambling for the orange or penny that a good-natured gentleman sometimes throws. It would be easy to tell the field in which pigs had run round. It would resemble a field I had ploughed. There would hardly be a patch of green to be seen, but all over the ground craters two or three feet deep, from which the dry clay was blown by the wind. When the new potatoes arrived in quantity in August the skeletons would be taken in and covered with fat.

Pigs are healthy creatures. Nature has arranged it so, because bottling medicine into a pig is almost as good as shooting it. The only way it can be done is through the toe of an old boot. There were plenty of old boots about our house.

Some time previous to the time of which I am relating, a neighbour had a sick pig. The man was poor and had only one pig, so that its illness gave rise to a lot of neighbourly sympathy. My father called in to inquire after the invalid.

'How's the pig?' he asked its owner.

'It's just in it and no more,' the owner said.

They looked at the pig, and the owner mentioned the old-boot method of giving a dose. Father cut a hole in the toe of an old boot. The day was Sunday. Sunday was a good day for bottling sick animals; there would be a crowd of idle boys knocking around the roads. A number of the boys were collected. Father agreed to dose the pig while the boys held it. That was the first and last time father experimented with an old boot in a pig's mouth. The pig in question dropped dead chewing the toe of the boot.

'The medicine went the wrong way,' one of the boys said.

There was a bit of a laugh at father. For weeks afterwards I would be asked: 'What did yer oul fella do to Malone's pig?' It was nasty. When any of our pigs fell sick after that we put the medicine through its food and let it take pot luck. As I have said, when we had five pigs the fifth one always died. Then there would be talk.

'It's a loss, Mrs Kavanagh, it's a loss, for it's not the day a baste dies that ye miss it.'

The pigs which we had on the present occasion were good thrivers. They were a wonder in the country. Visitors to our house before they entered first went to view the pigs. Shortly after the first man left another man crossed our yard towards the pigsty. Mother and I went out to speak to him.

'Bedad, but it's you has the knack of puttin' up the pig,' he said; 'sure, ye must feed a terror.'

'Not a thing them pigs got,' mother said, 'only praties and cabbage.'

'Arrah, howld yer tongue, woman,' he said. 'Looka the back of that pig,' and he laid his stick across its back.

'*There's* a light pig,' mother said. The man surveyed the pig.

'Be me safe sowl that's no bad pig,' he declared, 'it's short of its back, but looka the gut of it: throth, that's far from bein' a bad pig.'

'They're only five months of age,' mother said.

'Only five months,' the man exclaimed, 'that's a livin' terror.'

'We bought them the March fair of Carrick,' mother said.

'That's a holy dread.'

I believe the pigs throve on such talk: ours certainly did in any case.

'When are ye goin' to give them the hammer?' he inquired.

'Monday next, please God,' was the answer.

Pig-butchering was a good trade in those days. There were two famous pig-killers in our district – Magee and his partner Roddy. Magee was a red-headed fellow about six feet tall, and along with his skill with a pole-axe he had an eloquent humour. His partner was a stocky fellow of great strength.

I remember I went to Drumcatton Mass the following Sunday morning. Outside this chapel the pig-butchers accepted orders. Drumcatton was about two miles from our house; it wasn't quite as modern as the Inniskeen chapel, and as a result was more interesting. The road to Drumcatton led through Rocksavage and was known as Baragroon – the gloomy road. It wasn't a gloomy road. As there were no houses on this road, it was a favourite rendezvous of courting couples. I once overheard a girl say to her father: 'Oh, daddy, I love Baragroon.' High trees and thorn-hedges lined the road, and at one point the elms arched across, convciting the road into a tunnel of green darkness.

At a place known as the Briary Turn I caught up with the tin-whistle player and his wife. He hadn't the tin-whistle with him as he was going to Mass. The wife of the tin-whistler was a wizened little woman who always told the truth when a lie

177

wouldn't fit. She wasn't a malicious liar, but rather in the tradition of the great artistic fibbers. Her husband's job, when he wasn't playing the whistle, was to prove beyond doubt or cavil his wife's fantastic tales.

'It was somewhere around here,' she said to me, 'somewhere around here that the ghost of Hughie appeared to us.'

'Just down here at the crab-tree he appeared,' the tin-whistler said.

The tin-whistler and his wife had a sentimental regard for Drumcatton, for it was there the woman's heart had been piped away by the sharp falsetto of a tin-whistle.

The smell of weasels came from the dank undergrowth along the road; there were other smells more pleasant, but I do not remember. Rabbits were playing on the quiet road ahead of us. We met a fox with a rooster on his shoulder. We shouted at him, but he turned in a gateway with large unconcern; he knew that we were harmless folk. The tin-whistle player kept taking out his watch.

'We have lavings of time,' he said.

Near the chapel we came up with the Mass-goers. They were speaking in quiet tones and looked like people at peace with God and the world. And why shouldn't they? Prices of farm produce were none too bad. The chapel bell rang. 'That's the last bell,' the tin-whistler said, taking out his watch. We quickened our step.

Outside the chapel groups of men were lounging and chatting dispassionately. Magee stood tall and straight against the chapel-wall. Around him were a crowd of his customers. 'I'll kill for you at three o'clock to-morrow mornin',' he told one.

'Be damn to it,' the customer said, 'could ye not make it a little later?'

'What time will you come to us?' I asked.

'Four o'clock to-morrow mornin'.'

Anthony Magee had a large trade and often killed pigs during the Sunday, all through the night and next day, for the Carrick market which was held on Tuesday.

Through the open chapel door the priest's voice could be heard saying morning prayers.

'O God, who did so love the world.'

'I'll do yours at seven o'clock.'

'What kind of a team have yez for the game with Donaghmoyne?'

That was somewhat how the voices of God and the world blended. Nobody among us was anyway anxious to enter the chapel. It was a pleasant morning in late spring and the spirit of God's beauty was in the fields and among the bushes.

'Say, chaps, what about goin' in?'

'Come on, then.'

We sprinkled ourselves with holy water at the font. Most of our company went no further than the porch. I would have gone in if I could, but the chapel was crowded and I was compelled to stay in the porch. Around me were men, some of them kneeling on one knee, some others standing up against the doorposts, talking or chewing tobacco, and more than a few outside altogether. I liked the pagan piety around that chapel porch. Anyone that so wished could pray. I should have preferred the inside of the chapel, not because I was pious, but because there was a fine stained-glass window over the altar. I had seen the light come through it once and one didn't need to be a poet to appreciate the stained sunlight. I was kneeling on one knee myself with my handkerchief under it to save my trousers.

'Yez are killin',' a man beside me said.

'We are,' I whispered.

'Sure yez feed a terror.'

The priest turned round. 'Dominus vobiscum,' he murmured.

'Et cum spiritu tuo,' I answered involuntarily, remembering my Mass-serving days.

'Ye should be a priest,' a fellow remarked.

'Would you go to hell,' I said.

At the last Gospel the congregation started to leave. We had barely time to get to our feet before they crowded upon us. They pushed like Rugby scrummagers.

'You'd think a mad dog was after ye,' was how Father Pat saw it.

'What time are they comin'?' was a first question shot at me when I returned home.

'Four o'clock,' I said.

Father didn't mind; he was an early riser and could jump out of bed at any hour. During the Sunday afternoon we made all preparations for the killing of the pigs. We carried forty buckets of water from the bog, the ropes from which the dead pigs were to hang were fixed up in a wooden shed. Before we went to bed the twenty-gallon pot had been filled with water and hung over the fire.

Next morning I was awakened by the rattle of the wheel of the fan-bellows: father was blowing up the fire. I jumped up, mother was getting up, too. I looked at the clock which, rightly or wrongly, said twenty minutes to four. It was a lovely morning, if a bit thin. I went out to our yard and listened and stared. Silence, except for the hum of the fan-bellows' wheel and talk in the house. Then from a blackthorn clump below our potato-pit there came a sharp note like a note played in agony or the cry of new life. After that a blackbird turned his note at a right angle.

'They'll be here any time now,' I heard father saying. And he was right: in a few moments I heard the hollow sound of boots crossing the railway sleepers.

'They're coming,' I called.

'That itself,' mother said. 'We have the water boilin', anyhow.'

I was in good humour and full of delightful anticipations for I don't know what. Perhaps I do know. These men were travellers. They would have travellers' tales to tell. From the remote places of Donaghmoyne where the poteen was made, and from the secret archives of peasant-minds of which no official document has ever been made, they would bring the dark truths to our view.

They burst into our kitchen and laid their hammers and knives against the wall. Immediately Anthony Magee went straight to the fire and dipped his finger in the water.

'Mad boilin',' he said.

'Mad boilin',' father agreed.

'This is the only place where we are never kept waitin',' Roddy said.

They moved briskly about. They went outside and I followed. In the wooden shed Roddy swung from the ropes to test them.

He was over fourteen stones weight. They examined the table on which the pig-carcasses would be laid to clean. Everything was in order.

'Let yez come in for a sup of tay,' mother called.

'Aw, wait till we have the pigs hung up first,' they said.

One by one the pigs were dragged out by a steel gaff and killed right beside our front door. Nobody felt sick or squeamish. It was all matter of form and fact.

'The boilin' water here.'

We carried out the boiling water; the bucket splashed and got into my boot. My brother and sisters were up now.

It was a memorable morning; the blood of dawn was being poured over the hills, and of that other blood we only thought how much black pudding it would make. Our talk had the romantic beauty of reality. We were as close to life and death as we could be. I was part of that existence. Although I had been writing verse for some time, I had not become a denizen of the literary world where only spectres flit. I was never more than half a poet.

'We killed eight for Lucky Tom,' Anthony Magee said.

'And fourteen for Jack Brady,' Roddy added.

'Wonderful men,' father said.

We turned the pig on the table. Magee sharpened his knife on the steel.

'Larry Flynn's daughter is gettin' married,' he said.

'Musha, to who?' mother asked.

'She's gettin' a good take,' Roddy said. 'The boy is well-to-do.'

'Frank Smith,' Magee said, 'one of the best-doin' farmers in the country, keeps a pair of horses and four cows.'

'Be the mortal day.'

'Larry is givin' a hundred and fifty ballads with her.'

'He is in me eye. Where would a scrapin' farmer like Larry get a hundred and fifty?'

'He had good childre,' Roddy said, 'they sent him lashings of money from the States.'

'There's a man on his last,' Magee said.

'Who?'

'Peter Farrelly.'

181

'Givin up by priest and doctor,' Roddy supported.

'Poor Peter,' mother said, 'we'll have to pay offerings on Peter.'

'The same offerings should be done away with,' someone else suggested. 'What must the Protestants be sayin'?'

'Aw sure, the priests have to get a livin' anyhow.'

'That's right, the priests have to get a livin'.'

When the four pigs had been cleaned and hung up we washed our hands and shook the water from them. We gave the pork a final look over.

'Four good pigs, I wish ye luck of them,' Magee said . . .

'What weight would they be now?' mother asked.

'Ye have eight hundred if ye have an ounce.'

Tea, bread, and two eggs for every man, woman, and child; it was a gala day. The pig-killers told us their plans for the day, not forgetting to add a fictitious tail to their really wide practice.

'Ye must be iron men to stand it,' father said. The pig-killers laughed. They hurriedly scooped out the bottoms of their eggs and gave us our final instruction the while.

'The market starts at eight o'clock; put the lightest pigs on top of the load.'

Light pigs were most in demand.

Schoolboys passing our house on their way to school, on seeing the blood, called in for bladders. They would fill the bladders with air and make footballs of them. Father was old now and had given up going to the market. I was doing the business, strongly supported by my mother. She was a good business-woman and I was about the world's worst in fair or market.

We got the loan of Carr's ass and cart. On Tuesday morning we were all up at four o'clock. We knew that it is better to be an hour early than a minute late. My mother, my brother, and I had three pigs safely loaded and the fourth one between us ready to put in the cart when the ass moved on. 'Woa, Charlie, woa, Charlie!' we pleaded. It was no use, the ass had sighted a large thistle which grew beside the yard gate about ten yards away. With the heavy carcass of the pig in our arms we had to wait till one of my sisters came out to bring back Charlie.

I was sprinkled with holy water. I was off to the pork-market.

There was a long line of carts before the market crane; I cut in on the row and enjoyed the benefits of an hour's earlier start. The pork-buyers stood with sullen faces outside a pub that faced the market. We looked at their sour faces and said among ourselves:

'This'll be a bad day.'

'Don't mind them,' a fellow told me, 'it's all part of the game. If every man sticks out we'll get a good price.'

'But will every man stick out?' I asked.

'Indeed they won't,' he said, 'that's the kind of the unfortunate oul' farmer.'

It wasn't a bad market. I sold three times. The market rose sixpence after I had sold first time, so I rubbed out the pencil mark and sold again; the market rose another sixpence and I repeated the trick. Mother arrived then. I handed over the contract note to her and buried myself in the football results of the day's newspaper.

I was over twenty years then and according to the standards of many countries a man fit to assume responsibility. But this was Ireland, where every man's a gossoon till the day of his marriage at fifty-five or sixty. In this very market was a man of eighty and his unmarried gossoon of close on fifty. I could be proud of the stripes I had; this fifty-year-old gossoon had no more say in his father's pigs or affairs than the horse that pulled the load.

'Give me a shillin',' I overheard the son ask the old man.

'Now what would ye be wantin' with a shillin'?' the father said. He put his hand in his pocket, but he kept it there.

We stabled the ass, came back, and got paid, and then went to an eating-house. Most of the farmers went without a dinner, but none of them came home with 'the curse of the town'. The pubs did a fair trade. To come home without going into at least one pub was to come home with 'the curse of the town'.

I bought some leather in a shop. The clerk – I heard afterwards – thought I was a bit touched.

Mother paid all the bills. I got five shillings for my day.

For many years I repeated this day in the pork-market. I

recollect moments of wonderful happiness. The market-places sometimes exuded the flavour of a primitive world where men were simple and childlike and close to God. The fresh wind of youth blew through the files of carts in the little town, and moments big as years were mine to squander while the clock on the Protestant church-tower counted out the miserly minutes of an adult world.

24 The Grey Dawn

A county council quarry was opened in our vicinity. Among the quarry-men was one man named Bob. He was a stout fellow of thirty, brown-eyed and very quiet. For three months he passed our house on his way to work before we spoke to each other. He was usually reading a book – an Irish grammar. He was studying Gaelic.

Then one evening he came in to have his boot repaired. Bob was a flame. He touched the damp wood of my mind till sparks began to dance.

He talked on unusual themes. He mentioned Canon Law, syphilis, and irregular verbs. He recited verse, bad verse by critical standards, perhaps; Longfellow's *Evangeline* and a translation of Dante by – I think – Cary.

He had tried his skill at verse-making himself. One poem of eleven lines he gave me; there were meant to be twelve lines, but he couldn't get the last line. 'For the past six months I've been trying to find that line,' he told me.

'Beside an Irish rath,' was the nearest he could get.

'It's a great poem as it is,' I told him, 'a real masterpiece.' And I thought so at the time. We were then standing in the shadow of Rocksavage wall, close to the crossroads from which the wild laughter of young men came. It was a moonlit evening in October and the air was filled with the fragrance of over-ripe blackberries and alderberries.

'Aren't they the gets?' I said, referring to the boys at the cross-roads.

'They're true Irishmen,' he said.

Bob gave me a long lecture on the beauty of *Alice in Wonderland* and *Gil Blas*.

Down among the slabs of basalt rock, when Bob was in the quarry, thought took wing. The listeners in this academy of stone hunger were fed.

'What is God?'

'God's a man.'

Bob's conception of God, whatever it was, must have been a million-forked tongue of truth.

'What would the priest say if he heard us?' some fool was sure to say. And Bob would tell them that their conversation was truly religious. Bob was asked a long time afterwards who was the cleverest man he had ever met; he said I was. Lucky for me I didn't hear of this opinion till my mind had developed a resistance to vanity.

A neighbour of mine – a young fellow who lived alone in a fine house – had a large stock of inherited books. I used to visit him in the winter evenings. He loaned me books. We would sit by his fire long hours discussing literature. I did most of the talking, and I shudder when I think of the flood of poetic silliness I let loose on my friend. We agreed that *The Siege of Corinth*, by Byron, was sublime. I it was who suggested the word 'sublime'.

'Sublime, that's exactly the word,' my host said. I envied this fellow his stocks of books. The fine old volumes lay blue-moulded around the floor and on tables. Burns's poems and a huge history of Rome stood on the hob. On top of a bag of flour lay – in the company of some copies of the *Wide World Magazine* – Shelley's *The Cenci*. It was the fashion in fancy houses to have a big book on the parlour table. This man had several big books on his parlour table, but it wasn't for vanity.

Two is company, three is a crowd, the saying goes. There is deep intimacy when two men sit by a winter fire. When a third enters – though he be of close spiritual kindred – the whole fabric of familiar sweetness and innocence comes to pieces.

This often happened to us. Some fellow was sure to come rumbling in his hob-nailed boots up the cobbled yard to our door. A bull to the china-shop of the angels.

'Anybody inside?'

'Come in.'

If the fellow who entered had leprosy or was a lunatic with a gun I wouldn't be half as vexed. And he would more than likely be breezy with good humour. He would be entirely unconscious

that he was treading on holy ground. He would be sure to lift a
book and turn over the pages before he sat down.

'Aw, holy fiddlesticks! What the divil does that mane?'

It might be Milton's *Paradise Lost*, for that chunk of poetic
theology was in my friend's library.

We wouldn't tell him what the book was.

'Take a sate,' the man of the house would say.

Then the talk would turn on the loud wheel of present day.
I could talk that kind of talk, too, but it went against the grain
of my soul. So that when I talked everyday talk I was the most
vulgar man in the company.

This man's house was quite close to my own. I was lucky, for
had it been miles distant I should have gone there to read the
books, and more than that to unload myself of my poetic
whimsies. There were so few to whom I could talk.

He gave me the works of Pope. In this edition the poet was
given as Mr Pope. I liked Pope. His essays on Man and on
Criticism were good strong truths in rhyme. At the cross-roads
on Sunday afternoon I recited with enthusiasm to a crowd of
farm-folk:

> 'Of all the causes which conspire to blind
>   Man's erring judgment and misguide the mind,
>   What the weak head with strongest bias rules
>   Is pride, the never-failing vice of fools.'

My hearers understood and appreciated this. Some of them were
very eager for knowledge. We might have had some very metaphysical debates if there were not always in the crowd one of
those ridicule-making fellows whom poor Ireland still continues
to produce.

My sister was attending the convent school. She had many
books dealing with the craft of verse.

Intermediate Poetry and Prose, by Father Cocoran, D.Litt.,
was one I remember. I thumb-marked that book. I studied
iambics, trochees, rhyme, and stanza. I counted the feet in the
verses I read. I tried to write verse myself, but the number of
feet per line varied to break my heart. Once I wrote a complete
poem and sent it to a weekly paper which had a Poet's Corner.

I was in wonderful humour the next week when I saw my initials among the list of those whose poems had been rejected. It was recognition. I never imagined that the editor would as much as recognize that my writing was verse, even for the waste-paper basket. I was getting on.

I made a lot of ballads. I sang them at dances, and part of one at a wake. I remember at the wake how I had just the first verse sung when the Rosary broke out in the room of the corpse.

> 'Thou, O Lord, wilt open my lips
> And my tongue shall announce Thy praise.'

We all dropped on our knees.

Some of the girls at the dances got romantic about me. I really believe that one of them fell in love with me. The boys laughed at my songs, though not all. Some of them said I 'was the makings of a very good comic'.

My first song celebrated the drinking of a half-barrel of stout. I remember four lines.

> Farrelly fell over the barrow
> At the gable-end of the house
> And the singing and ructions were awful
> Around the half-barrel of stout.

To relations in America I wrote letters in rhyme. 'I see you have a new Tom Moore,' one of the Yankees wrote to my father.

As I wandered about the roads and fields I composed my verses.

I was spreading dung in drills for turnips in a field belonging to Red Pat. Red Pat was not at home. I was alone. I got my tea in the field. Sitting beside a heap of steaming dung I drank the tea and afterwards felt in great poetic form. I had lately been reading of a poet who made a poem about a telegraph pole. I started making a poem on an old wooden gate which guarded a field I knew. For every drill of dung I spread I made a line of verse. I kept adding to the poem till it was of grand size. I sent it to the editor of the local paper. The next week my poem appeared.

Address to an Old Wooden Gate

Battered by time and weather, scarcely fit
For firewood. There's not a single bit
Of paint to hide those wrinkles, and such scringes
Tear hoarsely down the silence – rusty hinges.
A barbed-wire clasp around one withered arm
Replaces the old latch with wanton charm.
This gap ere long must find another sentry
If the cows are not to roam the open country.

There was a whole column of similar quality. I cannot remember the rest. It wasn't too bad. The readers of the paper didn't like it. They wanted sentimental verse about the gallant sons of Erin or something like that.

Everyone who had an old wooden gate – and that was half the parish – claimed that it was *their* gate I had slandered.

I sent some verse to the Poet's Corner of a Dublin paper. It was published. Part of the rules of the Corner was that the author's address as well as name must be at the bottom of each poem. This rule left the poets open to a lot of fan-mail. I got books of tickets to sell for charitable purposes. From priests and nuns these tickets came.

An Irish woman in Wigan, England, wrote asking if I would do some research into her family history for her. Her mother's people were natives of Monaghan, she said, and she would love to know if there were any of the name in the place now.

A fellow wrote to me from Chicago:

Dear Friend,

I read your poem entitled 'A Memory' in the Irish paper. I have never found this sense in writing before.

The weather here is very bad for the past two weeks, but I think we will have a dry spell soon.

Wishing you great success in your writing.

I remain,
Yours sincerely,
Harry J. Millin

I replied to this letter. Then my distant admirer began to flood me with letters and piles of comic papers. Some days I got half a dozen letters from him. He sent me a Sunday-school paper in which he had inserted an advertisement in praise of me. It was a double-column advertisement about six inches square:

Greetings:
From Harry J. Millin to Patrick Kavanagh,
Poet, Ireland.

It was headed thus in heavy black type. There was a lot of small print which said big things about my poetic genius. I was suffering from chronic poverty at this time and I wrote to H.J.M. for money. I had hopes that he might be a mad millionaire. He replied:

Dear Friend,

This is the first letter of this description I have ever received. I can only afford to send you one dollar. I am only a poor lift-man in a hotel at fifteen dollars a week.

Yours sincerely,
H. J. M.

I lost contact with him shortly afterwards.

Verse-writing was getting a grip on me. It grew unawares like an insidious disease. But I wasn't satisfied. There was something dead and rotten about the verse-world in which I moved.

Of Yeats I had not heard. Not one of the contributors to our Corner had heard of him either. Yeats, A. E., Colum, Stephens, and all that crowd, if their names ever came through the dense wall of prejudice to us, would have been just a gang of evil men who were out for a destruction of the Catholic Faith. No nun or priest would send books of lottery tickets to such men.

We were very pious poets. Many of the poems in the Corner were religious. The blessed Virgin, Saint Patrick, Saint Bridget, the Sacred Heart, and others of lesser nimbus power provided themes for our verse. From Brian Boru to Dan O'Connell we sang the praises of the saints of Irish Nationalism as well.

We were the biddable children of Kathleen Mavourneen – but for me at least the grey dawn was breaking.

It was the last days of August nineteen-twenty-seven. We had grass-seed for sale. I had cut the hay with a scythe and scutched in on the bottom of a tub. It yielded me four bags, which I had sieved and winnowed in the breeze and sun. I was proud of my grass-seed – it was white and clean. My father, who was in his second childhood then, seemed as proud of me as I was of the grass-seed. Second childhood is like that.

'Ye'll be takin' it to Dundalk,' he said.

'To-morrow,' I answered.

Selling the grass-seed was my special prerogative. I could do as I liked with myself and the money.

A man passing looked at the seed. 'Very dirty,' he said, 'a lot of hair-grass in it.'

This after all my sieving.

I went to get the loan of Carr's ass on the evening of Sunday – the market was next day. The ass was already promised.

'The "Charger" has him,' I was informed. 'Charger' was the nickname of a neighbour.

'Get Maggy Quigley's ass,' they advised me; 'he's a very good stepper.'

Maggy lived up a long lane. Her ass was an old creature and the cart was still older. 'It's a danger to be safe in Maggy's cart,' people used to say.

'We don't lend the ass to anybody,' she stated when I declared my business. She waited till the importance of the ass and cart should have time to sink into my mind. 'But on account of who ye are we'll let ye have Darby.'

The ass was lying before Maggy's door with his two forepaws stretched out in front and his eyes closed. He wasn't a promising beast to drive to Dundalk.

'Do ye see that pole there?' Maggy said, pointing out to me a long pole laid across the gap in the stone ditch. 'If Darby gets an aisy day he jumps that pole during the night, but if he's abused he lies out there on the rock.'

I promised to treat Darby well.

It was considered a good-stepping horse could make Dundalk from our district in two and a half hours. I left at five o'clock in the morning as I calculated getting in around nine. I over-rated Darby's powers; he was nearly as bad as the ass of the song:

> With blood-stained powers
> It took him two hours
> To travel each mile of the road.

191

Darby wasn't just as bad as that, though he was bad enough.

Sitting on top of my four bags of grass-seed, I jogged down the Mucker Road between the tall poplars at a pretty speed. I had given the ass two full porringers of oats, a temporary rejuvenation to his old blood. He cocked his ears and swayed pleasantly between the shafts. It must have been an early harvest that year for much of the corn was gathered, and in one or two haggards the threshing mills were set up.

The morning was chill, still, and the crevices of the land were grey. There were two stars in the western sky. When I turned eastwards for Dundalk, leaving the poplar-lined road, the dawn was before me, a grey dawn breaking above the Irish Sea, and in my mind a grey passionate dawn was breaking too. I was becoming aware of new beauty.

For the first two miles Darby travelled on the steam of the oats. Then the weariness of age returned to his bones. It took him half an hour to climb Mahera Hill. I got down and pushed at the tail-board.

'Foolish fella,' a man who was yoking a horse to a cart said when he saw me. 'Don't ye know,' he explained, 'that the more you push the less the ass will pull?' I might have known, for I had wide experience of the ass-temperament. The man who spoke was getting ready for the market himself.

'How's the time going?' I inquired.

'It's hittin' round half-six,' he said, 'but ye'll have lavings of time.'

Darby trotted down the hills passing out horse-carts drawn by hairy-legged Clydesdales. Short and sweet like an ass's gallop, is a good saying: the hairy-legged Clydesdales recovered the lost ground and passed out of our sight on the top of the next hill.

The sun was up before I got to the town. A double row of carts laden with grass-seed was queued up in Park Street. I tried to get in before a woman who was holding an ass by the head. She looked quiet enough but was far from it as I soon found out.

'Ye brat,' she sort of squealed, 'is it tryin' to knock dacent people outa their turn ye are? People that's after losin' a night's sleep.'

'I have only the bare four bags,' I pleaded.

'Four or twenty-four, it's all the same to me,' and she pulled on the rein to narrow the gap between her and the cart in front. There was nothing for it but go to the end of the row and learn patience.

The rows of carts moved very slowly towards the market crane because of late arrivals, whom well-wishers were letting cut in further up. Around me people were complaining. 'It's a damn shame, that's what it is.'

I strongly supported the speaker. 'It's all that,' I said, 'and a good deal more.'

There was a lot of talk about politics, and right behind me two young men were confabing about last night's dance.

'I think I could go with her if I went all-out.'

'I think you might.'

'I seen Tom on the job again.'

'Aye, the oul' clown, some people wouldn't know when they were insulted. Paddy Kirk tried his hardest for Josie Duffy and he might as well be idle.'

'No go for Paddy.'

I came opposite a newsagent's shop, and was glad. 'Keep an eye on that ass,' I told the fellow before me.

Searching among the papers on the counter I came across a periodical dated a few weeks back. 'What kind of a paper is this?' I asked the newsagent.

'Something like *John Bull*,' he said.

It was the *Irish Statesman*. Returning to my ass I opened the paper and read.

The first thing my eye fell upon was a review of a book by Gertrude Stein. I read a quotation and found it like a foreign language, partly illuminated by the Holy Spirit. There was mention of a man called Joyce. I was a little surprised to find that his Christian name was James and not P. W. or Robert Dwyer. P. W. Joyce had written a History of Ireland which I had read at school and his brother Robert Dwyer Joyce, whom I knew from a song of his – three lines of which I remember:

> Where the stream leaps down
> From the moorland brown
> And all on a May-day morning.

'Any stir on the paper?' a fellow asked me.

'Plenty,' I replied. 'Gertrude Stein is after writing a new book.'

'Quit the coddin'. How's the markets goin'? My sowl, this looks like a bad pit to-day.'

> They shall sink under water
> They shall rise up again,
> They shall be peopled
> By myriads of men.
> Paris and Babel
> London and Tyre
> Re-born from the darkness
> Shall sparkle like fire.

I didn't understand A. E.'s poem except, in a vague way, the last line: 'Shall sparkle like fire'. Later I heard from A. E. himself that that poem had a commonsensical meaning, but for me on that August morning in Dundalk Grass-seed Market it had a meaning and a message that had come from hills of the imagination far beyond the flat fields of common-sense.

On that day the saints of Ireland, political and theological, lost a strong supporter. I never wrote for the holy poets again. How I fared with my four bags of grass-seed hardly matters. Sufficient to say I sold it, afterwards visited an eating-house, viewed the sights of the town from the gaol to the distillery chimney and down to the quays, bought a packet of cigarettes, yoked Darby to the cart and gave him his head. How long it took us to get home I do not know, for I was wandering among the hills of a timeless world. It was an Eden time and Eve not violated. Men were not subject to death. I was happy.

> Paris and Babel
> London and Tyre
> Re-born from darkness
> Shall sparkle like fire . . .
> Færy shall dance in
> The streets of the town
> And from sky headlands
> The gods looking down.

25 The Poet

During the following winter and many winters after that, the fall of dark found me in my den up to my knees in scribbled paper. The corner of the room upstairs in which I worked was the North Pole of our house. It was often very cold.

'Come down before ye get yer death of cowld,' I would be advised.

I never heeded.

I used to sit on an old black chest opposite the table of an old sewing-machine on which a lighted candle dropped its grease. A hundred times at least I tried to write a poem on the candle but never got beyond the first line. On the walls of my room hung five holy pictures: 'The Virgin and Child', 'Pope Leo XIII', with his red robe and bald head, 'The Little Flower', carrying a bouquet of roses or carnations, 'Saint Anthony of Padua', wearing a wide halo, and last, but not least, our own 'Saint Patrick' prodding the snakes with the ferrule end of his crozier.

Down below in our kitchen visitors and customers were talking. Their conversation intruded a little at times on my mystic reveries. Johnnie of the Parables was there, relating the most profound metaphysics to the most homely parable. I thought Johnnie a bad construer of parables till now when I am trying to invent ones of my own to replace his which I have forgotten. He could tell a story to illustrate the working mechanism of an airplane engine or the movements of stardom.

'It's just like a wheel-plough on a rocky ridge,' he would begin, or: 'Ye might compare it to a man that was after comin' from America.' I never could see any comparative points. His other listeners would say: 'It's just like that, that's exactly how it is.'

Apart from his parables Johnnie was a pleasant talker and I should have been pleased to listen to him from any place other than the ivory tower.

Girls laughed in our kitchen and sometimes I caught enough of the joke to make me want to join the company.

The outside door rattled and a voice I recognized spoke. 'Paddy in?'

'He is, come on inside.'

'I wanted to get a heel on me boot. Where is he?'

'Patrick, Patrick, are ye comin' down? There's a man here wants a heel on his boot.'

I didn't answer.

'Are ye dead or alive?'

I rattled my boots on the floor to express irritation.

'Hello, hello, will ye throw a heel on this oul' boot? It'll not take ye five minutes.'

At that very moment the last line of a poem was dangling within my reach and now it was gone into the limbo of all unwritten things.

'Very well,' I said, 'I'll be down with you in a minute.'

'So that's what I was called for,' I said, examining the boot. 'That boot's first-class.'

'Listen,' he said. 'I've a great piece to tell you.'

I didn't want to hear. Like the little dog that destroyed Newton's life-work, this man didn't know the harm he had done. Six good lyrics are the price of immortality and perhaps one-sixth of immortality had been lost to me for the sake of an old boot.

'Troth, ye ought to stick to the trade,' Johnnie of the Parables said.

'That's what I do be tellin' him,' my mother added in support. Father was then going quite simple and took little interest in the talk.

About this time, too, a new farm was purchased for me; my mother's heart was in the land and her greatest wish was to see me set up as a strong farmer.

I bought an old bicycle and every week rode to Dundalk for the *Irish Statesman*: sometimes I missed it and came home ready to fight or do anything nasty.

'As sour as a buck weasel,' was how my household described me on such occasions.

Once in the harvest time when I was working for a neighbour, I left the harvest field when we got the call to dinner. I rode to Dundalk in record time, got my paper and came back happy, though I had missed my dinner. One of the harvest men took the paper from my coat pocket where it lay among the sheaves. He turned the pages over.

'Begod,' he exclaimed, 'what the hell kind of a book is that?'

The roar of the reaper coming down the ledge blotted out my blasphemous reply.

As my name no more appeared in the Holy Poet's Corner, the neighbours concluded that I had given up the bardic game. The light in my window was a bit of a puzzle to many. Some said I was studying to be a policeman, which theory wasn't so far-fetched as you'd imagine: that very time a fellow called Crooked Paddy was being coached two nights a week by the local school-master for the examination to the Civic Guards. A few others thought I might be doing puzzles. My own household knew what I was up to, but they kept it close as it wasn't considered a respectable occupation. My mother being a practical woman said to me time and again:

'I'm not against you writin' if I could see ye makin' anythin' of it.'

'You wait,' I told her. 'I'll be rich yet.'

'I don't see much signs of it now,' was all she could say.

'Christ,' I explained, 'sure I'm only at it a year or so. Shaw only made ten pounds before he was forty and now he's a millionaire.'

'Troth if ye'd mind yer little place it would fit ye better.'

'£. s. d.,' I cried, 'the only measuring-stick you peasants have is the one marked £. s. d.'

'The next thing is the people will be callin' ye "the bard",' one of my sisters said.

'Shakespeare was called the Bard of Avon.'

'You and yer Shakespeare.'

I sent a few poems to A. E. and in about a week got a reply. He liked my verses, he said, and though he couldn't accept these, advised me to send him some more. A month later he accepted a poem from me; only the half of a poem in fact – the other half was written on a second page and got lost in the crowd.

I didn't see that poem in print till two years later. I missed that week's *Irish Statesman*. I got a pound for the poem, which came as a pleasant surprise. I never expected payment: I was quite innocent.

'Patrick, Patrick, the cows are after breakin' into the turnips,' I heard cried loudly.

I was sitting on my black box with a clean sheet on my knee. I felt that a magical poem was hovering near, ready to stray into my net of words.

'Aw, that's the lazy, lazy oul' divil.' Writing wasn't counted work. 'Will ye come down, I tell ye, before they destroy all the turnips?'

If it wasn't the turnips it was the pigs were after breaking loose, or a hen they wanted me catch for the fowl dealer.

At nine o'clock the word came up to me:

'Come down, we're goin' to say the Rosary.' After waiting a few moments they sent me a second call: 'We're on our knees waitin' for ye to come down. If ye don't come down we'll start it without ye.'

'Well, start away,' I snapped.

'There can be neither luck nor grace in the house with ye, ye oul' Protestant ye. Go ahead, we'll say it without him.'

> 'Thou, O Lord, will open my lips
> And my tongue shall announce thy praise.
> Incline unto my aid, O God:
> O Lord, make haste to help me.'

The beginning of the Rosary was very good poetry, had habit not for me worn the keen edge off its surprise.

I came down and, kneeling beside a stool, threw my head on the stool and fell asleep. I am sure that should I ever have an attack of insomnia I need only have somebody start the Rosary and I'm cured. The Rosary in our house had been growing, growing steadily like a snowball, collecting prayers and pious ejaculations, till by the time of which I write it was a mile long. I mightn't complain too hard, for in other houses longitudinal additions to Rosaries had proceeded at a much greater speed. Litanies to this saint and that, prayers for intentions special and plain. I suggested on many occasions cutting the unwieldy end of our devotions, but my suggestion was vetoed as being grossly irreligious.

My brother Peter, who was now grown up, became my critic. Ablaze with the fire of creation I would come down and show him my latest poem. He read it quietly while I fidgeted about the floor waiting for the momentous decision.

'I think you have written better,' he said.

'For God's sake,' I cried, 'don't talk such nonsense. Read it again.'

'Read it for me,' mother said. 'I'd be able to give you a better opinion than you think.'

During this period father died. I wasn't really sorry, though my love for him had been very warm. His mind for two years before his death had been all mixed up. Names of people and things would dangle in his brain just beyond the rim of recollection. For instance, one day he thought of something that was associated with a spire or tower. I had become expert in this trouble of his: I ran up and down all the likely names and sounds connected with towers and churches. I used the word 'damn' – it occupied a prominent place in my vocabulary at any rate. Immediately father said, 'I have it – campanile, a campanile tower.' When his mind was clear he compared his condition to Swift's. The Parish Priest – when I went to him to arrange for the burial service – said father was a lunatic. I told him he knew nothing about mental processes or psychology. The Parish Priest withdrew into the snailbox of dogma and refused to be drawn to discuss such a heterodox subject.

Father died in autumn. It is a fine thing to die when the leaves are falling and not when the cry of spring is among the hills. The earth that fell upon father's coffin covered in its fall one of the kindest, most self-effacing, self-sacrificing of fathers and husbands. I remembered with joy the beatings he gave me. They had helped to make me pliant and resilient in a world where proud things get broken. I remembered the pally talks we had together, comparing lists of the stupidest men in the parish: my list corresponded with his in every name. Father told me how great was his *wanderlust* when he was young. He stayed at home to take care of his old mother. His care of his mother was one of the things for which he was famous in the district. I am not virtuous by my own good works. I am virtuous by nature. I have inherited my father's good works.

Peace to his soul.

Though no mortal woman has danced for me the angels of the sun have: upon the wavy skyline their silver slippers sparkled.

I was twenty-two years old.

Often on summer evenings when all the young people were dancing at some cross-roads I wandered in petulant loneliness among the innocent of flower-land and tree-land. True, I sometimes was found among the mortal dancers in later years when I tried to have life both ways and had it neither. But in these rare moments of sweetness and light I remained true to myself, and poetry and vision were mine.

Old men and women colloguing in groups along the poplar-lined laneway would suspend their conversation as I passed. Across the conversational breach they would hang a suspension bridge formed by the word 'and', 'Aaa... nnn... ddd'. Through the wide eyes of this bridge they would survey me with puzzled looks.

'And ... as I was sayin', she came up to me. ... Is that Paddy Kavanagh? Would he be gettin' a bit odd of himself?'

Or some old farmer would stop to talk to me: 'The praties are doin' fine. 'Twill be a good year for the world. Yer not at the dance?' I was tempted to answer, yes, but I merely said: 'I didn't feel like it.'

'And yer far better off; this dancin' is all a cod. I never knew a good dancer was worth his grub to a farmer.'

From the tone of his speech I guessed that he thought me foolish in my wisdom.

I had just been writing a poem and it had come off, so I took a walk among the poplars as a thank-offering to the gods, but more because I had achieved something and was happy.

The gods of poetry are generous: they give every young poet a year's salary which he hasn't worked for; they let him take one peep into every tabernacle; they give him transcendent power at the start and ever after he must make his own magic. While he is learning the craft of verse and getting ready his tools they present him with wonderful lines which he thinks are his own.

In those days I had vision. I saw upon the little hills and in the eyes of small flowers beauty too delicately rare for carnal words.

'Do you see anything very beautiful and strange on those hills?' I asked my brother as we cycled together to a football match in Dundalk.

'This free-wheel is missing,' he said and he gave it a vigorous crack with the heel of his shoe. 'Is it on Drumgonnelly Hills?'

'Yes.'

'Do you mean the general beauty of the landscape?'

'Something beyond that, beyond that,' I said.

'Them hills are fine no doubt.'

'And is that all you see?'

'This free-wheel is missing again,' he said. 'I'll have to get down and put a drop of oil on it.'

We got moving again. 'What were we talking about?'

'Beauty,' I said.

And just then another football-follower caught up with us and the talk changed to such things as centre-forwards and half-backs and the prospects of the game. I was a football fan. Some of the pleasantest hours of my life were spent watching a game from the top of a wall near the Dundalk football ground. There were usually on this wall a dozen penniless followers of the game. We called it the Vincent de Paul grand-stand.

Another day I mentioned this beauty to a bearded man: because he was bearded I thought him a mystic.

'Of course, of course ye can see things,' he said, 'sure any man that's a Catholic can see the Holy Ghost.'

I knew I had blundered, and I tried to change the subject, but the bearded one went on:

'When a man's confirmed, doesn't the Holy Ghost come down on him? Sure the bishops can talk to the Holy Ghost any time they like. And the priests too, if they want. Why, man, it's as simple as kiss yer hand.'

He said a lot more, till I swore that never again would I mention visions. Yet I did mention them.

Two men were leaning across the river bridge at Inniskeen. I think they were cattle-jobbers waiting for a train. Of their appearance I can only remember that they wore bowler hats and that one of them had a round patch on the upper of his boot. I was in the village for the morning newspaper. I stopped on the bridge and opened up a conversation with the two men. They were anxious to talk. A cattle-jobber out of a cattle-market is the silliest creature you could imagine, and this pair were no exception. They were weak on metaphysics.

We talked a long talk on religion which was relieved at intervals by some incongruous remarks on passing girls, the trout leaping in the stream below, and the price of cows.

'Can a Protestant get to Heaven?'

'Why not?' I said.

'And in that case one religion is as good as the next.'

'I heard a missioner to say,' the second jobber said, 'that he wasn't prepared to deny that there were some Protestants in Heaven.'

'That cow of Mullens' had a blind teat.'

I spoke of the beauty beyond beauty.

'I always said Inniskeen was as nice a spot as Rostrevor,' one of the jobbers claimed.

Towards the end of our talk the jobber in the bowler hat mentioned Shakespeare. I imagine he thought Shakespeare was at least a third cousin to God. As a schoolboy he had read *Othello*, he said. He read the play aloud to his father. His father wept and tore his hair, crying: 'Oh, if I could only get my hands on that scoundrel Iago!'

From that day forward I grew wise, but my innocent vision was gone. I had learned from Miss Cassidy's catechism that there was only one unforgivable sin – the sin against the Holy Ghost. Now I understood.

The Holy Ghost will not enter a soul that has not within it a secret room, free from vulgarity.

Yet though my candle of vision had been snuffed and the *Irish Statesman* no more, I still continued to write.

Having knocked and knocked and knocked at the door of Literature it was eventually opened, and then I did not want to enter. The clay of wet fields was about my feet and on my trouser-bottoms.

I was not a literary man. Poetry is not literature: poetry is the breath of young life and the cry of elemental beings: literature is a cold ghost-wind blowing through Death's dark chapel.

I turned from the door of Literature and continued my work among poetry, potatoes, and old boots.

26 The New Farm

As I have said, another farm had been purchased for me during
the early period of my apprenticeship to poetry. We had now
nearly twenty acres of land. To be the owner of a twenty-acre
farm was all glory. A farmer who could keep a pair of horses
would be looking for a fortune of a couple of hundred pounds
with a wife. There was some people who thought my younger
brother would be getting one of the farms. 'Yerself and yer
brother have a farm apiece,' an old-fashioned lad said to me
shortly after the purchase. He was merely repeating what he had
heard others say.

The new farm was situated in the townland of Shancoduff –
black Shanco. Its fields faced the north, little hills which hung
like pictures on the black northern wall.

I wrote a poem about those hills, the first verse is:

> My black hills have never seen the sun rising,
> Eternally they look north towards Armagh.
> Lot's wife would not be salt if she had been
> Incurious as my black hills that are happy
> Where dawn whitens Glassdrummond chapel.

There were good names on these hills even though their soil
was sticky and scarce of lime. Poets had surely put the names
on them. Translated from the Gaelic they were: 'The Field of
The Shop', 'The Field of The Well', 'The Yellow Meadow',
'The Field of The Musician'.

'The Field of The Musician' was a triangular acre under the
shadow of the Rocksavage Forth. The sun hardly ever saw it.
It grew a kind of tough grass, like wire. Something strangely
mysterious seemed to hang around the Field of The Musician.
It was like a place where fairy-gold might be hidden. It sounded
hollow underfoot.

I don't know who the musician was that gave this field its

name. I have a vague notion that it was no mortal music he made. This field had one thing which might or might not appeal to a player of sweet music; an echo which repeated and repeated till lost in the briary hollows of Donaghmoyne.

The Field of The Well had nothing surprising in it or about it. It was the best and least perpendicular of all the fields. It had a well in the middle. Because the well was ours I should praise it. I should say that its waters were the purest and coolest of any well in the country. It was the tradition of the people to praise their own wells and in a quiet way to dispraise all others.

'In nineteen hundred and eleven, when every well in the parish ran dry, that well of ours never went down an inch.'

I have heard this said about at least twenty different wells.

The well after which our field was named was nothing to sing about. Its waters rose through yellow clay and had a soft taste. As far as I could see, it was the headquarters of the frogs' association. Whenever I knelt down on its flagged brim, one of the frogs was sure to plop in just where my lips were preparing to go. It was a useful well to a thirsty ploughman or to hay-makers. It was awkward, situated as it was in the middle of the field. When the field was under tillage, at least three square perches of good land around the well was waste. Not com-pletely waste, for these perches grew the finest, strongest, tallest buck thistles you ever saw.

The well was built and roofed in such a way that the animals could not drink or contaminate the waters without gravely risk-ing their lives. Animals are shy of dangerous drinking places. A foolish young calf of ours did on one occasion try to quench its thirst at the well – it was found standing on its head, drowned, some hours later.

The Yellow Field was true to its name; in wet weather its soil had the consistency and colour of putty, in dry weather it be-came hard and cracked like a canyon. Rushes ten feet high grew in this field. As it was a sort of plateau the tall rushes were on view to half the parish. People passing on the road half a mile away looked up and inquired who owned the rushy field. I was often asked why I didn't cut the rushes.

'They put the appearance of the devil on the place,' I was

told. Rushes aren't an economic crop. They used to be used for thatching houses and corn ricks, but in my time rushes for thatch had gone out of fashion. I did afterwards cut the tall rushes and ploughed the field. I broke two scythes, at the mowing; the tuft foundations of the rush-clumps looked like the stumps of felled trees. I ploughed the field myself, as no self-respecting plough-man could be got to take on with it.

'When I couldn't plough it dacently I wouldn't plough it at all,' they told me.

The Field of The Shop was a long briary garden as ill-shapen as ever puzzled the schoolmaster's chain and brain. It was on this field that the dwelling-house of the previous owner of the farm had stood. One of the out-houses attached to most old farm-houses was usually known as 'the shop'. The shop was a particularly clean barn in which were stored such delicate tools and things as scythes, rakes, sieves, winnowing-sheets, and perhaps in it, too, would be kept bags of oaten meal or a few sides of home-cured bacon. The walls of the old houses were still standing. The thatched roof had only caved in during our occupation of the farm. The man who lived in the house was indeed dead only a few years. When the fire goes black on the hearth of a thatched house, the roof soon comes down. I had attended the wake of this very man and a boisterous drunken wake it was.

I remember seeing stones being thrown through the open window at the old man's corpse. It was on a chilly morning in April. The old man died childless, and the sorrow and tears at the wake of a childless man or woman are few and far between.

I didn't imagine then that I should ever be the owner of that wild house, and those bleak acres.

MacParland was the name of the old man. He lived well enough on his poor farm. When he died he had money in the bank, and a lot of people thought he had some more money hidden away in the walls.

I often searched among the holes in the masonry, but all I ever got was the shanks of a few clay pipes.

In spite of the poor quality of the farm's soil it had many things to recommend it. The view from the top hills was fine if rather dark. If there weren't fairies there, then there are no fairies in Ireland. I heard tell of ghosts that were seen in the vicinity. I never saw one myself, though I am a night-coward and full of tremulous faith in uncanny things.

I could sit under the Forth in the corner of the Field of The Musician and listen to what music vibrates in the mystic imagination of an Irishman. I shouted in that field and heard my shout go travelling towards the Pole Star. I had dreams.

Men in the little fields below looked up at my lazy dreamer and were filled with shame and disgust that such a 'useless animal' should have come into possession of land. I was a bad example.

'Fit him better to be makin' drains or trimmin' the briars,' they said.

Perhaps they were right. A young girl once crossed the fence to me where I sat in The Musician's Field. She wasn't a fairy.

I wasn't always dreaming. When I worked I worked hard. For about an hour I would delve and slash, compressing a day's work into an hour.

My neighbour, Johnnie of the Parables, said to me one day, 'You have a whole lifetime's work before you in MacParland's farm.' He thought this was something to make me glad. And so it should have been if I had been an artist as a farmer. For an artist, whether poet or farmer, must find glory and exultation in struggling with the crude ungainly crust of earth and spirit.

MacParland's black hills were an epic subject for a poet of the plough and bill-hook. Any true farmer would have joyed in making of those fields good tillage land.

'A life's work,' my neighbour had said. It is a great thing to have found a subject that can serve a man his lifetime. On either side of me were men who had made good land out of bad soil.

'Look at the Dooleys,' my mother said to me. 'See the way they're gettin' on.'

I looked often enough but I didn't see: I was blind as an old rat.

The place was a sanctuary for hares and rabbits. I didn't disturb their briary haunts.

I worked on this farm for seven or eight years. It grew good crops for me. More by good luck than good guiding, as the saying goes.

If anyone goes around those untrimmed hedges to-day, he will find stuck among the forked branches of the stunted ash-trees the faded leaves of many a highbrow magazine. I stocked every fence with a book or paper of some kind. As I walked around the hedges, bill-hook on my shoulder, I might feel an inclination to read a poem or a short story. I knew just where to find what I wanted. The hedges were the shelves of my library. I had not my literature card-indexed, but I had a plan of my own as good. I could say: in the second ash tree from the top end of the Field of The Musician is a poem by Yeats or A. E. There is a short story by A. E. Coppard at the root of the boor-tree beside the gap in the Field of the Well.

It was a spacious library. Often enough my literature disappeared. It might be some mentally-starved ploughman who had caused the paper to vanish. I never grudged it to him, nor did I over-much grudge the blackbird the luxury of a good poem as binding for his nest. Rats, too, are rather fond of paper pillows for their beds. On the rim of a rat-hole I found one day a scrap of paper which bore in my handwriting:

It is very cold, we are drifting north by the North Star,
The night had fallen,
The water is turned to stone in the scooped jars.

It was a poem by Archibald MacLeish which I had transcribed out of some periodical. The rats had used the remainder of the poem, but they left a few good lines untouched.

27 The Kicking Mare

To work our spreading dominions it was necessary that I should get a horse and cart and some farm implements. My mother thought that an old horse would suit me best. She said: 'If he gets a wild young animal he'll let it run away and break its neck while he's dreamin' or readin' a book.'

One evening a wandering farm-labourer came to our house. He had news of a horse and cart and harness which were to be had cheaply. The horse was old, but a good quiet baste, he said.

'Just the thing we're lookin' for,' my mother said.

The fellow told us that the horse, cart, and harness were to be sold by public auction next day in Carrick fair.

The horse, cart, and harness were put up in one lot. The auctioneer stood in the cart. I bid seven pounds.

'Seven pounds bid,' the auctioneer shouted. He had the hammer up.

'And going at seven pounds,' he added, striving to give dramatic tension to his words. Slowly, oh so slowly, the hammer came down. It was within an inch of the auctioneer's book. The tremor of a gambler passed through me.

'Going, going, going,' the auctioneer repeated. And then:

'Five bob more,' someone at the back of the crowd bid.

The hammer went up again. I bid seven pounds ten. Again the fateful hammer began to descend.

The suspense was a terrible torture. The fellow who was bidding against me waited till the last second before putting on his five-shilling bid. And so it went on till the bidding stood at my twelve pounds.

That auctioneer was an expert at slow-motion hammering. For fully five minutes he held the hammer within an inch of his book.

'Are you all done?' he said at last. Silence, silence, silence. Then 'tap,' the hammer had fallen. The horse, cart, and harness were mine. Men gathered round to congratulate me. I thought I discerned a trace of irony or ridicule in their felicitations.

'Ye bought Wood's oul' bay mare,' one fellow came up to me and said.

'Aw, she's not dog ould,' said another, to take the harm out of the first statement. The two men fell to argument on the mare's age.

'She's about thirty years.'

'Aw, begod she's not passin' twenty-five at the outside.'

'Thirty years, that's her age. She was sowl' a five-year-ould in the fair of Dundalk the year after the Boer War.'

Another well-wisher came and shook hands with me. 'There's a good season in her,' he said.

Around the mare and cart were gathered a large crowd of horse-judges and neighbours. They examined the beast: back, belly, and sides. They looked in her mouth and in her eyes. They tapped the cart-wheels with their sticks, and shook the side-boards.

Out of the gabble a few illuminating phrases emerged.

'Her teeth's a foot long, she'll grind no oats with them spikes.'

'She has a spavin.'

'Looka the two pockets over her eyes, ye could put a pint of water in each of them. The rale sign of oul' age.'

'There's a damn good straddle.'

'It is that. Pity to have it on such a scram.'

'The cart-wheels are a bit dished. I wouldn't like to chance them over a bad pass.'

'That's a bleddy good axle.'

They rattled the cart to test the soundness of the axle.

I paid the auctioneer. I asked him for a luck-penny.

'You got a very good bargain,' was what he said.

I got in the cart, caught the reins and ordered the mare on. Nellie was the mare's name, but the people around me called her Brown Bess. They gave me an inglorious cheer as I drove off.

Of all the mare's faults, not one of the critics had named the only one for which she was justly infamous. She was a kicker. She'd kick the stars out of the sky, was the local description of her kicking prowess.

In a cart she was as quiet as a dog, but in a plough beside

another horse she was the queen of kicking mares. She would plough very well by herself as far as willingness was concerned. The best single horse in the world can only do very middling ploughing, and Brown Bess was far from being the best horse in the world.

On the evening of the purchase, when I drove her into our yard for the first time, my mother and sisters and brother gave us the family equivalent of a royal salute. It was an evening in January, nineteen hundred and twenty-nine, I think. It was pitch dark when I got home. There was a stable-lamp hanging on our yard gate to light me in. All my people were in great good humour. The mare and turn-out looked remarkably well in the lamplight. Her blemishes and the cracks of the cart were veiled in darkness. Nobody could see the pockets over the mare's eyes and her spavined joints. She was just a horse standing in a cart. A bright-painted and new cart would not have looked better then. It could be heard as it came up the road, but not seen, and the sound its axle made was a good sound. Indeed so solid did the axle rumble that my mother thought it was Cassidy's cart. Cassidy's cart was famous for its axle – we knew it miles away.

My mother was smiling: she was proud of me. I was as famous coming from the fair as Goldsmith's Moses was going to it.

'We're better loose her out of the cart,' my brother said.

I brought her to the tub for a drink. Someone else got oats, and others were pulling hay out of the stack for her. She could eat oats though her teeth were long. She could eat hay. She could eat anything that was good for a horse. That same evening Michael put his head in the stable door while the mare was eating her oats. He shook his head and smiled.

'Live horse and you'll get grass,' he said to the mare. 'I never knew the meanin' of that sayin' till now,' he said, addressing me.

'Live horse and you'll get oats,' he said, varying the saying to make its wisdom clearer.

'What do you think of her?' I asked.

'She's all right, she's all right,' he said.

There were many ways of saying a thing was all right. The particular inflection which Michael used meant that the mare was all wrong. You must not take the statements of our people at their face value. Englishmen, and other foolish people, often do, and are laughed at behind their backs afterwards.

'Well, what do you think of Patrick's bargain?' Michael was questioned when we straggled into our lighted kitchen.

'He made a good bargain,' Michael said. 'Why, man alive, when that mare gets a few feeds of oats you won't know her. I wish yez luck of her.'

'Thank you, thank you,' we all replied.

Tea was made. We drank to the health of myself and the mare. Suddenly in the middle of the tea we heard a great commotion in the stable where the mare was. We rushed out. The mare was lying groaning in pain on the stable floor.

'She has a pain,' Michael told us. It was a platitude, still we looked at Michael with respect, for his diagnosis. Then he elaborated. 'She got too much oats, I'd say, and she wasn't used to it. She'll over it, I think, so long as it isn't a water pain.'

'Is a water pain bad?'

'It's the last.'

The mare recovered.

Next day I brought my mother in the cart to Inniskeen. The neighbours who met us all saluted us and wished us success in our purchase.

We were now numbered among the big farmers. We had a horse and cart as good as most of them.

Old George wanted to see the mare. I led her over to his house. He leaned on his crutches in the doorway.

'She's a well laid-down little article,' were the exact words he said.

George turned to his son who stood by and asked his opinion. I didn't quite catch what the son said, but from the tone of his speech I gathered that he was admitting the creature was a horse-beast and nothing more.

It was the beginning of the ploughing season. The question was, who would be my joinsman for the season. Every pair of one-horse farmers joined forces at the start of the ploughing season. Such co-operative connections were of a very fragile nature and hardly any two consecutive seasons found the same pair of farmers joined. A borrowed horse needs hard hooves, and so does the horse which is tied in the plough with a neighbour's horse if the owner isn't present. There were fairly well-founded beliefs in that country that the strange horse wouldn't get the best of fair play in its owner's absence. It wouldn't get its share of oats. The belt on the double-tree could be shifted to throw an extra pull on the beast. This was known as 'putting an inch on the horse'. It was done with soft young horses, but this was legitimate.

Often enough a join would be broken right at the height of sowing time. There would be high talk in low fields then and perhaps black eyes over white sheets.

'Yer makin' my horse do too much.'

'Yer a liar, sir.'

You could tell a plough which was being drawn by a joined team: there would always be two men following the plough. A man whose stock of farming implements didn't include, say, a harrow tried to form a join with a man who had a harrow.

When we began to consider who would be our joinsman most of the other one-horse men had come together. All that remained were the hard cases, the contrary men whose horses were either kickers or biters or rusters. Or whose land was rocky and hilly, or who had poor implements or none. We looked about us. Many of our neighbours were also looking about for us. The end of it all was I joined with George's son for the ploughing season. Nobody in the vicinity was aware of the mare's vicious nature. Otherwise I should have had greater difficulty in making a liaison.

The bad habits and faults of horses are kept very quiet. 'Say nothing till ye get rid of her,' was the guiding principle. And even then the late owner would say nothing. There was a second reason why Brown Bess's conduct in the plough was hardly known. For many years she hadn't been put in the plough: she was used as a cart-horse to draw gravel for the roads. Her owner for the past ten or fifteen years had been a road-mender.

28 The Ploughing-season Combine

George had a strong slate-coloured horse. Its name was Glug because of a watery sound that came from the beast's belly when he trotted. Glug was a good plough-horse: he was a bit lazy, but that habit was overcome by a liberal use of the stick and plough-rein.

George always spoke of Glug as 'me horse'. His son also said 'me horse', but seldom in his father's hearing. One day he did slip up in his father's presence.

'I think I'll go out and feed me horse,' he said.

George became furious; he was a most excitable old man.

'When in the name of God did *you* get a horse?' he cried. 'Sure that's none of your horse!'

Relations, as you see, between George and his son were not always the best.

The son did the plough-work. The sum-total of farming implements about George's was an old swing plough and a six-bull harrow. The son had a large contempt for me because we weren't traditional farmers. Neither had we plough or harrow as he had. Nobody would wish to join up with a fellow who had no farm implements. The blood of cobblers is inferior to the fluid in the veins of a five-acre farmer. The man who would join with us would have to be in desperate straits. And so it was with George and son. They had rung the changes on all the one-horse combines so often that now the only hope was a newcomer as I was.

On the morning that I first brought Brown Bess into the acquaintance of Glug she behaved like a pet lamb. Until we had her coupled to Glug and almost completely yoked she looked like an angel of horsedom.

George's son was carelessly hooking up her outside chain when without a note of warning she let fly a sixty-mile-an-hour kick that just grazed the forehead of the ploughman. We pardoned her this first kick as we believed it was due to impatience and free from malice. Fred – that was the name of George's son – looked at the mare.

'I don't like the set of her ears,' he said. Brown Bess had her ears down like a mule in anger. Fred made another attempt to put in the crook and succeeded. Then the kicking started in earnest. For a creature of her years she had wonderful agility in her hindquarters. George came to the doorway of his house and shouted wildly:

'Good God, loose out me horse or she'll break his leg.'

Fred paid no heed. He was determined to make the mare work or know for what.

'Lead her by the head,' he said to me.

I caught the mare by the ring of the bit. She eased off in her kicking. Glug was taking this display of passion in a very stoical manner. He edged away as far as he could from the mare. We commenced ploughing. While I held the bit she didn't kick too bad. She was inclined to rush forward.

'Aisy mare, aisy mare,' Fred kept saying soothingly from the handles of the plough. I patted her on the jaw, and for the length of the one-acre field all went beautifully.

'Aisy mare, aisy pet,' Fred continued.

Then the plough struck a rock; the handles leaped up out of Fred's hands. The single-tree hit Brown Bess on her heels. She gave a repeat-performance of her kicking act. And worse than all, the place she chose to do it was in an exposed place where all the neighbours could see. Around on all the little hills men and women were standing watching the sport. This enraged Fred. He got furious with the mare. He kicked her, and we both kicked her. She lay down like a moody ass. We could hear laughter rising from the little hills.

A helpful neighbour came up to us.

'Don't abuse the baste,' he advised, 'she's just a bit nervous.'

We got her going again. The helpful neighbour walked up and down alongside us. I noted that he was closely studying all the rascally tricks of Brown Bess. He wanted to have first-hand information of her doings. It was the makings of a good story by some bright hearth.

We got on much better than the mare expected.

'I'd make Oul' Nick himself plough if I could get the traces on him,' Fred boasted.

During the ploughing-season, like all other joinsmen, we had many rows. Whenever a dry week came both of us wanted to be labouring our own land. Ploughing in the wet is bad work: it sours the soil.

We kept a tally of our work for one and other. My partner had a good memory, it was indelible as ink.

'I have three days on ye,' he said once. I looked in my book and found he was right.

Between us we had ten acres to plough. Fred had one acre and a half for potatoes and turnips, three acres and a half for oats. Our complement of tillage land worked out much the same. But while George's land was flat and dry and kindly, ours on MacParland's hills was hilly and stiff, a comparison which Fred often pointed out. Each morning at eight o'clock I led my mare up to George's front door. None of the household would be up. It would be near ten o'clock before we got started. Fred claimed that he could take the last out of any pair of horses from ten in the morning till six in the evening. I disagreed with him and quoted the saying of Faylee MacFadden:

'If a man don't get up in the mornin' and fodder his horses, he can't expect to do a good day's work.'

Fred was for ever telling me of his great deeds in various ploughing fields. Up in the County Louth he had worked for the big farmers. I heard George, his father, telling him to shut up.

'Sure what were ye but a yard-man,' he said.

'I was a ploughman, I tell ye,' Fred replied.

Fred held the plough-handles as though there were great pressure needed. His great gnarled hands trembled with nervous power. Fred had a long spade jaw and wild eyes like his father. He stared in front like a visionary who was seeing things. I walked alongside Brown Bess, but out of her range. We could never be sure when she'd take a fit. We got wise to her ways. Though we couldn't cure her of kicking we could read the delicate signs of an oncoming attack. She would switch her tail ever so slightly, and perhaps let down her ears.

We carried on during what is known as the first ploughing. No day passed without a kicking display. And we were never without an audience no matter how urgent the rush of work.

Kavanagh's kicking mare was known all over the parish.

To give the beast her due, she never, I think, deliberately aimed a kick at the other horse.

'Does she kick in or out?' was the first question everybody would put.

'She kicks out,' I could answer.

'Aw, then there's a chance with her. If she kicked inwards ye might shoot her.'

As the days lengthened the fire in Brown Bess's veins mounted. Before we had the last of our acres blackened she was kicking with a fury that was something splendid.

Just as we were beginning to cross-plough the land for potatoes the trouble came to a head. While turning on the headland my mare lashed out and scored a direct hit on Glug's hind quarters. Fred turned pale.

'Loose out yer bleddy kicker,' he cried, 'loose her out afore she does harm.'

I hesitated. Fred ran up to the mare's head and untied the coupling reins. I loosed the chains and led her away. Once out of the plough innocence began to sweeten in her eye. She looked real innocent like a cooey woman.

Fred continued ploughing with one horse. Cross-ploughing land that has been winter-ploughed and loosened with frost isn't such a very difficult job for a strong horse. As I was leading the mare home I met a neighbour-man.

'Did she buck up on yez?' he asked.

I said she was no worse than ever she was.

He knew of another man who was in a similar predicament.

'Yez ought to join for the rest of the season,' he suggested.

I thought it a good idea.

As I dragged the mare after me over the whitening spring road I was feeling humbled. My genius has been of a ridiculous turn. I sensed the joke and laughed back into the mare's face.

The man whom I was advised to join had not a horse, but a jennet, a white jennet, whose pace was about one yard per minute.

It had exhausted the patience of every horse and horseman in the country. It was a bad proposition but there was no alternative. The spring day was in it, as the people say. It was no time for finicky selectiveness.

From the very first Brown Bess took a particular dislike to the white jennet. While alongside it her hind legs were oftener in the air than on the ground. To make a bad job worse the jennet wouldn't work in the furrow and it was towards the ridge the mare's kicks were directed. The owner of the jennet wasn't easy to get along with, and at the end of a week we came apart like cement from a piece of timber.

My mother thought that I had done enough joining for the time being.

'We'll get Hamills to put in the crop,' she said. I could do the carting of dung and such work with the mare.

During the summer I drill-harrowed the potatoes with Brown Bess and ploughed the plot for turnips. This plot was the steepest part of MacParland's hills. The steepness was an advantage. I went up idle and ploughed down. It was brilliant weather towards the end of May. On the top of the hill after each 'scrape' I sat down to let the mare get her wind.

The headland was hard and warm and creative as a poet's stool. Beside me on the bank the primroses grew. It is a fine thing to be alone with flowers. When I looked north Slieve Gullion filled my eyes. I could see the busy people in the little fields beneath me. There were two girls weeding thistles out of corn, beyond that a man shovelling sand out of a sand-pit. The parochial house among fine trees was the only grand house on my horizon. I could see priests coming in and out: there was to be a party in it on this day.

Holding the handles of a rusty old plough that was drawn by a kicking mare, I made a poem:

> 'I turn the lea-green down
> Gaily now
> And paint the meadows brown
> With my plough.
> I dream with silvery gull
> And brazen crow

A thing that is beautiful
I may know.

Tranquillity walks with me
And no care;
O the quiet ecstasy
Like a prayer.

I find a star-lovely art
In a dark sod;
Joy that is timeless! O heart,
That knows God!'

A. E. printed it in the *Irish Statesman*. I could not help smiling when I thought of the origin of my ploughman ecstasy. A kicking mare in a rusty old plough tilling a rood of land for turnips.

We had the mare for four years. The second season I managed to get a joinsman in spite of my mare's reputation. A fellow called Dinny B—— who was after purchasing an old horse.

Dinny had every implement that ever was needed in a farmer's place. Dinny joined with me for no reason connected with land or horses, but because I would listen to his stories of old Ireland. Over and over again he had inflicted the story of Tara on me. He would lean on his gate and talk. His voice, like a sad woman's, still sings in my ears.

'And Saint Rudin went round Tara and he cursed Tara and he prayed that there wouldn't be left in Tara a stone upon a stone.'

And it might be a piece taken verbatim from the lectures of Father Tom Burke. He had great respect for books. Father Burke's *Lectures and Sermons* was for him the masterpiece of Irish writing.

Dinny employed a man to do the ploughing for him, a professional ploughman who could deal with all kinds of horse villainy. This ploughman was a wizard after horses. Brown Bess behaved splendidly.

My job was to sit beside old Dinny (he was old and lame) on a heap of stones beside his front gate and listen to his lore. I liked my job well.

Father Tom Burke's *Refutation of Froude* was dinned into my ears. Tara of the Kings was plainer history to me than the 1916 rebellion. I knew the wise sayings of King Cormac. I knew all Dinny knew: he emptied himself into me.

All the while Tommy the ploughman was turning the brown earth up. He kept a tight firm rein on his team. When he could come close to where Dinny and I sat he would say:

'Who said that mare was a kicker? Why, she's as fine a plough mare as ever wore a trace.'

'Be careful,' I advised.

'And Saint Kevin lay down on his bed,' Dinny would say. I don't remember what Saint Kevin did when he lay down.

The neighbours couldn't believe that Brown Bess was keeping quiet. Some of them visited us.

'Bedad, yez are gettin' on gallant,' one man said.

'We are that,' the ploughman agreed.

> 'Go sleep with the sunshine of fame on thy slumbers
> Till touched by some hand less unworthy than mine.

And a hand less unworthy came when in Ireland's lays appeared the immortal Thomas Davis.'

Dinny was quoting from Father Burke. The ploughman and the visitor didn't pay any heed. They were talking of more poetical things: such as the price of fat cattle, local romances, if any, or the condition of the plough-irons.

'Yes, it could be doin' with a new sole-plate.'

But Saint Rudin was at that moment cursing Tara, and the condition of the plough's sole-plate held no interest for Dinny.

We got all our crops planted – all save a corner in one of Dinny's fields in which we intended planting some carrots. In an hour or two we should have wound up the season.

Brown Bess had won for herself the name of 'a great wee baste'.

As Tommy was turning his plough on a very narrow headland, without any warning the mare raised her hind hooves. She had a new set of shoes and the iron glistened in the sun; like two flashes of fork-lightning they were. What kicking she had done during her thirty years of existence was mere horse-whimsy compared to this outburst. She kicked a circle clean round her, she knotted herself up in the chains and reins. Dinny and I were sitting together in the beam of a drill-plough. Spiritually we were reclining in the Banqueting Hall of Tara.

Tommy shouted. I ran to him. The two horses were inextricably mixed up in the chains and were struggling together on the ground. I had no hope to see ever again that tangle of horseflesh and tackle righted.

Tommy was taking it cool. He was an experienced ploughman. There is a good deal of showmanship about a horse-row.

'In another hour we'd have finished,' Tommy said. 'She blotted her copy-book. Isn't that the spite.'

The horses came clear of each other in the long run. Dinny enjoyed the piece. He laughed heartily. Maybe this display recalled for him some great heroic struggle of ancient times.

'We'll keep it quiet,' Tommy said, 'and nobody will be any the wiser.'

But did we keep it quiet? Before night the whole country was laughing at the story. And the story was adorned with a thousand fantastic flourishes.

29 A Visit to Dublin

For a long time I had been imagining that literary people would
be interesting to meet. I wanted to meet A. E. and any other
of the Dublin writers with whom I might be able to connect.
But greater than my desire to meet the exalted beings of Literature
was the road-hunger in my heart that cried out for dusty romance.
I had listened to the journeymen shoemakers, common tramps,
and uncommon tinkers. I had read Jim Tully and Patrick Magill.
The blood of tramps was in my veins: my father's father had
come from the West; he had taken the road Queen Maeve took
when that cattle-fancier was on the chase of the Brown Bull of
Cooley.

On the nineteenth of December, nineteen thirty-one, I said to
my mother:

'I'm going a bit of a journey.'

'Musha where?' she asked in surprise.

'As far as Dublin,' I said.

She thought I was mad.

'What nonsense are ye up to now? 'Twould fit ye better to be
cleanin' the drain in the meadow and not have the flood drive
us out of the place.'

I was aware of the condition of the drain which was making
a lake of our meadow.

'I'm walking to Dublin,' I said, 'and I don't care if the flood
in the meadow rises high as the Flood that floated Noah above
Ararat.'

She took it in good part and gave me all the change was in
the house. My brother was privy to my adventure – he was
fifteen years old then – and gave me good practical advice.

I had in my pocket exactly three shillings and fourpence
ha'penny.

I wore my working clothes and boots. On my trousers were
the tramp-necessary rectangular knee-patches, my jacket was

down to beggar standard, my boots were a hob-nailed pair of my own making. I made a great mistake in not taking a second pair of socks, or at least one clean pair.

I was off. I was going down the road of my dreams. I had intended keeping a diary of my journey, but after a few entries gave it up.

It was a beautiful morning, bright and crisp, one could almost imagine spring in the air. Spring was in my imagination at any rate. I remembered how the women used to call after us on our way to Carrick fair: 'God be with ye on the Dublin road where nobody ever had luck.' I walked at a brisk pace for the first five or six miles. I knew this part of the road too well and the road and its people knew me. I wanted as quickly as possible to get on to the strange roads where Romance wearing gold earrings was waiting for me.

'Good mornin',' a man near home saluted. 'Where are ye bound for?' he inquired.

'A little bit of a journey,' I said.

Ten miles from home I was in a strange country, among folk who wouldn't know me. I decided that it was time to test my skill as a beggar. I looked about me and selected a snug, well-kept house a few perches off the main road. It was a white-washed thatched cottage. An ideal house, I said to myself. I never imagined it could be so difficult to break into the beggar trade. For half an hour I stood on the road trying to screw up my courage to the sticking place. I walked up the laneway to the house and turned back again. I was finding it very difficult to get rid of my peasant-solid pride.

I went to the door at last and leaning over the half-door muttered something. A woman came. She was a nice woman of about thirty years and turned out to be one of those creatures of whom tramps dream but never encounter. Spiritually and physically she was tender as a sheltered leaf.

'I want a sup of a drink,' I said.

'Come inside,' she invited.

It wouldn't require a great detective to guess that this was a young woman married to an old man. I was never a cold-blooded lover of the brazen images set up by poets in the name of Woman. But adultery is not for tramps: it is a respectable, well-fed sin.

As I entered, the kettle on the hob broke into a sweet song.

She set a chair for me near the fire and rinsed the teapot. I love the music the lid of a teapot makes.

'A sup of tay will do ye no harm,' she said.

'You're too dacent,' I said.

I told her a tale of glamorous grief. I said I hadn't tasted a morsel of food for the past twenty-four hours and that I had walked from Newry.

'Me poor fella,' she murmured, three short words more eloquent than a bookful of godly sermons. I was an impostor. She put before me a blue mugful of strong tea, four thick slices of brown bread well buttered, and to crown it all a pair of duck eggs. I should have wished to stay a longer while in that house but I was a tramp and must travel on.

My feet were feeling a bit tender, though I had only gone ten miles. A granite milestone along the way told me it was forty-five miles to Dublin: the chiselled letter-grooves were filled with moss and I had to trace the letters with my finger like a blind man reading Braille. These were the miles that were made in old gods' time when good measure was in fashion.

My belly was full but my starved soul had still to break its fast. I touched a kind-faced gentleman who was standing outside his fine house: I touched him for money. He whistled and not a pleasant tune – he was calling the dog. I didn't look back, like Lot's wife.

Just not to deliver judgment on fine-housed gentlemen I went up to another hall door that had a chromium-plated knocker. A low-set woman answered my knock; when I saw the face that was on her I knew she was a torturer of tramps.

'Give me a couple of coppers,' I said. The slamming of that massive hall door generated an electrical current about my eyes. As I walked down the steps from that hall door I pronounced my final judgment on all well-housed people.

'A bad lot.'

The evening was thickening about the view, and I had so far not added to my three and fourpence halfpenny.

I entered a blacksmith's forge. The smith, a big, round-shouldered man with a neck of red folding fat, was making shoes for hunters. I talked him to generosity. He was surprised when he heard I was on the road.

'Be the mortal day you could very nearly be a schoolmaster,' he said. He searched in his trousers pockets and I imagined that I heard the sweet tinkle of silver. Then he went to his coat that hung on the vise and searched again.

'I'm sorry,' he said, 'but that's all I've on me, two pence.'

I took it and thanked him. As I moved off I overheard him say to himself: 'He's not right wise, he doesn't look all there.'

It was quite dark now. I was travelling through grass-land, 'Meath of the pastures,' and the small houses I wanted were few and far between. I came up with a young man who had been seeing his girl. He was as decent and generous as men in love are. He gave me sixpence and after we parted he called after me.

'Wait, there's a few fags in this packet you might like.'

Six cigarettes. I sat down on a bank of darkness and had my first smoke of the day. The smell of bacon and eggs being fried came to my hunger-acute nostrils. I followed my nose and called at the door whence came the smell. 'We can't accommodate you,' was the answer I got.

'I don't want accommodation,' I said. 'It's a meal I'm asking.'

'We can't accommodate you.'

Not far from this house was a smaller one. I pushed open the door. An old, half-blind woman was sitting by the hob all alone.

'What d'ye want?' she squealed.

'A bite to eat, woman, if you can spare it.'

She hobbled over to the dresser and from the cupboard extracted a crust of white bread which would have attracted the attention of an archæologist. She gave me the museum-piece and I walked out. I had scarcely swung my coat-tail free of her door when she most ungraciously, and with a loud click, turned the key in the lock.

I was wondering if I'd have to be content with a soldier's supper, when prosperous goodness appeared like a new star in the December sky.

I spoke to a young boy who was standing outside his gate listening with cocked ear. I told him how it was with me.

'My father and mother is in the fair,' he told me, 'and the divil a one is in the house but meself.'

I went in, and between the young boy and myself we produced an excellent supper. The clock standing in the back window said it was ten o'clock.

'Give no heed to that oul' clock,' the boy warned me, 'it never toul' the truth in its life.'

The rattle of a cart reached our ears.

'That's thim,' the lad said.

I left. I passed through Slane, the place I had often seen from the hills of my childhood. There were numerous hay-barns here. By the light of matches I groped my way round one; it was filled to the top and I had to climb up a twenty-foot standard to bed.

I didn't sleep well. Between midnight and two o'clock a shiver ran through me. Bury myself as I did in blankets of sweet-smelling hay, I couldn't get warm. I was up early. When I put my hand in my pocket I had no money – lost in the bedclothes! I tossed the hay back, and my luck was in – I found all the money save the halfpenny. No doubt it had gone to seek its comrade in the till of some ladies' draper.

Here and there curly columns of smoke were rising from big chimneys. I got an excuse for a breakfast in a labourer's cottage – dry bread and weak tea. The woman of the house kept saying: 'God help ye, me poor fella, or anybody has no home.'

The weather was perfect, like a May day. I washed my face at a road-side pump. I wrote in my diary.

'Am now twenty miles from Dublin, left foot very sore, can get everything but money. Have just talked to two children going to school, a boy and girl. Cromwell was their name.'

I broke a branch from an ash tree and made of it a walking stick. I passed through Ashbourne village at eleven o'clock. A crowd were gathering to see the meet of the Meath Hounds. I build these facts from another entry in my diary.

I gave up begging for money, it was a hopeless quest. I got tea in another cottage. The woman there had a twinkle in her eye.

'Yer not a tramp,' she said.

'To my grief I am,' I replied.

'Yer up to some cod-actin',' she declared. 'I'd know a real tramp.'

I put two slices of bread in my pocket, disregarding the rule in my native place: 'Eat your fill and pocket none.'

Nothing of importance happened to me between Ashbourne and Dublin. The road was giving me very bad value.

I arrived in the city at half-past two. I was more helpless than a bull in a mist. Tramps should keep clear of all cities and Dublin in particular. The Dublin police are the scourge of tramps – worse than blisters. I kept fairly free from their strong grip and inquisitive tongues. I went to the National Library, as I was quite sure that the people there would know the whereabouts of every literary man and woman. I was mistaken.

'Where does A. E. hang out?' I asked. They didn't know, though they tried to give the impression that they did. They knew where he used to live – in Plunket House.

'Sure I know that myself,' I told the fellow with the goatee beard who stood behind the counter. I called the office table the counter when speaking to them and that made them laugh.

'Maybe you could give me the address of some other poet,' I said.

A woman searched in a book and after a long time extracted one address, that of Oliver St John Gogarty.

'Is that the best you can do?' I queried. And that was the best they could do.

When I was in the library I thought I could take advantage of the fact and get a book to read. Eliot's *The Waste Land* was being talked about at that time. I asked for *The Waste Land*. The man with the goatee beard wanted to know if it was a book on drainage, and before I could explain was almost on his way to procure one of that type for me. I should have said that I asked specifically for *The Waste Land* by T. S. Eliot, so that left the joke a far finer one.

I turned for Gogarty's house in Ely Place. Near the National Gallery I inquired my way of a man who was speaking Gaelic to a boy, evidently his son. The man was the Minister for Finance in the Free State. I knew him by eye-sight as he was the Member for my own county. Close on the Minister's heels was a detective with whom I chatted when I had parted with the keeper of the State purse.

I mistook Gogarty's white-robed maid for his wife – or his mistress. I expected every poet to have a spare wife.

'Are you a patient?' she asked.

'Devil a that,' I said.

She didn't understand my language but understood my clothes.

'I want to see the poet.'

'Well, wait till I see if the Doctor is in.'

She turned her back and as soon as she did I turned and ran up Ely Place with the sidelong gait of a thief.

I tried Plunket House. I knocked and a girl down under spoke to me. 'Who are you looking for?'

'A. E.,' I said.

She knew his address.

'You're a topper,' I said. 'You know more than the chaps in the National Library.'

A. E. opened the door to me, and not merely the door of wood on his house in Rathgar. I was afraid of that man. He looked like a man who had awakened from a dark trance. His eyes stared at me like two nightmare eyes from which there was no escape. He appeared quite certain that I was a beggar. I regretted not having a fiddle under my arm to add a touch of wild colour to my drab tramp.

When I had explained who I was he gave me a handshake as warm as I've ever got. I sat on a chair that was too comfortable. I wasn't used to easy chairs. If I had been travelling respectable I shouldn't have minded so much. My hob-nailed boots as I watched them grew bigger and bigger. The patches on the knees of my trousers, because I sat on a low seat, stood up like two pictures on exhibition. I cursed, inwardly, those boots and those dark patches. I was partly aware, too, that my shin-bones were visible.

A. E. started to talk in a voice that was musical as evening over ploughed fields. He talked while I interjected an odd word for decency's sake. He told me all his stock tales and pet philosophies. I was bored and tried, like the hypocrite I was, to affect deep embarrassment in the presence of genius. I wasn't listening to A. E. I was worried over the poor impression I was making. I was hungry – for poetry? Yes, but I was also physically hungry, and an empty stomach is a great egoist, and a bad listener to anything save the fizz of rashers on a pan.

I was a peasant and a peasant is a narrow surveyor of generous hearts.

He read me Whitman, of whom he was very fond, and also Emerson.

I didn't like Whitman and said so. I always thought him a writer who tried to bully his way to prophecy. Of Emerson at the time I had no opinions to offer. I found him out later to be a sugary humbug. His transcendental bunkum sickened me.

When A. E. told me how sorry he was that his girl was out I was shocked. Satisfaction for my appetite in a café would shatter my capital on the reef of bankruptcy.

He plopped to the floor and searched among the lower shelves for books. He kept picking out volumes till my eye was full. I didn't judge those books by their covers or by their contents, but by their weight. They would weigh four stones if they weighed an ounce. Emerson's works and Whitman's were in the pile as a matter of course. Victor Hugo was represented by his masterpiece *Les Misérables*. The emotional warmth of Hugo appealed to me. There was a book by a modern Syrian prophet which for many years helped me to prattle glib lies that looked like truth. George Moore's *Confessions of a Young Man*, the only book of that author I could ever stomach. There were two books by Dostoyevsky, *The Brothers Karamazov* and *The Idiot*. These two books were worth more than all the rest together. I read *The Idiot* twenty times at least. Of the books of verse I got two volumes by A. E. himself. A. E. wrote some poems that I like, even now in maturity. I got James Stephens collected in a beautiful binding. I read Stephens for a short while and tossed him aside for ever. I daren't read him as I would find myself imitating his beautiful rhythms. Stephens was one of my favourites and I had to ban him. I got a good anthology compiled by a Japanese professor, Mahata Sargu. The printer's errors in this book were beyond counting and often made hash of a lovely poem.

I put the books on my back and left A. E. I didn't call on any other poets or writers on that day.

Night was in the city when I left A. E. with my load of literature.

I moped around Nelson's Pillar. The newsboys and hard cases talked very intimately to me. I was one of themselves. I was looking for a cheap lodging-house. One fellow suggested a St Vincent de Paul night shelter.

'Chroist, don't go there,' another advised me, 'they'd make ye pray there.'

To one of the worst slum lodging houses in Gloucester Street I was directed. I paid sixpence for my bed. There were six other beds in the room which was at the top of a three-storied house. The stink of that room and those beds has never left my nostrils. My room-mates were the derelicts of humanity. There was a blind man, a lame man, a horrible looking young fellow with no nose, only two little holes under his eyes, there was a deaf but not dumb man, and another with a look of the criminal. The communal sanitary convenience was a rusty bucket which hadn't been emptied from the night before, and had apparently never been scrubbed: it had a scum of many layers.

I laid my books beside me covered with the ragged quilt.

The next day was a fast day. I went to a café and – taking a dispensation from the fast – ordered a breakfast of rashers and eggs. I had a long journey ahead of me and I knew that a man travels on his breakfast. As soon as I got clear of Dublin I sat down on the road-side and opened one of my books, *The Ring and the Book*. I couldn't read Browning. A motor-car passed by and a curiously amused face peeped out the back window. A girl from our country who recognized me. I was upset for she was a nice girl.

Forward again. People who saw me took me for a purveyor of heretical Bibles and shook their heads. A priest mounted on a beautiful bay horse pulled up and was all edge to know what kind were the books. He was interested in books, but not in Russian writers.

'Books by the great Russians,' I told him I carried. The name of Russians was associated with barbarism and grizzly bears.

'Books by Russians?' he said. 'That's strange.' He trotted his horse off and I continued my journey north.

The only entry in my diary relating to my homeward journey was written here. This is the entry:

'Have just overheard two men talking about me. One of them said to the other: "I wonder who yon kinat with the load of books would be?" The other answered: "Some lazy Rodney, I suppose, that wouldn't do a tap of honest work."'

My journey home was a two-day misery. It was pouring rain as I crossed the Hill of Mullacrew. I passed safely through the village of Louth where the fairies had led myself and my mother astray. I was home.

Although I had seen A. E., had got books, and had tasted the road, I have always regretted going to Dublin. I had lost something which I could never regain from books.

I got to know Dublin much better later on. It is a city overrun by patrons of poetry and art who praise the poets and secure the jobs for their own relations. A Government – since – to whom poet, prophet, and imbecile are fellows with votes.

With the death of A. E. the only true friend of the Irish poets had passed. His genius was his generosity and – whether born of vanity as some say it was – it was practical, and not the soft-mouthed admiration that A. E.'s critics were in the habit of bestowing.

One of the best of the young Irish poets, F. R. Higgins, once told me that there was, he believed, more dishonesty in the literary city of Dublin than in any other quarter of the globe. Shelley said that poets were the legislators of the world. Dublin must have changed a lot since Shelley knew it.

Irish writers leave Ireland because sentimental praise, or hysterical pietarian dispraise, is no use in the mouth of a hungry man.

30 Tramping

In the spring following my visit to Dublin I again took to the road. It had been a dry spring and the first rush of setting and sowing had been got over by the first of April.

There would be a slack period of six weeks or two months till the sowing of the turnips started.

'You'll never get a better chance,' my brother said.

I agreed with him but I was suffering from the common vanity that I was indispensable to our farm and home.

'If you were dead you'd be done without,' my brother said.

I had five pounds in my pocket. That winter I had been most successful at the poetry trade. At least five per cent of the verse I sent out failed to come back. In three months I had made twenty pounds out of my poems.

I turned west: a tramp needs to be going somewhere till he gets used to going nowhere. I was bound for Connemara. I stayed two months on the road, though when I told the story I always said two years. My experience of tramping convinced me for all time that the road as a career is no better than verse-writing.

I had five pounds with me as I've said, but I had left behind me my imagination, and a wanderer without imagination is a blind man in an art gallery.

I passed through County Cavan, the best place in the world for a beggar. Generous are the Cavan folk. There is only another place in Ireland runs Cavan generosity close and that is South Armagh, in the vicinity of Slieve Gullion.

The Cavan lake-land between Shercock and Cootehill is beautiful as Killarney. If only some American Jew would write a song about those lakes the tourists would pour into Cavan. On the island in the lake I saw the blue and stately heron-cranes. There were buds on the blackthorn trees and the black sallies on the edge of the lake were dropping catkins – like caterpillars – on the calm water, I should have preferred a later period of the year when the land would be dressed from bonnet to shoes in green and silver. As it was I might be thankful enough: perfect weather kept up with me, and the wind – like a private detective – was always behind me.

In the town of Cavan I felt doubtful about the road to Galway and went into a garage office to inquire. The middle-aged woman in the office was most deferential. She led me to a large road map on the wall and with a pencil traced the road to Galway and also roads that led to Limerick, Longford, and other places. I said I'd like to travel via Carrick-on-Shannon and through north Roscommon.

'For goodness' sake,' she warned, 'don't go that way: the roads are terrible for motoring.'

'Still it would be rather interesting,' I said.

'Terrible roads, terrible,' she said. 'If you have any respect for your tyres go through Longford.'

She escorted me to the door: 'Where did you leave your car?' she inquired.

'Just around the corner,' I said as I dashed around the corner in a hurry lest my acting talent should let me down.

I made it my business each day while my money lasted to have one good meal at an eating-house. I made a discovery in the matter of eating-houses. The dirty ramshackle ones in the back lanes were the most expensive and the cooking such as would upset a pig's digestion. The well-kept eating-houses had fewer customers; the farm-folk didn't like dining-rooms where there were pictures on the walls and white table-cloths on the tables.

'It's us has to pay for the pictures and fancy linen,' they would say.

After a few visits to the dirty houses I made the pleasant and economic discovery. I went by Carrick-on-Shannon in spite of the garage woman's advice.

I slept in a bedroom in Carrick-on-Shannon in the company of four journeymen tailors. The landlady's nephew, a young schoolboy, occupied the bed in which I was to sleep. She put the lad to sleep with one of the tailors in a double bed, when I arrived. The price of the bed was one shilling. All the tailors were sitting up in their beds smoking pipes when I entered the bedroom. They wore no shirts. Just to show that I wasn't out for the first time I took off everything. A tramp always slept in his naked skin, I knew that much from the journeymen shoe-makers. Disease germs and fleas, it appears, are men of honour and will not attack the unprotected body.

We sat smoking and exchanging notes. The tailors were travelled men, they knew every parish in the Four Provinces. I had a good idea of the lie of Ireland. I had learned geography and history from the wandering scholars who frequented my father's cobbling benches. One of the tailors had worked in the parish of my birth.

I stayed a week in Connemara and was disappointed with the scenery and the people. When you have seen one bit of Con-nemara you have seen it all, and it is all stones. The folk there were inclined to laugh at me. They spoke Gaelic and yet I felt that the English-speaking peasants of my own country were nearer to the old tradition. There was no culture in Connemara, nothing like County Monaghan where the spirit of the old poets haunted the poplars.

I stayed with a Gaelic-speaking family in Rossmuc. I told the woman of the house that I'd be liable to stay six months as I was studying the language. I thought I'd get it cheaper on this account. 'How much a week will you charge?' I asked, in the worst of bad Gaelic.

'Well,' she said as she fingered her red petticoat, 'I had a priest here last summer and he paid me two pounds, and I had a doctor the summer before that and he paid me two pounds five.'

She wasn't making little of me.

'How about fifteen bob?' I said.

And fifteen shillings it was to be.

A few barefoot children looked in the door. I spoke to them in Gaelic – or what I thought was Gaelic – but they laughed at me.

The roar of the Atlantic lulled me to sleep for three nights. I thought the place unbearably monotonous.

I regretted having left it. My regret started when I was a few miles south of Galway. Should I go on or go back, I mused, as

I stood on the road. I turned about and stopped again. I should have stayed longer and, on the other hand, I should not.

I went up to a man's gate, he was putting a ridge of onions. I put my case before him.

'If I thought I was lavin' somethin' important,' he said. 'I wouldn't go, and sure yer as well here as where ye are.'

That wasn't very helpful. The reasons for my going back or going on were equal. And there I was for the best part of two hours perched on the horns of indecision's dilemma.

Throughout the period of my pilgrimage the weather kept fine except for one evening. I was heading for Tullamore when down upon my unprotected optimism the rain started falling and the night as well. My funds were running low at the time, though I had striven hard to conserve them. As I trudged along miserably in the rain, I searched the road-sides for some sort of shelter, but I seemed to be travelling in a nightmare land where the devil trips the runners. It was the first days of May. The hedges and trees were only half-roofed. No houses anywhere. I felt rotten and ready to give up, and if only I was a hardened sinner I'd have lain down and begged the cold wet stones for mercy. I thought of the eerie crypt in a graveyard near home known as the 'skull-house': I remembered the dozens of old skulls whitening to dust in it, and smiled thinking of the poor heroes who entered the skull-house at midnight. A person suffering from scarlet fever – I think – had had only to go to the skull-house at midnight and drink out of a skull to be cured. I thought of that eerie vault and laughed at its petty ghosts; confronted by a down-and-out and rain-drenched tramp they'd have put up a poor show.

It was quite dark now. The rain was whistling in the skeleton bushes. There wasn't an eye open in sky or earth window.

And then while I mused at the gate of Hell, the light of Salvation appeared. A light from a window winked out at me. Here was a house of some kind or other; I couldn't make out its outline for a moment.

A dog barked and then ran at me. I hit him with my stick and he ran squealing towards the door of the house.

The house was a castle, a great grey medieval castle with turrets and long louvre windows. The door was modern enough;

it had a knocker which I rattled vigorously. The door opened a
little bit and a woman's face peered out.

'Is that you, Henry?' she asked.

'It's a desperate wet night,' I replied, 'and I'm a stranger.'

Before she had time to say yes, aye or no, I was within the
castle. I felt that after long wandering I had at last stumbled on
romance and I meant to hold death's grip of her.

The woman looked me over edge-ways as if she were afraid,
but my youthful face reassured her.

'In the name of God who would you be?' she inquired in a
voice too sweet and polite to be wholesome.

I told her that I was going for the doctor for a poor sick
woman down the way.

'What's the woman's name?'

'Judy Callaghan,' I said. The only name I could think of was
the title of a song. She never heard of anyone of that name,
but all the same I was permitted to move out of the hall-way
into the kitchen – if the ante-room of a castle may be so called.

The kitchen or ante-room was appointed to receive the lord's
bards, or beggars of any century. A great turf fire burned in the
grate, an oak table stood within leg-stretch of the fire, laid with
china as if somebody was coming to tea; on the centre of the
table stood an elaborate brass lamp which looked as if it had
been a present from Queen Victoria. I suppose an expert would
have called that room smug or snug and not at all medieval. It
was smug and snug I admired that night, and not the roofless
tree of Clifford, or Grace O'Malley.

The woman was alone as far as I could see, unless I counted
the black buck-cat that gave me a side-look as I entered and then
lay back in peace on the hearth rug. She was a fat rosy-faced
creature, very spick-and-span-looking in her check apron and
elastic boots. The woman, I mean – not the cat, whose side-look
at me suggested a proud cynic.

I told her bluntly that I wanted to sleep there that night and
she just as bluntly told me I wouldn't.

'Ah, damn its sowl, woman,' I said, 'have a heart.'

'It wouldn't answer us,' she said: and by this I knew that she
was not alone.

While this talk was going on, the pad, pad of stockinged feet sounded on the stairs. A man came down, an old soft-mouthed man – he would be called a slob of a man – one of those fellows whose whole charity is in the mouth.

'Wants to sleep here,' the woman said.

'The poor fella,' the man said.

'And sure we'd keep him only it wouldn't answer us.'

I sat down on a chair by the fire to dry my clothes while the man and his wife looked me over.

'Maybe you'd take a cup of tea,' the woman said.

'I will and welcome,' I said.

During the tea I learned that they were merely caretakers of the old castle, and daren't take in strangers.

'Isn't it a holy terror,' I said, 'a holy livin' terror that I a man can speak the Seven Languages can't get a bed for all my learning?'

The pair of them were quite unmoved in the face of this learned lie. I knew then they weren't true Gaels, only some poor couple from England, maybe an ex-soldier and his wife, who in lieu of a pension or a lump sum got the caretaking job.

I ate and drank and warmed till I was in a fit condition to have mystical visions.

I sat in a deep arm-chair flanked by my host and hostess; I sat tight knowing that I was sitting on nine points of the law. 'Out of this I will not go,' I said to myself, 'not till compelled by force.'

'Wait till we see what the night's doing,' the woman said, going towards the door.

'Well?' her husband called with the back of his head.

'It's a grand night now,' she said.

I could hear the rain pelting on the cobbles outside the door, and the poor dog crying in some angle of the walls.

'It's a grand night,' she addressed me when she returned.

I said nothing, I kept looking up at the oak rafters trying to find the wonder-nicks that counted the sensations of a feudal lord. I saw nothing, I was only a common peasant after all.

'I fought through the war,' I told the man with the soft mouth.

'You did?' he said. 'And so did I.'

237

He smothered me in war stories until I turned off his gramophone by again asking as an old soldier if I could get a bed.

'It wouldn't answer us,' the woman repeated for the third or fourth tantalizing time.

At about ten o'clock the rain eased off. Through the diamond-shaped window-panes I saw a star or two in the southern sky.

As I stood outside that old castle I cursed it – pure affectation, but I wanted to be kept in the tradition of the old poets.

That night I slept in a police barracks. Decent fellows were those policemen. They bedded me on a shake-down in the day-room.

'In the black hole I should be puttin' ye,' the sergeant said.

The policeman on night-duty went to bed. Right above my pillow was a photograph and a minute description of one John Smith.

Wanted for Sodomy, John Smith. He was described as a man of five feet eight in height and with two teeth missing from the front upper row. That is all I remember except that in the neighbourhood of Clonmel I had fallen in love with a charming girl. How I regretted not being travelling respectable; women are great sticklers for respectability. I managed to reach home by the first of June in time to sow the turnips.

'How did you do?' my brother asked. Everybody else asked me the same thing, and expected me to have a wonderful tale to tell.

I told them the stories of the roads out of the books of Patrick Magil and Jim Tully. To my brother I told the truth. To myself I repeated the quotation I had heard somewhere: 'The wise man stays at home.'

Among my own little hills and poplar-lined roads was all the romance. For there my imagination had planted in childhood the seeds of whimsical poetry.

Connemara, Dublin, castles, and far roads, I mused, all dead things. I was cured of my *wanderlust*.

31 Between Two Stools

My chin is weak. I find it hard to make decisions. For years I had been caught between the two stools of security on the land and a rich-scented life on the exotic islands of literature.

I wasn't really a writer. I had seen a strange beautiful light on the hills and that was all.

In my heart I wanted to live the simple life of my people – to marry, found a family and find immortality as a peasant finds it.

The true artist is homosexual, spiritually if not always physically. George Moore and Oscar Wilde are examples. From Nature to Art I shifted petulantly seven times each day.

There was the excitement of primrose time, the music-filled silence of little fields in March and April. I could be free and human following a narrow furrow on a hill.

By turns I was ecstatically happy. I was living in the living present.

Standing on the top of one of my little hills one day in May I looked across at the sun-flecked plains of Louth and Meath and knew how fine a thing it was to be alive. The green fields and the simple homes and the twisty primitive folk told me of the unchanging beauty of Ireland. At my feet were primroses and violets, a magic carpet on which I could journey over the Baghdads of dreamland.

In the hollow a man was hoeing potatoes. Now and then he would look my way and I knew he was slightly angry with me. He thought me a lazy good-for-nothing.

As usual my reverie was violently disturbed by one of the men who appear so innocent at a distance, and at close-range are savage godless creatures.

'What the hell are ye dramin' about?' he shouted in a harsh voice.

I was angry. I thought him no better than a pig or cow. All

my dreams of the innocent country-folk were shattered. He talked about the weather.

'A sup of rain would do no harm,' he said.

'Who wants rain?' I replied.

'Sure the cattle are starved for a mouthful of grass,' he said. He produced a cigarette from his waistcoat pocket.

'You wouldn't have a match on ye?' he said.

This man, one of my neighbours, was a realist, and realism untouched by the imagination is a sordid petty thing. He made me feel that I was just a lazy fool, that all my dreams of beauty and love were only codology. By the heels he pulled me down from the stars and made me a worm-cutter.

'Yer an awful man doesn't trim them hedges,' he said. 'Why, man alive, ye could plough in three yards farther if them briars were cut.'

'To hell with the briars,' I said.

When the man had gone I took out a book and began to read. It was Dostoyevsky's *The Idiot*, a piece of beautiful insanity packed from cover to cover with the rare jewels of a neurotic angel. An Irish hill was not a good setting for such a book, and I soon put it aside. It should be read by lamplight.

During that summer I fell in love – or to speak more truly – I threw myself into it on top of my head as a suicide would leap into a lake. I believe I could have saved myself from this fall. I had the prudence of a peasant. As the old Gaelic poet had said: 'A wise woman did nurture me.'

She was not particularly pretty, but she was young and slender and gay.

She hated me, and didn't scruple to tell me so.

To complicate the matter my best friend turned out to be the third side of the triangle. Between myself and him ensued a romantic war which lasted a year and a half. Against each other we used the poison gas of calumny and every vile and deadly weapon of heart and brain.

I depended on my reputation as a poet to bring me victory. All vanity! On the battle fields of romantic love, fame or wealth are as useless against a foe as a poem read by Edward Thomas in the trenches in France would have been against the Germans.

I made poems in praise of that girl: all bad poems because I was too close to the emotion. Only one poem, which I wrote when the fire was dying down, has survived the critical breath of my cold day.

> And though her passing was for me
> The death of something sweet
> Her name's in every prayer, her charm
> In every face I meet.

That was the final verse. She passed out of my life, though not entirely. Even yet when I am in her presence a melancholy note echoes in my subconscious mind.

I might add that my rival also failed: he had taken her too seriously, and that is a bad mistake for a lover to make.

Occasionally I went to Dublin to see some literary friends. A. E. had gone away. I knew Frank O'Connor, Sean O'Faolain, F. R. Higgins, Seamus O'Sullivan, and a couple of villainous journalists. The latter never missed an opportunity of putting a lurid paragraph in the Sunday newspapers about me. I must be an interesting character, I thought. So I decided that in future if I was to be exploited I should do the exploiting myself.

After A. E., Frank O'Connor was the next of the writers I met. He had a powerful, though not subtle, mind that flashed immense vitality. I liked his short stories very much because they had artistic and intellectual honesty – and there was a great deal of humbug writing being turned out everywhere. He had the knack of conserving his power, a wisdom I could never learn: he knew when to keep silence.

Sean O'Faolain was the clever academical writer down to the ground. And yet, he had in him the essential fool on which all poets are built. His book of short stories and one of his novels were not considered holy enough for circulation in Ireland.

F. R. Higgins was a softer and perhaps more Gaelic writer than either O'Connor or O'Faolain. His verse had always charmed me, especially *Meath Men* with its merry ending.

> Now in this half-way house my song is set,
> So shut your mouth and let me kiss the barmaid;
> For Brinsley MacNamara you dare not forget
> The poets and their privileges at Tara.

241

Seamus O'Sullivan I had not met in the flesh. Of his verse I knew some lovely lyrics. One beginning:

> I whispered my great sorrow
> To every listening sedge;
> And they bent, bowed with my sorrow,
> Down to the water's edge.
> But she stands and laughs lightly
> To see me sorrow so,
> Like the winds that laughing
> Across the water go.
> If I could tell the bright ones
> That quiet-hearted move,
> They would bend down like the sedges
> With the sorrow of love.

One day during the harvest my friend Tommy Lennon said to me:

'A fellow I knew in Glasgow has written a prize play for the Abbey Theatre. He's home in Blackrock on holidays and we should go to see him: you'd be interested.'

The dramatist's name was Paul Carroll.

With Tommy Lennon I cycled to Blackrock the following Sunday. Between us we possessed in cash one shilling.

Blackrock was a seaside resort near Dundalk, afterwards to achieve fame as the place where kissing wasn't allowed. A boy and girl were brought up on the local court and fined for kissing on the beach at Blackrock.

During the time of which I write Blackrock was not so famous. It was frequented mostly by old men and women in search of health and an unobtrusive glass.

When the tide goes out at Blackrock it goes out very far. I overheard one humorist saying that when the tide was out at Blackrock you could almost walk across to England.

When we got to Blackrock the tide was in; we accepted this as a favourable omen.

We walked up and down the promenade, Tommy Lennon on the look-out for his friend the playwright, while I was taking in the beauty of the seascape and the comical gestures of the half-drunk country-folk trying to be merry in a modern way. I broke into a song I knew because the first line bore some relation to the scene.

> 'I try to be merry but it's all no use,
>   My case is very hard;
>   She left me as silly as a farmyard goose
>   And got married to a railway guard.'

'Good man, Tommy,' I heard.

It was Paul Carroll speaking to my friend. I was introduced. We adjourned to a pub. Over our glasses we talked enthusiastically of poetry and the drama. Although Paul Carroll had never heard of me I had heard of him. He also had been a contributor to the holy poet's corner with which I was once associated. I remembered reading one of his poems years before. He laughed when I mentioned the poem. Apart from my intellectual delight I was also pleased that two pilgrims in the desert of poverty should have come upon an oasis of green generosity.

We had food and drink and cigarettes and still possessed our original fund of a shilling.

Paul Carroll thought me a great genius. He was surprised that a poet such as I should be compelled to work in the fields.

'My God!' he exclaimed, 'to think of you dragging dead cats out of drains!' He advised me to break away and quoted Shakespeare: 'Security is mortals' chiefest enemy.'

With Paul Carroll I formed the warmest attachment, which lasted for three years. It was indeed too warm, which was the cause of its disruption.

In the winter I combined poetry and cobbling – but my customers were getting fewer every day: I was a bad careless cobbler. I had some pretty girls among my customers and some not so pretty. Among the latter were two oldish girls who were still trying their luck in the marriage lottery. I read the cards for them and never failed to fish up a husband.

When the visit of these two girls coincided there might be loud unmaidenly talk around my cobbler's bench.

It could be started in this way: someone might remark: 'I hear Mary Hanlon is gettin' married.'

The mere mention of a girl getting married was gall to this pair.

'Aw, is she indeed?' one of them would say.

'Well, she's not much and the fella that's marryin' her must be a fool.'

'Sure, some girls would take anyone.'

'I wonder is she gettin' married decent.'

'Just.'

This word 'just' was much more eloquent than it appears on paper. It was steeped in the venom of a thousand repressed desires.

There is a knock on our door.

'Come inside.'

A man enters. He has a pair of old boots under his arm. He is a migratory farm-labourer.

'Will ye throw a pair of half-soles on them boots?' he asks.

I look at the boots. Noting my critical eye, the fellow explains: 'I let them go a bit too far, I know, but...'

The conversation had died down, all have become listeners.

I rise from my bench without giving the man a direct answer, and adjourn to my den.

As I sit struggling with the enemies of rhyme and rhythm the man's final query is heard.

'Will ye do anything to them oul' boots?'

I am in another world now and do not reply.

I was deeply interested in Modernist poetry. I read the work of Ezra Pound and Hopkins with delight. Walter Lowenfels, a poet who made queer verses about machinery, gave my imagination a lift forward. But it was in the American poets I was chiefly interested. Horace Holley, 'H. D.', Gertrude Stein, and all the Cubists and Imagists, excited my clay-heavy mind. Gertrude Stein's work was like whisky to me; her strange rhythms broke up the cliché formation of my thought.

As I sat in my den, unable to get a line written – and with the hum of kitchen-gossip in the next room – I would open a secret drawer and take out a bundle of newspaper and magazine cuttings. These cuttings were my real library: every one of these cuttings contained a poem that was important for me: there was one among them could vitalize the moment's mood. I had then never read a complete book by the poets I have mentioned; as I have said, I used only the newspaper cuttings. And I found out later on that the single poem read by itself possessed far more power than when included in a volume. I seldom read a book through; when I had found and read the significant word or phrase, I would close the book, feeling that to read further would only do harm. I had been baptised again by fire and the Holy Spirit.

'Patrick, come down, we're going to say the Rosary,' I am called.

'Christ Almighty! Sure, it isn't that late,' I reply.

'Come down or we'll start without ye.'

'Start away,' I cry.

'Listen to that fella,' some of my household says, 'how can there be ayther luck or grace in the house he's in? The oul' haythen.' I make one last desperate effort to recover the Promised Land, but the dream has been completely shattered. Around me is the litter of old papers, and on my knee an unfinished poem:

O Pagan poet, you
And I are one
In this – we lose our god
At set of sun.
And we are kindred when
The hill-wind shakes
Sweet song like blossoms
On the calm green lakes . . .

I may find the remainder of that poem to-morrow, I think as I move into the family circle for a good night prayer – but not the blackbird's.

Spring came round again with its magic and innocence. And still I was one of the people. The land, when once it gets a grip on a man, will not easily let him go. The land is jealous of literature, and in its final effort to hold a poet offers him, like a despairing lover, everything, everything.

The crops I so carelessly had planted flourished in every field; my cattle throve; the trees my father planted put on their richest foliage and were filled with song-birds. But not all this blandishment could win me back now. My poems had been published by Macmillan; and while the people admired they felt that I was a stranger within the gates. I know some of them were afraid; in the country places of Ireland writing is held in certain awe: a writer was a dangerous man from whom they instinctively recoiled. It was a big surprise to many people when they discovered I was a poet: I had kept my art more or less secret, and those who knew I aspired to poetry thought that meant a writer of Come-all-ye songs.

One neighbour-man was rather bitter about my supposed reputation: he thought me a rival for his girl. He said I was a madman, and suggested that it would fit me better to mind my farm and not have the cattle breaking into the turnip-field.

One day I had a row with another neighbour over a march-fence. March-fences have been a source of much bitterness in Ireland: many a lawyer has made a pile of money over the ownership of a disputed thorn bush.

I was cutting a limb of a boor tree when this fellow came up on his own side of the fence.

'Damn ye to hell's blazes, what do ye mane?' he roared.

'What's wrong?' I replied simply, as I continued to cut.

'That's none of your hedge,' he cried, 'the roots of the bushes are growin' into my land.'

'The back of the hedge is to me,' I said.

'Begod then, ye'll not cut it, I'll see to that,' he said. In a lower voice he went on: 'It's not the value of the bleddy ditch at all, but the greed and the maneness of some people that would take the eye outa yer head and tell ye ye were better without it.'

It was a clear calm day, and the sound of our voices carried delightfully to many an ear eager for gossip. I lost my temper.

'I'd cut the head off you,' I said. The man pulled off his coat.

'Come out and try it,' he challenged.

'I wouldn't think it worth my while,' I replied.

Then I realized that I was doing a foolish thing in becoming angry with a man who might yet be one of my characters in a novel.

On a Sunday afternoon as I sat in my room, a man called at our house: a man of about sixty-five, with a high blood-pressure bloom on his countenance.

'Does the poet live here?' he inquired when I went to the door.

I told him he was face to face with the poet.

'I'm glad,' he said as I led him in. 'I was afraid ye might be out.'

He flopped to a seat and wiped the sweat from his brow with a red handkerchief.

'It's a very hot day,' he said, 'and I'm after walkin' ten miles.'

'My goodness,' I said.

He looked like a man who wasn't too sane.

'What can I do for you?' I asked.

'Ye can do a great deal for me,' he answered. 'I'm an unfortunate man livin' among the worst of bad neighbours; night, noon, and mornin' they have me persecuted. I want ye to make a ballad on them, a good, strong, poisonous ballad.'

I was charmed. Here was a twentieth-century survival of the ancient faith in the power of the poet.

'I'll give ye the facts, and you'll make the ballad,' he said.

'I'll make the ballad,' I assured him.

He gave me the facts. He told me the names of his neighbours and their nicknames. He told me which of them had bastard blood in their veins and which of them had been accused of theft.

To be accused of stealing is in Ireland for a man a crime which most lowers him socially – it is worse than murder. For a woman, of course, the giving birth to an illegitimate child is a stain on herself and her family that will be revived in three generations to come.

'That should make the bones of a good ballad,' the man said when he had finished. 'What would you charge me for a ballad like that?'

This was sweet music. From the beginning of our encounter my only fear was that the fellow's obvious madness mightn't produce a reflex-action on the muscle-strings of his purse.

I tried to look as professional as possible.

'Ten shillings a verse I usually charge,' I said.

I didn't like the look he gave me, the fire left his eyes which stared at me empty and unresponsive.

Perhaps I had asked too much.

'I'll do it for three pounds,' I said. He shook his head.

'I might just as well go to a solicitor,' he remarked in a melancholy tone.

'Well, how much would you be prepared to give?' I asked.

'I thought ye might do it for the price of a couple of bottles of porter,' he said.

It was a big come-down for my pride. A couple of bottles of porter as remuneration for a poet. I dismissed my customer as gently as I could.

It was a very hot day in mid-July. I was mowing a meadow with a scythe. I had taken off my shirt so as to get the full benefit of a sun-bath.

A girl who saw me from a distance gave a sweet, ironical cheer.

'Come over here,' I called to her.

'What for?' she asked.

'To rub my back,' I said.

It was very indelicate of me to say this, but then, I was a peasant – almost – and so the remark was in good taste.

The scent of the new-mown hay was in my nostrils, the hum of bees vibrated in the hazy blue air. The pulse-beat of life was sharp and intense. On such a day Art might hide in dark corners, for the great sun would have none of it. Cattle, goaded by flies, were dashing with their tails up across a field. The corn was still green; it would be a late harvest. Slieve Gullion, the mountain of my childhood, wore a veil of sun.

I should have appreciated the quality of this beauty much better if swinging a scythe wasn't such hard work.

As I was lying on a bed of sweet hay taking a rest a man stepped through the gap beside me. It was Paul Carroll. At the same time my tea arrived – a ten-glass bottle of tea corked with a piece of newspaper. As there was no cup, Paul Carroll and myself took turns at the bottle.

His plays were having a bad time, but he had a new one written in which he had great hope, *Shadow and Substance*; it was afterwards a great success at the Abbey Theatre and in New York.

I also was full of hope in spite of a trail of failure. We were therefore kindred.

I remember this meeting more vividly than anything: a visual

memory only. I do not remember what we said. We sat there in
the meadow under a strong sun, swopping disappointments while
we drank tea out of a large wine bottle.

Summer passed, the golden harvest flowed in like an easy tide.
I mowed our three acres of corn with the scythe.

The blackberries came in with the harvest. I liked this black,
juicy fruit, a taste which my dog Sam shared. He would stand
on his hind legs and, with his front paws, pull down the fruit-
laden briars.

All the time my brother, who was now a schoolteacher, kept
saying to me: 'This life is all right and fine in its way, but it
will get you nowhere.'

I agreed with him in a sentimental way.

'Maybe next year,' I said.

'Next year is never,' my brother said, 'now is the only time.'

But my nostalgia for country life and virginal innocence among
green fields kept me sitting a little while longer on my insecure
seat between two stools. It was threshing-time now, and the
clank-clank of steam threshers was heard on many a narrow
road.

Threshing-time was a fine time. Threshing labour was got by
a system of swop. I went around to the neighbours and they in
turn came to our threshing. Carrying sacks of corn was my
favourite job. It wasn't always easy; there was one notorious
bag-packer in the district. The sack filled by him had no wrinkles
in its sides. He was the farmer's friend, but the mill-owner's
enemy. The mill-owner was paid per sack.

Around to all the threshings came the marriageable girls of
the district – to cook. At one threshing I counted seven cooks in
the kitchen. They appeared very busy when I called at the door.
Seeing that it was only myself was there they slowed down a bit.
If I had been one of the strong farmer bachelors who were so
numerous in the place they would not have raised their heads.
They had the tables set for dinner, two long deal tables laid end
to end in the middle of the kitchen. At each of the four corners
was a chair, and from chair to chair were placed long boards as
seats.

Twelve mugs of buttermilk stood on the table. The large pot

of potatoes was boiling over the fire, and beside it simmered another pot of cabbage already boiled.

'Have yez much help?' one of the girls asked.

'Fair,' I said.

'Will yez be done before tay-time?' the woman of the house asked.

'We may,' I replied.

'That would be great,' her daughter said; 'we won't have the trouble of makin' tay if we keep back the dinner.'

Such a scene and such talk was common in the country, yet I had not observed its humour before. Now I was the half of one remove from the people and developing a sense of perspective.

The weather was perfect. The wet weather which ordinarily would be enough to drive the most patriotic Irish poet out of the country kept away. It was Nature striving to hold me to herself, jealous Nature.

The potato-harvest arrived and I assisted at the work.

Though it was mid-October scarce a leaf had fallen from the trees. It was an Indian summer, a second youth in which to sing and dance and love.

As we picked up the tubers the smells rising from the dry brown clay were a tonic to revive the weariest body, the loneliest spirit. Turning over the soil, our fingers were turning the pages in the Book of Life.

We could dream as we gathered the potatoes, we could enter in the secret places where all unwritten poems lie. It is true that my metaphysical wanderings had a bad effect on my skill as a potato-gatherer. Someone suggested that I was leaving half the crops behind me. A man crossed the fence to where I worked.

'Ye have fair good ones,' he said as he eyed the drills.

'Not too bad,' I agreed. 'How is yours?'

'They're a holy livin' dread,' he said. 'Do ye think will there be a price for them?'

'God knows,' I said.

And then the poet that still survives in the Irish countryman got the upper hand. We were idealists. We talked of women, the beautiful ideal women of the mind, minxes of unreality.

'She's a nice one,' the man said.

'The nicest in the parish,' I replied.

'She's apt to be at the dance.'

'I think you have a notion of her,' I suggested.

'What put that in yer head?' he said with affected surprise.

'I wouldn't walk the side of the road she'd be on.'

'We'll see,' I said.

As he recrossed the fence he called back: 'Will ye come to the dance in Culliville on Sunday night?'

'I might,' I answered.

'Don't forget,' he added as a parting shot.

I should not have gone to dances. I was a bad dancer. Most poets I know are bad dancers. Poets, because they can write about love, are considered great Don Juans. This is a mistake, at least in these times, for a bad dancer wins no fair women. The finest poet who couldn't dance wouldn't have an earthly in a romantic struggle in a country hall against a good dancer. Perhaps this is only half the truth, but it is my experience. I might make a good, solemn serious lover in a Faustian way, as a flirt I was hopeless. I went to the dance as my neighbour had suggested. I entered the hall filled with hope. I was going to conquer.

At the end of an hour my hope began to fade. I drifted to a corner among the older men who talked politics and sport.

My companion came to me at the end of a dance.

'It's a rotten dance,' he said.

His ideal wasn't there. I suggested going home.

'Wait for one more dance and I'll be with ye.'

Beside me the men were talking about dogs. A short distance apart from us were two fellows who were going to smuggle a bag of brown sugar over the Border when the dance was over. The dance-hall was in Northern Ireland; the brown sugar was used in the making of potheen.

I overheard part of their conversation:

'We'll go the Crooked Road.'

'The customs officers are away with two women.'

'That's good.'

My companion still lingered on in hope till the very last dance was announced.

'Let's get to hell outa this joint,' he cried sourly. 'I never was in a worse oul' hole.'

Going home together my companion told me how he fared. First of all he asked me how I had succeeded, but did not wait for my reply.

'I don't want to be braggin',' he began, 'but I could go with Bridgie Reilly if I had gone all out.'

'I'm sure you could,' I said.

Then he went into the complicated business of dance-hall clicking in all its moods and tenses.

I bore with him as best I could; no man likes to hear another boasting of his successes in love.

As my brother had said, this life was fine and pleasant in a useless kind of way: it would get me nowhere. The dancing and the light loving were enervating in the long run.

I survived through the winter, knowing that I must soon make a decision. I could not have left both ways. In the spring I collected what money I could.

I decided to go to London. Ireland was a fine place to day-dream in, but London was a great materialist city where my dreams might crystallize into something more enduring than a winning smile on the face of an Irish colleen – or landscape.

I broke with the land. With a blue, torn suitcase in my hand I walked to the railway station, a Dick Whittington without his cat, bound for London.

32 In London

Leaving my native place I experienced neither exultant joy nor tear-moist regrets. To Ireland I bade no patriotic emigrant's farewell; towards London I did not turn hope-wide eyes in vision. I did not care, I was going half against my will. I was a fatalist drifting inconsequently on the winds of Chance, and I did not care whither they blew me.

Only this, I had deep faith in Her who guides the wanderer, and as the boat swayed in the choppy Irish Sea I remembered She was litanied Star of the Sea.

When I arrived in London I had in my pocket two pounds four shillings, and to make a poor man poorer my pounds were Free State pounds and only worth nineteen and sixpence each.

It was just four days before the Coronation – a bad time to lay siege to London. Most of the *literati* had left town. I did not blame them, for the decorations – from the slums to the pasty-faced Angel of Peace on Selfridges – were enough to drive an æsthete mad.

The streets, even at the early hour of my arrival, were thronged with sight-seers. The enthusiasm was mob-enthusiasm. Every pick-pocket, chancer, and beggar from the four winds of crime had come to London to wallow in the wake of generous hysteria.

From Rowton Houses they radiated. I also radiated from a Rowton House. I had been advised to go to one of these cheap lodging-houses. It was an interesting experience. There I met the artists of the *demi-monde*. Not all the denizens of Rowton House, Camden Town, were of this class, though. But all were quaintly individual, and these I've always loved.

On the fourth landing of the stairs I spoke to a man who was leaning over the balustrade, a melancholy-looking fellow with a cast in his eyes. He told me he was a writer.

I remembered A. E.'s philosophical theory, expounded in *The Candle of Vision*, that as men float down the stream of Life those who are kindred come together. As I spoke to the man I liked to think that he was not kin to my king's house. He was a sentimental dilettante who was unconscious of his own foolishness.

'I'm writing a book,' he told me, 'it's my own life, and Cherry Kearton of Jarrolds has promised to publish it. Heavens, if I only had leisure to write I could do big things.'

I told him I was an illiterate Irish navvy in search of work.

'I know Ireland well,' he said. 'I was stationed for three years in Athlone with the Royal Field Artillery. I could always get along well with Paddy,' he added after a pause.

One evening as I passed along the corridor I heard something drop at my feet. I stooped to pick it up; it was only a piece of cardboard. When I got to the end of the corridor I noticed that the writing-pad I had under my arm was gone. I rushed back along the corridor querying everyone if they saw a writing-pad. Nobody saw one.

The pad was only worth sixpence, but I was worried about a very private poem I had written on it. It was titled *A Private Despair*, and that is all I can recall.

Many Irish boys made Rowton House, Camden Town, first stop from Mayo. The soft voices of Mayo and Galway sounding in that gaunt impersonal place fell like warm rain on the arid patches of my imagination.

These boys were true peasants. They walked with an awkward gait and were shy. To me they looked up as to a learned man and posed me crooked questions which I couldn't answer.

I wasn't greatly interested in these boys; I had seen too much of them in Ireland. Their characters, impressionable as wax, were soon to wear the impress of common vulgarity.

In Rowton House there was a gentleman called Mister Boot, a man with an academic beard and a very exalted appearance. He wore spats and was such a man to whom simple folk in Ireland would raise their hats.

I never found out what his line of business was. I saw one of his associates selling cure-all medicine under the Irving statue in Saint Martin's Place.

Mister Boot would have fitted perfectly into the environment of any West End restaurant. I saw him ordering his supper in

Rowton House. It consisted of a plate of the cheapest soup – twopence-worth.

But Mister Boot, he was the grandest-looking man you could see, a man of personality and charm. In olden days such a man would easily fall heir to a vacant kingship. And here he was in Rowton House, Camden Town, looking out, like myself, on a world that had forgotten true aristocracy and was crowning a new king.

One evening a washy lad with an artificial leg, aged about twenty-five, attached himself to me. He had come, he said, on a lorry from Leeds to sell Coronation stuff. His Coronation stuff was the poorest catch-penny of all: a few hundred post-card pictures of the Royal Family.

I told him he would get few to buy the cards. He didn't agree.

'The simpler your coronation stuff the better,' he said. 'I'll get a shilling each for them, and with luck maybe half a dollar.'

As I appeared very interested he instructed me in his business methods: a sort of Guide to Careers in the underworld.

'I'll go to the West End in the evening,' he explained. 'Should trade be bad I have another way of doing business. I'll take off the artificial leg and take my place as a war veteran.'

He produced from his pocket a bunch of war-medals and ribbon decorations.

'Would you like one?' he asked.

I didn't mind.

'It won't do you any harm to wear this,' he said as he fixed on the lapel of my coat a Mons Star or Military Cross. We neither of us knew rightly what it was. I am certain my medal was one of the highest decorations which must have rewarded great gallantry.

Having invested me with a high order he went further and invited me to share good business with him the same evening.

I had some misgivings about being a partner in this very limited company. I was afraid Wooden Leg might not scruple to pick a pocket should trade prove bad. However, I agreed to try it.

We went to Oxford Circus by Underground, he very decently paying the fares. We did not display our war medals on the train:

we were not gallant soldiers till the sale of our cards should prove a washout.

On the train Wooden Leg talked most intimately to me; he pressed his dry lips close to my ears and shouted into them above the roaring of the train. I should have preferred if he would keep more to himself; he looked a down-and-out, and I was still half-brother to Respectability.

We struggled through the dense crowds of people on Oxford Circus. We were to take up positions in Bond Street or Regent Street, whichever might be the best.

All the streets in the West End were thronged with sightseers. Crowds of people with their mouths open were staring up at Selfridge's Angel of Peace.

'It's wonderful,' I heard them saying.

'And why shouldn't it be,' was the answer, 'it cost forty thousand pounds to decorate Selfridges.'

'That's an awful atrocity,' I said to my partner. He had no æsthetic sensibility. He ignored my comment, being far too intent on business to have any heed in the finicky echoes of a poet's palate.

Having listened to Wooden Leg's rosy tale of good business I had imagined that our company would have few rivals. I was greatly surprised to find vendors of Coronation stuff on every yard of the pavement, and Coronation stuff a hundred times more gaudy and more plausible than ours.

I expressed my surprise.

'Don't mind that,' he reassured me, 'see the crowds there are. We'll easily be worth two quid a man for the night.'

I had ma doots.

He took his stand on the edge of the pavement.

'Watch me,' he said.

Then he began to cry out.

'Coronation souvenirs, Coronation souvenirs.' When anyone showed the slightest interest he would lean to them and as man to man point out the uniqueness of his ware.

'Lovely stuff, nothing like it to be had; you'll never forget the Coronation. See how charming Princess Margaret Rose looks,' etc.

I watched him for some time and, as I watched, his pitiful failure awoke in me a form of curious wild laughter; it was all too tragic for tears.

He had wonderful patience, he was willing to wait and want and suffer. Of such humble endurance is the kingdom of million-aires. The profession was overcrowded, I thought, worse even than literature. In Charing Cross Road there was a poet in every bookshop, in this street there was a vendor of Coronation stuff on every yard.

Wooden Leg gave me a bunch of the cards. I didn't offer them; seeing how he with experience had fared, I couldn't face the crowds.

After half an hour's vain appeal he came to me. We moved into a doorway. He took off his artificial leg. There were air-holes on the leg.

'Is it moth-eaten?' I asked.

'Ventilation,' he explained. 'You take care of the leg,' he said, 'while we try this other plan. Stick up your medal.' He himself was already busily converting his poor T.B.-wasted body into a war veteran's. I put up my medal: he was more hero-glorious than Earl Haig on his horse. Then he picked up his crutches and, positioning himself in an old-soldier pose, he began to call out in a broken sergeant-major voice: 'Help an old soldier, wounded in the head at Mons, lost the leg at Wipers. God Save the King and Queen.'

I saw one woman giving a very critical glance at Wooden Leg's decorations. She gave him a coin all the same.

I made no effort to play the old soldier, I hadn't the neck to do it, and I was afraid of being arrested: it was an Irish fear.

Wooden Leg's back was turned to me now, and I heard him relate how his wife and children were starving and he had no disability pension.

I cannot remember how it happened, but when the man whom I took to be Wooden Leg turned round it wasn't him at all. I had the artificial leg in my hand. I walked up and down in search of my business partner and – to use an Irish expression – if the Divil took him I couldn't find him.

I was tired. I was cold. The lights of London twinkled like a galaxy of stars, but in that godless firmament I had no interest. I left the West End carrying an artificial leg under my arm.

I handed the leg to the porter at Rowton House and got a ticket for it.

I had a good sixpenny supper of Bovril and sandwiches and went to bed.

Next morning I met Wooden Leg.

'My leg,' he exclaimed.

I gave him the ticket, which he snatched with nervous fingers.

'I was afraid I'd never see you again,' he said.

We sat on the bench in the corridor and talked while the lodgers passed up and down.

'How much did you make?' I queried.

'Two quid, odd,' he replied. 'What happened to you?'

I told him.

'You got turned round,' he said; 'that often happens to a stranger in a city.'

'Did you really make two pounds?' I asked.

'I made ten bob,' he said. I was more inclined to accept this statement after having seen the state of the cripple-market.

Among the inhabitants of Rowton House was a Ceylonese cook. He sat apart from us on the bench, as indeed he sat apart from all white men. I moved in his direction because he looked so down in the mouth, and my self-pity was taking the form of pity for others.

He was suspicious of my advances and not inclined to be communicative. The warmth of my address eventually thawed the frost of his silence. I didn't blame him for his bitter aloofness after I had heard his story. He had been getting the dirty end of the stick of life for a long time.

He said he knew six European languages as well as his native lingo.

'You should be teaching at the University,' I said. He smiled wanly. He dismissed the idea that linguistic accomplishment was any use to a coloured cook.

'If you were in Ireland . . .' I began.

'I lived in Dublin,' he broke in, 'nice people, the Irish, but the English, rough, rough, rough, cruel people, the English.'

I thought how perfect an Irish patriot he would have made.

'You don't like the English?' I said.

'Hate them, hate them, hate them,' he repeated.

He was a private cook, unemployed. I suggested that he might easily get a job in a restaurant.

'Restaurant,' he scoffed, 'me never work in restaurant, private houses. Restaurant, dirty, vulgar place.'

He had lived fifteen years in Paris, all the time with the same family. He loved Paris. 'Gentle, gentle Paris.'

On the day before Coronation Day I took a room, a mean room in a mean street. I couldn't stand the institutional atmosphere of Rowton House.

The rent of my room was eight shillings and sixpence a week, to be paid in advance. Having paid out the money, I counted what remained and found myself with one pound four shillings. I was feeling pretty desperate. My money was running out and my prospects in the literary world were nil. Sitting in my room, I took pen and paper and began my first literary work, the writing of six begging letters.

Only one ship picked up my S.O.S. The Irish poet, Seamus O'Sullivan, who sent me a guinea by return of post.

I took little interest in the Coronation. The crowds, I thought, had too much of the hysterical vulgarity of an all-in wrestling audience. It was a wet morning, and the man who would call the coat I wore a waterproof wouldn't be telling the truth. My coat let in more rain than it kept out. Somewhere out in the town I noticed an advertisement outside a door.

'Umbrellas From Sixpence Up.'

I bought an umbrella for sixpence; it had a broken handle but the cover was good. I lost that umbrella the same day.

I stood outside the barricade in New Oxford Street among the crowd. To many of these people being shut off from a view of the Coronation procession must have been the anguish of those darkened souls shut off from the Beatific Vision.

A man with an improvised periscope was selling views of the procession at a penny a peep; he was doing a good trade. Three women were trying to climb a lamp-standard; before the policeman hauled them down they had achieved a height sufficient to give us all a very demoralizing view of white lingerie.

In the midst of it all the clear-voiced propagandists were shouting out.

'*Daily Worker*, one penny.'

'*The Blackshirt*, one penny.'

I bought the *Daily Worker*. There was an article by Shaw and one by C. Day Lewis, or Auden. The cold winds of reason blew through the sultry swamps of emotion.

The man with the periscope gave a running commentary on the procession as it passed.

'The Grenadier Guards.'

'Not at all,' another periscopist corrected. We who were shut out could give no opinion. I didn't mind. A young woman beside me tried to climb up on my shoulders; I shook her off, and she wasn't too pleased.

A hush fell on our crowd except for the sharp cries of '*Daily Worker*, one penny'. I knew the Royal carriage was passing. I thought I had seen and heard enough. The temper of the place was similar to many an Irish fair green. The street was as muddy as Ireland's roads. I went home to my room and fried herrings on the gas-ring.

The landlord, when he came home, caught the smell of fried fish. He was furious and half-drunk. Normally he appeared a very polite fellow, but now he swore.

'Leave this room when your week is up,' he said.

'Okay,' I said.

Fish, and herrings in particular, are supposed to be good for the brain. I needed something good for the brain; I needed to have my wits about me if I was to survive in London.

I tried to write an article for the newspapers. I couldn't write a line, and I don't know how anybody could whose next week's food was no more than an astral hypothesis.

I had the addresses of two literary people. I decided to try one of them – a man – the other was a lady.

This man was a once-upon-a-time poet who had taken refuge in the last refuge of spent poets – journalism and anthology-compiling. He was in, but not in to me. He was sitting in a pleasant front room in a pleasant part of the city, very busy writing. He opened the window and spoke to me. I told him who I was. He looked puzzled.

'I had a poem in one of your anthologies,' I said.

'There are so many poets,' he began. I didn't wait.

'Damn you, you're no poet, anyway,' I shouted as I strode out, banging the gate after me.

Bang went sixpence: it cost me threepence each way on the train. As all my dreams seemed going to Hell, I spent another shilling of my funds on a second-hand copy of Chekhov's short stories.

I went to my room, stretched myself on my back on the bed, and read far into the night. Beautiful stories, these by Chekhov, they brought me into a world made, not by a radiant creator, but by a brilliant technician.

Next morning I walked to Charing Cross Road, the Road of the Books, where things happen. I was prowling around Foyle's bookshop, fingering volumes that I couldn't afford to buy.

In the poetry section I was startled to hear my name spoken. A slight-built fellow addressed me.

'You're Patrick Kavanagh?' he said.

'Are you a member of the Yard?' I returned.

'You're the Irish poet?'

'How did you know?' I said.

'I heard your broad Irish brogue when you spoke to the assistant; I saw you were interested in poetry, and these two facts for me spelled Patrick Kavanagh. I'm Gawsworth.'

'John Gawsworth, the poet,' I said.

I was delighted to find that my name had penetrated so far into the jungle of literature.

We went to a café and over cups of coffee praised each other. Before we parted, John Gawsworth loaned me five shillings.

I went into a newsagent's and bought an Irish newspaper. In the paper I read that the statue of George II had been blown up in Stephen's Green, Dublin. That was an idea. I would go to one of the newspapers and sell a cock-and-bull story which I duly did – to the *Daily* —.

My story was that I had been one of the men engaged in the

blowing up of the statue, that I funked the job and had to leave Ireland in a hurry.

I first tried *John Bull*. There was nothing doing. That journal had already gone to press, and next week the news would be stale, I was told.

Next I tried the *Daily Mail*. I sent a note up to the News Editor which read 'Blowing up of George II statue, inside story.' The man who interviewed me knew a great deal more about the lay-out of Dublin than I did – and about explosives too.

'How far is Stephen's Green from Nelson's Pillar?'

'What size are four stores of gelignite?'

'How was the mine put off?' and a lot of other puzzles he propounded, to all of which I gave replies that wouldn't take in a two-year-old child, not to mention a London newspaper man. If he wasn't satisfied he was at least sympathetic.

'Try the *Daily* —,' he advised me with a knowing wink, which, as they say in Ireland, would have been enough for a blind donkey.

I sent up my note to the — editor as I had done at Northcliffe House. It drew the editor at once.

I was feeling more confident now. The gruelling I got from the *Daily Mail* man was a real education on the subject.

Going up in the lift, the name I had given on the slip completely left my mind. The interviewer saved me the foolishness of appearing not to know my own name.

'Good evening, Mister Conroy,' he said.

To make a long story short he accepted my story and printed it next morning at the top of a page.

I called for my money, and not without much trepidation of soul: I was afraid Scotland Yard might be on the trail of such a dangerous fugitive.

I got a guinea for my lie and would probably have got three if I hadn't been so much afraid.

The boys in the — office, the young boys, looked at me, and I knew they thought me a two-gun Pat in the flesh, and they wouldn't think twice of getting my autograph. I was on the top of the world. The tide of my prosperity being at the full, I took a train to the second address I knew.

Miss Helen Waddell was in, and in to a stranded poet. She received me as the Prodigal Son was received.

It was she suggested my writing this book, and introduced me to the Promised Land.

At the end of the week I changed my digs. I secured another room, also a mean room in a mean street. I made it part of the contract that fish was to be allowed.

This street was not in a residential area; it was loud with street criers and children. At one end was a pub, frequented by sensual drinkers and low-priced prostitutes. I have no actual knowledge that these women were cheap, but as a judge of feminine allure I should say they weren't too expensive. London is the loneliest place I have known: this loneliness is the only holy thing in the city. I have always thought loneliness holy. I wrote for four hours each day. My leisure time hung around my neck like a millstone. I found some escape in going to the pictures.

London, I noticed, has ceased to worship God and has substituted the cat. Tom Cat was the Supreme Being everywhere. Outside the windows of pet stores were always idolaters.

'Oh, isn't that a lovely tortoiseshell?' I heard a well-dressed woman say. She waggled her pink-nailed finger at puss and tapped the window-pane.

London is a pagan city, and it is not the poetic paganism of blackbirds. After the chaste paganism of Ireland London's materialist immorality terrified me. There was no shyness, no shame, and London's god, the cat, didn't care.

There was little innocent courting: on Hampstead Heath I saw them copulating like dogs in the sun.

I became acquainted with a fellow who seemed to have a dame in every street. He reminded me of the character in Chekhov's story who went among his women like a panel doctor visiting his patients.

He invited me to some of his clients' flats. In each of these was one pretty dame and one ugly one. The ugly one was for me, but I wasn't having any . . .

Like these were my experiences in London; a trifle comical, the image of my soul.

My story is finished.

The Green Fool

I had been five months in London. From the noise and excitement I passed. The roar and surge of the tide of Commerce was in my ears for a long time, like the after-effects of 'flu.

I returned to Ireland. Ireland green and chaste and foolish. And when I wandered over my own hills and talked again to my own people I looked into the heart of this life and I saw that it was good.

READ MORE IN PENGUIN

In every corner of the world, on every subject under the sun, Penguin represents quality and variety – the very best in publishing today.

For complete information about books available from Penguin – including Puffins, Penguin Classics and Arkana – and how to order them, write to us at the appropriate address below. Please note that for copyright reasons the selection of books varies from country to country.

In the United Kingdom: Please write to *Dept. EP, Penguin Books Ltd, Bath Road, Harmondsworth, West Drayton, Middlesex UB7 0DA*

In the United States: Please write to *Consumer Services, Penguin Putnam Inc., 405 Murray Hill Parkway, East Rutherford, New Jersey 07073-2136.* VISA and MasterCard holders call 1-800-631-8571 to order Penguin titles

In Canada: Please write to *Penguin Books Canada Ltd, 10 Alcorn Avenue, Suite 300, Toronto, Ontario M4V 3B2*

In Australia: Please write to *Penguin Books Australia Ltd, 487 Maroondah Highway, Ringwood, Victoria 3134*

In New Zealand: Please write to *Penguin Books (NZ) Ltd, Private Bag 102902, North Shore Mail Centre, Auckland 10*

In India: Please write to *Penguin Books India Pvt Ltd, 11 Community Centre, Panchsheel Park, New Delhi 110017*

In the Netherlands: Please write to *Penguin Books Netherlands bv, Postbus 3507, NL-1001 AH Amsterdam*

In Germany: Please write to *Penguin Books Deutschland GmbH, Metzlerstrasse 26, 60594 Frankfurt am Main*

In Spain: Please write to *Penguin Books S. A., Bravo Murillo 19, 1°B, 28015 Madrid*

In Italy: Please write to *Penguin Italia s.r.l., Via Vittorio Emanuele 45/a, 20094 Corsico, Milano*

In France: Please write to *Penguin France, 12, Rue Prosper Ferradou, 31700 Blagnac*

In Japan: Please write to *Penguin Books Japan Ltd, Iidabashi KM-Bldg, 2-23-9 Koraku, Bunkyo-Ku, Tokyo 112-0004*

In South Africa: Please write to *Penguin Books South Africa (Pty) Ltd, P.O. Box 751093, Gardenview, 2047 Johannesburg*

READ MORE IN PENGUIN

Published or forthcoming:

A Confederacy of Dunces   John Kennedy Toole

A monument to sloth, rant and contempt, a behemoth of fat, flatulence and furious suspicion of anything modern – this is Ignatius J. Reilly of New Orleans. In magnificent revolt against the twentieth century, he propels his monstrous bulk among the flesh-pots of a fallen city, a noble crusader against a world of dunces. 'A masterwork of comedy' *The New York Times*

Giovanni's Room   James Baldwin

Set in the bohemian world of 1950s Paris, *Giovanni's Room* is a landmark in gay writing. David is casually introduced to a barman named Giovanni and stays overnight with him. One night lengthens to more than three months of covert passion in his room. As he waits for his fiancée to arrive from Spain, David idealizes his planned marriage while tragically failing to see Giovanni's real love.

Breakfast at Tiffany's   Truman Capote

It's New York in the 1940s, where the Martinis flow from cocktail-hour to breakfast at Tiffany's. And nice girls don't, except, of course, Holly Golightly. Pursued by Mafia gangsters and playboy millionaires, Holly is a fragile eyeful of tawny hair and turned-up nose. She is irrepressibly 'top banana in the shock department', and one of the shining flowers of American fiction.

Delta of Venus   Anaïs Nin

In *Delta of Venus* Anaïs Nin conjures up a glittering cascade of sexual encounters. Creating her own 'language of the senses', she explores an area that was previously the domain of male writers and brings to it her own unique perceptions. Her vibrant and impassioned prose evokes the essence of female sexuality in a world where only love has meaning.

READ MORE IN PENGUIN

Published or forthcoming:

Seven Pillars of Wisdom T. E. Lawrence

Although 'continually and bitterly ashamed' that the Arabs had risen in revolt against the Turks as a result of fraudulent British promises, Lawrence led them in a triumphant campaign. *Seven Pillars of Wisdom* recreates epic events with extraordinary vividness. However flawed, Lawrence is one of the twentieth century's most fascinating figures. This is the greatest monument to his character.

A Month in the Country J. L. Carr

A damaged survivor of the First World War, Tom Birkin finds refuge in the village church of Oxgodby where he is to spend the summer uncovering a huge medieval wall-painting. Immersed in the peace of the countryside and the unchanging rhythms of village life, Birkin experiences a sense of renewal. Now an old man, he looks back on that idyllic summer of 1920.

Lucky Jim Kingsley Amis

Jim Dixon has accidentally fallen into a job at one of Britain's new redbrick universities. A moderately successful future beckons, as long as he can survive a madrigal-singing weekend at Professor Welch's, deliver a lecture on 'Merrie England' and resist Christine, the hopelessly desirable girlfriend of Welch's awful son Bertrand. 'A flawless comic novel . . . It has always made me laugh out loud' Helen Dunmore, *The Times*

Under Milk Wood Dylan Thomas

As the inhabitants of Llareggub lie sleeping, their dreams and fantasies deliciously unfold. Waking up, their dreams turn to bustling activity as a new day begins. In this classic modern pastoral, the 'dismays and rainbows' of the imagined seaside town become, within the cycle of one day, 'a greenleaved sermon on the innocence of men'.

BY THE SAME AUTHOR

Selected Poems

One of the major figures in the modern Irish poetic canon, Patrick Kavanagh (1904–67) released Anglo-Irish verse from its prolonged obsession with history, ethnicity and national politics. Instead his poetry, written in an uninhibited vernacular style, focuses on closely observed images of rural and urban life, where 'ordinary things wear lovely wings'. The first comprehensive selection of Kavanagh's poetry to be published, this volumes offers a timely reassessment of a poet unfairly neglected outside Ireland.

'These poems ... make you feel all over again a truth which the mind becomes adept at evading ... "You must change your life"'
Seamus Heaney

Tarry Flynn

A man's mother can be a terrible burden sometimes. For Tarry Flynn – poet, farmer and lover-from-afar of beautiful young virgins – the responsibility of family, farm, poetic inspiration and his own unyeilding lust is a heavy one. The only solution is to rise above it all – or escape over the nearest horizon

'Any man who wrote *Tarry Flynn* is entitled to throw down his hat and offer a challenge to the wide world. *Tarry Flynn* is a work of art' *Irish Times*